16 FOREVER

LANCE RUBIN

HARPER

An Imprint of HarperCollins*Publishers*

HarperCollins Children's Books, a division of
HarperCollins Publishers, 195 Broadway, New York, NY 10007

HarperCollins Publishers, Macken House,
39/40 Mayor Street Upper, Dublin 1, D01 C9W8, Ireland

16 Forever

harpercollins.com

Library of Congress Control Number: 2025943557
ISBN 978-0-06-333036-8

Typography by Catherine Lee
25 26 27 28 29 LBC 5 4 3 2 1

First Edition

FOR KATIE

CARTER

I don't want to fall asleep.

I can't.

I know I've tried staying awake before, and I know it didn't work.

But I'm trying again.

Maybe this time I'll unstick.

Maybe this time I won't forget.

I pull the note out from its hiding spot and stare at what I've written.

1. If you haven't already, find Bodhi Chang. He's a junior. Close friend.

And then I think about her. What she said.

Why did she wait until *tonight* to tell me such crucial information? When it's too late to even do anything about it?

Maybe it's not too late.

I grab a pen off my desk and quickly scrawl in a sixth entry, then shove the note back into its hiding spot before I can change my mind.

Maybe we've already unstuck me.

Maybe tomorrow I'll be seventeen.

I look down at her text for the fiftieth time.

I'm sorry I didn't explain sooner. I wanted it to work. And maybe it will

Whatever happens I love you

But I really hope you Remember Me tomorrow

I'm not going to fall asleep.

I can't.

I won't.

I—

DECEMBER.

CARTER

My eyes are barely open, and already I AM PSYCHED.

The day's soundtrack kicks on in my brain, an upbeat song I am writing in real time entitled "Everything Changes Today Because Today Is Gonna Be the Best Day That Has Ever Been." Title probably needs work. But I don't care.

Because today *is* going to be the best day that has ever been.

It's my sixteenth birthday, baby.

Sweet sixteen!

Within hours, I will be acing my driver's test, finally getting my license—a *junior* license, sure, but I'll take it—and hitting those bad streets like a bolt of lightning in Dad's old Toyota Corolla.

I'm going to name it Rex.

I grab at the nightstand for my phone, ready for the requisite slew of celebratory texts, GIFs, and DMs. Or at the very least a message from my best friend, Manny.

But the phone's not there. I peek under my bed, on my dresser, under the pair of jeans I left on the floor. It's nowhere. Probably left it on the couch last night.

I press onward, bounding out of bed and tripping over the very pair of jeans I just looked under. I somewhat gracefully recover, barely saving myself from face planting. "Noice!" I shout as I glide into the bathroom.

Unlike every other day that has ever been, my younger brother,

Lincoln, and his gigantic mop of curly hair don't appear in the hall to engage in a pointless argument about who gets to shower first. I appreciate this birthday gesture. He may be annoying in at least a dozen ways, but he has a good heart.

Hot water pulses on my back as I belt out lyrics to my new hit single. "'Everything changes today! Because today is gonna be the best . . . day . . . that has ever . . . BEEEEEN!'" People have called me tone-deaf on many an occasion, but I think I make up for it with confidence and gusto. You don't have to sing well when you're trying to be funny. Plus, it's impossible to get the tune wrong when you're the one writing it.

I move into the bridge ("'There have been . . . so many days in history . . . but none of those days . . . can compare . . . to the day . . . that is happening . . . NOOOOOOW!'") giving myself the birthday gift of a long-ass shower, no matter how much it might make Lincoln squirm. Kind of weird that he hasn't engaged in his usual progression of passive-aggressive knocking to active-aggressive knocking to straight-up screaming through the door for me to finish up. Should probably check on the kid, make sure he didn't die in his sleep.

But first: five more minutes of deliciously hot water.

Oh, how good it feels to be sixteen!

When I sense my bathroom time has crossed over from annoying to cruel, I flip the shower off, wrap a towel around myself, and deodorize before popping my head into Lincoln's bedroom to smugly give him the green light.

"Yo, bro, it's all yours. Thanks for—"

Lincoln's not in there.

And his bed is perfectly made. The entire room looks weirdly untouched, like he did a thorough clean after he woke up.

Which would be . . . odd.

But also hilarious.

Could this be some kind of prank?

I mean, that's more my thing, but maybe that's the whole idea. Turning the tables on the b-day boy, giving him some of his own medicine.

And I have to give Lincoln credit for his commitment. Skipping a shower in the name of a prank is hard-core.

I choose my clothes with a little more thought than usual because this is going to be my birthday suit. *Heh heh.* I'm obviously not going to my driver's test—and school after that—naked. Too many people would pass out from excitement. I grab my favorite new purple plaid button-down from the closet. The fabric feels kind of worn-down, which is funny because I just got it. There are also a few shirts in the closet I don't recognize at all. Maybe hand-me-downs from my cousin Ben that Mom snuck in there.

Once I'm dressed, I pop back into the miraculously still-empty bathroom to throw a little wax in my hair and spike it up in different directions. Then it's downstairs to the kitchen, where Mom is at the table with her mug of coffee and Dad is standing by the counter staring into the toaster and Lincoln is . . . nowhere.

"Good day to you!" I say, and it's almost like my parents flinch.

"Happy birthday, sweetie!" Mom says, her smile somewhat forced.

"Yeah!" Dad says at the same time that the toaster dings. "Happy day, bud."

"Um, thanks," I say, confused by their lukewarm vibes and the absence of one family member. "Where's Lincoln?"

Mom's smile crumples, and she lets out a sob. "I'm sorry," she says. "Carter, don't— I said I wasn't going to. . . . But every time it's—"

"I know," Dad says. He walks over and wraps an arm around her.

"Every time it's what?" I ask, alarmed by the insanity unfolding before me. "What happened to Lincoln? Did he go out last night? Where is he?"

Mom and Dad look at each other for a moment. Dad gives her a little nod and tells me to take a seat at the table with them.

"Just tell me what's going on." I stand firm near the kitchen entrance, my body going haywire, unsure whether to react with fight, flight, or vomit. "Did something happen to Lincoln? Is he dead or something?"

"No," Dad says with a sigh, rubbing a hand over his salt-and-pepper beard. "Lincoln is fine. He's totally fine. It's . . . more you."

"*I'm* dead?"

"No, no, you're— Could you please just sit down, Carter? It'll be easier to talk about this if we're sitting."

"I don't wanna sit!" I shout. "Where the hell is Lincoln?"

"He's . . ." Dad squeezes the edge of the round table as he stares at it, like he's expecting juice to come out.

"How old are you today?" Mom asks, rising to join Dad and me in the Land of the Standing.

"What?"

"How old are you turning today?"

"Mom, what the . . . ? Is this a prank?"

"I wish it was," she says. "I'm genuinely asking."

"Sixteen, right?" Dad says.

"Yes," I say, not enjoying this at all. "And if you need to ask that, I'd say you're failing at this whole parenting thing."

Mom puts a hand over her mouth to stifle another sob.

"Unfortunately," Dad says, "your answer is, uh, technically incorrect. Even though you believe it's your sixteenth birthday . . . you're twenty-two today."

CARTER

Have you ever had your parents say something to you that not only feels heinous and inaccurate but also like they might be losing their minds?

"Um," I say. "If this is a prank, it's a very bad one. It's confusing and not funny and seriously WHERE IS LINCOLN? Dude, if you're hiding behind the couch or something, you can come out!"

"He's not here, Carter," Mom says. "He's at college. His first semester."

"Ohmigod," I say, and, though I don't sit down, I do lean on the table and bury my face in my arms for a moment before resurfacing. "Guys. This is a noble try, very noble indeed, but you are absolutely terrible at pranking."

My family has always been this way. I keep waiting for them to evolve, to get better at it, but it's just not their thing. "There's an art to it, you know? And though I appreciate—"

"It's not a prank, Carter," Dad says. "We don't do pranks. You're the prank guy. And every year, you think this is us attempting a prank, and every year, we feel horrible that we have to explain it to you all over again."

"'Every year'? What does that mean: 'every year'?"

"It's been five years, sweetie," Mom says. A phone rings on the kitchen counter. I'm thinking maybe that's where I left mine, but Mom grabs it. "Here he is." She answers the call and stares at the screen. "Hi, Link."

"Hey," a man's voice says. "How's it going?"

"Oh, you know," Mom says. "I'll let you talk to him." She hands me the phone. "It's . . . Well, you'll see."

"Hey, bro," the man on the screen says, and I sort of want to pass out because he does resemble my little brother. He really does. But, like, a nineteen-year-old *man* version of him. His huge locks are gone, replaced by a short cut with a few bouncy curls dangling down his forehead. He's sitting in front of a white wall, a sticker that says Arlo Parks behind him. "Happy birthday."

I look up at Mom and Dad. "Who is this? Did you hire an *actor* to play older Lincoln? This is seriously messed up."

"I know this seems batshit, CT," the man on-screen says, smoothly incorporating Lincoln's nickname for me, "and it *is* batshit, but it's what we've all been dealing with for more than half a decade."

"What are you talking about? My brother is thirteen. Which is *less than sixteen*."

"No, I know," the Lincoln imposter says. "But you've been sixteen for six years. And every time you're about to turn seventeen, you don't. You flip back to thinking you're sixteen, and you lose all the memories and, like, physical changes from the past year. And it just happened again."

I stare at the screen for a long moment.

Then I start cracking up. "Dude, that is the stupidest thing I've ever heard. And so unnecessarily complicated." I look to my parents, who are both grimacing like they need to number two. "Mom and Dad, you have to keep a prank simple. Like, you could've rearranged the furniture or something, put all the kitchen stuff in the bathroom, so, for example, I'm about to pee, right? But then there's a microwave on the toilet. And I'm like, *Whaaaaaa?*

And you're like, *Ha ha!* And I'm like, *Ohhhhh*. That would be a good pr—"

"Our wrestling safe word is *Cheetos,*" fake Lincoln says.

I look back at the screen. "Come again?"

"We once accidentally broke the glass on Mom and Dad's wedding photo—the one where they're standing in a random meadow holding umbrellas—and Dad freaked out at us and said we were maniacs. We once wrote a play about being doctors in space doing surgery on an alien, and we performed it for Mom and Dad and Uncle Flip and Uncle Jed. Well, actually, you said you weren't a writer so I would have to come up with everything myself, but then you kept having all these great ideas."

My fingers are trembling. That is a lot of really specific information.

"Okay," I say, working extra hard to form the words. "So . . . clearly my parents prepared you well. But did they tell you what the *name* of the alien in the play was?"

"Ah yes!" the guy says, excited. "You asked me this last year, and I couldn't remember, so I dug up the play from the box in the basement. It's Flanghorn! The alien is Flanghorn."

He's right, dammit. The alien was Flanghorn.

I glance at my parents, and suddenly I see it: They look a little older than they did last night. Mom's black pixie cut is the same, but she has way more lines on her face. Dad's hair, on the other hand, has gone almost entirely gray.

Which is when it dawns on me:

This might not be a prank.

MAGGIE

He hasn't texted yet.

This isn't good.

But there's still hope. Right?

Maybe his parents took away his phone, thinking he would loop back, but then he *didn't*.

So he needs to get his phone back from them and *then* he'll text back.

Something like:

Success, Mags! It really worked!

Maybe he won't text. Maybe he'll call.

We should have discussed this ahead of time.

But, really, any kind of message coming through this phone will suffice.

Text, call, FaceTime, voice memo.

Even a single GIF, honestly.

Like, a dancing lizard in a party hat under the words *I AGED!*

My phone lights up.

YES.

It's Shana. Damn.

Any word?

This isn't good.

CARTER

The room spins.

"Whoa!" Dad says, grabbing me under the arms and steering me toward a chair.

"Link," Mom says, after sliding the phone out of my hands, "we'll call you back a little later."

"All right," Lincoln says. "CT, you can call me whenever to talk! I'm here. You're going to be okay! Love you!"

"Thanks, sweetie. Love you." Mom hangs up, and now she and Dad are sitting on either side of me at the table.

Dad puts a hand on mine. "Do you want to say anything? Ask us any questions?"

I shake my head, even though I feel like all the blood flowing through my circulatory system has, in fact, been replaced by questions.

"Here," Mom says, pulling up something on her phone. "Watch this."

Before I can protest, she's holding up the screen, and there I am, talking to the camera, delivering a message to myself.

CARTER

"Hey there, sexy," the me on Mom's phone says, filming himself in my bedroom, wearing the same purple plaid shirt as me. "If you're watching this, it means you're back to the beginning of sixteen. Damn. That sucks. And, unfortunately, this is not a prank.

"I know. You're staring at me saying these words, probably at the kitchen table with Mom and Dad, and thinking, *I can't ever remember filming this!* And that's not because I'm some, like, AI deepfake version of you. It's because you literally *can't* remember. The memories are gone. And you are sixteen again."

Mom rubs my back.

"*Again?* you're thinking. *I've never been sixteen!* Alas, you have. We have. I'm sixteen as I'm filming this! But every time we're about to turn seventeen, we wake up the next morning a couple inches shorter, several pounds lighter, the growing stubble on our face a little less . . . existent. And, of course, with no memories beyond the last night of being fifteen."

I feel the seed of a headache blossoming above my right eye.

"So now," the me on-screen continues, "the billion-dollar question is: *WHY?* Why is this happening to you? To me? To us?" He throws a hand into the air and shrugs, falling backward onto the bed. "Dude, I wish I knew! We all wish we knew. Because being stuck forever at age sixteen is . . . not ideal! We've gone to all kinds of doctors—neurologists, oncologists, blood specialists, aging experts—who've tried to figure out what's happening, how to get us to seventeen. Also healers and psychiatrists. Even a couple rabbis. No one understands it. Though some of them pretend to.

"And we've been seeing this therapist guy, Soren, since the second or third loop. He doesn't know why it's happening either, but he's good to talk to. Kind of a dweeb, but a helpful one who occasionally says wise shit. I'm sure there are some other experts we've seen that I'm forgetting to mention. I'm the Loop-Four Carter, so some of this happened before my time. And that makes you . . . the Loop-Five Carter."

"Loop Six, actually," Dad says. "You didn't want to make a new video this time around. You were hoping it wouldn't be necessary."

"So, yeah," Loop-Four Carter says, sitting back up in bed. "I know it's gonna take a lot longer than the length of this video for you to process all this. But, if you take away nothing else from what I'm saying, at least know this: It's real. Not a prank. I repeat: NOT. A. PRANK. The sooner you accept that, the better this year is going to be. Oh, also in the Good News Department: You already have your driver's license! You've had it for five years, so it's not even a junior license anymore. It's the real thing. Drive at all hours. With as many people as you want in the car."

"Well, within reason," Mom interjects.

"And you don't need to waste time taking a stupid driver's test on your birthday! Cheers to *that*!" Loop-Four Me takes a long exhale, taps his fingers over his mouth. "And that's basically the deal. This won't be as bad as it feels right now. It really won't. I'd tell you to reach out whenever you need me, but I'm you! So unfortunately that's not possible. You should lean on Lincoln, though. And Mom and Dad, obviously. We're gonna figure this out. We're gonna get to seventeen. And till then: Just know you're the same cool-as-hell Carter you've always been. We got this, baby!" On-screen Carter gives a peace sign. "That's kind of a stupid way to end this video. Ah, whatever."

The image of me on-screen freezes, a smirk on my face.

I'm numb.

And the headache has spiderwebbed out to the side of my skull.

"You okay, hon?" Mom asks, rubbing my back again. "We know it's a lot."

"Yeah, what're you thinking about all this, Carter?" Dad asks.

I'm thinking I've been hit by a metaphysical Mack Truck.

"I don't know what to think," I say.

Dad puts his hand on mine. "Well, like you said in the video, we're here for you."

"Always," Mom says, giving me a hug. Dad joins in too.

I awkwardly pat their arms.

"And, bud," Dad says, "we're still doing everything we can to find a cure. So that we won't have to do this all over again next year."

"Pete," Mom says.

"What?" he says. "We are."

"I know, of course we are, but we should also be prepared to just . . ."

"To just what?"

"To accept!" They're still hugging me as they have this argument.

"Sure, we can accept the situation," Dad says, "but that doesn't mean we don't keep . . ."

"Keep what?"

Dad has noticed the horrified look on my face.

"Let's . . . talk about this later. Sorry, Carter." He pats my shoulder and looks away.

"Yeah, sorry, sweets," Mom agrees, giving me one last squeeze before releasing the hug. "It's easy for us to . . . get caught up in our frustration. That this happened to you. But like you said in the video, this always feels the worst on the first day. It will get better."

"It does feel really bad right now," I say.

"That's normal," Dad says. "I mean. In its abnormal way."

I peer around at the kitchen, trying to spot differences from yesterday as if it's a puzzle in a kids' magazine.

"So what happens now?" I finally ask.

"That's up to you," Mom says. "You can stay home and adjust to this situation—Dad and I both took off work to be here with you—or . . . you can go to school."

"Can we go to the movies? What's even playing? Do movie theaters still exist?"

Mom and Dad look at each other. "We *could* go to the movies, in theory," Mom says, looking back to me. "They still exist. But maybe, for today, let's keep the options to either home or school."

I feel an overwhelming urge to move around, so I stand up and start pacing the kitchen.

"What grade am I even in?" I open the fridge. Mostly the same old stuff. There's a brand of oat milk I don't recognize.

"Well," Dad says, "up till yesterday, you were a junior. But you'll be moved back to sophomore year. That's how we started doing it in Loop Two. Just easier that way."

"Since you won't remember anything you learned as a junior," Mom adds.

"I see." I grab an apple from the fruit bowl and toss it into the air. I mean to catch it, but I miss—Mom gasps—and it hits the tiles with a thud.

"It's fine," Dad says, not so convincingly. "It'll still be good."

I pick it up and take a bite, accidentally getting some of the mushy bruised part. I pretend it's not gross. "So if this has been going on for six years, I've been going to Ridgedale High School for, like, a long time."

Mom and Dad nod sheepishly.

"That's kind of embarrassing."

"It's really not," Mom says, a little too emphatically. "Everyone knows about your condition. They're all very understanding."

I put my face into my hand and press on my closed eyeballs. "This is a nightmare. This is a terrible nightmare. I need to wake up. I need to wake up."

"We know, Carter," Mom says. "We—"

"Where's my phone?" My eyes are open again. "It wasn't in my room."

"Yeah, we have it for you." Mom gestures to Dad.

"Oh, right," he says. He goes into his office and comes out with a large black rectangle. "It's here."

"That's not my phone."

"Well, it's not the one you remember, no," Dad says carefully, as if he's ready for me to explode. "Phones are bigger now. Bigger screen, you'll like it."

"I don't care about a bigger screen, I want *my* phone. With all my photos and texts and everything on it."

"We don't have that phone anymore," Mom says. "It broke."

"It *broke*? What happened? Did it fall in the toilet or something?"

"It just broke, Cart," Dad says. "It was old."

"Okay, fine, fine, so what's on this new one?"

"Nothing," Dad says.

"Nothing?"

"It's a fresh start," Mom says.

"What if I don't want that?"

Mom and Dad exchange another look. "It's not really a choice," Dad says. "Your therapist, Soren, says it's too distressing and disorienting for you to see memories that you never experienced."

"It's worked out well this way so far," Mom says.

"Fine!" I snatch the phone from Dad's hand. "I'll take this stupid oversized garbage phone."

"The camera is pretty amazing," Dad says.

"Oh, very cool," I say, the flood of internally building sarcasm bursting whatever dam there was. "I guess today is actually pretty great after all. What with this camera and everything. Can't wait to snap some pics!"

Dad just calmly nods, as if he's expecting this. "Do you want some chocolate chip pancakes?"

"What?" I ask.

"For breakfast. A birthday treat. I already started putting together the batter."

"*You* did? Not Mom?"

"Your father has, uh, learned to cook in the past few years. And bake. He's actually quite good at it."

Dad gives a little grin, clearly so proud, and it's endearing, but I also want to smack it right off his face. Then a third feeling arrives and replaces the first two:

I am very hungry.

"Yeah, okay," I say. "Sure."

Dad nods and gets to work at the stove, and six minutes later, the three of us are sitting at the table eating together.

A fucked-up birthday breakfast feast for a fucked-up sixteen-year-old who will never turn seventeen.

The pancakes are excellent.

CARTER

I decide to go to school.

Because the idea of being home with my parents right now—as this itchy, restless fire burns through every cell of my body—sounds like torture. They both look different. Dad cooks now. It's disturbing on all the levels.

Turns out the Toyota Corolla I was ready to inherit from Dad was mine until I got into a fender bender during Loop Three, which effectively ended poor Rex's life, may he rest in peace. So now my car is a beat-up silver Honda Accord that my parents got used. They said I named it Toro. Well done, me. Sick name.

But that's not relevant at this moment since Mom wants to drive me to school in her white Prius. Probably a good idea—even though I technically have my license, I don't actually have any memory of driving on my own. Add to that how wigged out I feel, and I'd probably crash into a stop sign or something.

During the seven-minute journey from home to Ridgedale High, I continue to play my spot-the-differences game. Stop & Shop has been replaced by Whole Foods. Bed Bath & Beyond is closed. Best Bagels is now called Bagel Bagel. Chilling.

It's like overnight, everything has changed.

Also, I'm used to blustery winter weather on my birthday, but instead it's almost sixty degrees out. In December. Climate change has been evolving too, I guess.

At least my high school looks exactly the same.

Mom pulls into the parking lot and turns off the already silent engine.

"You ready for this?" she asks.

I'm glad she drove, but it's freaky looking at her all old and stuff.

I shrug. "Probably not."

We buzz into the lobby, and everything is so similar to what I expect that I can almost convince myself that maybe this really *is* a prank. A very involved and elaborate one.

Mom guides us toward the main office, where a Black woman in a pantsuit is waiting for us. "Hi there, Carter," she says, extending a hand, which I shake. "I'm Ms. Jones, the principal."

"Hi," I say.

Mom and I follow her into a separate office, even as my suspicion deepens. This woman could be an actor. I mean, Ms. *Jones*? That's like the most classic fake last name in the book. Other than Ms. Smith.

"Where's Mr. Nguyen?"

"He retired three years ago," Ms. Jones says, taking a seat behind her desk and gesturing for us to sit across from her. "Then I took over."

"Oh."

"You and I have known each other since then. We get along well." She gives me a wink. I know it's supposed to be comforting, but instead it's like I'm on the outside of my own inside joke.

"It's okay if this feels overwhelming," Mom says, eyes on me, like I might shatter at any moment.

"Yeah, there's no way for it not to be," Ms. Jones says, clasping her fingers together. "But I got your back. All of Ridgedale does, really."

I wonder if a school-wide email went out this morning.

Dear students, teachers, and parents,

Longtime tenth grader Carter Cohen once again failed to turn seventeen. His shitty-ass condition continues. Proceed accordingly.

With great Ridgedale cheer, Ms. Jones

"And if you decide you want to stay home today," Mom says, "ease back into school tomorrow, or even wait until after winter break, that's perfectly fine too."

It's a tempting proposition. I would also be open to *move to foreign country and assume new identity.*

"Absolutely," Ms. Jones says. "Yours is a unique situation, which means it often requires a unique approach. But it might bring you some comfort to know that, as you shift back to a sophomore schedule, your homeroom and English teacher will be Mrs. Destin, same as when you last remember being in school." She slides a stack of textbooks toward me. "In fact, we've kept your day as close to what you remember as possible. Unfortunately, some of your teachers are no longer with us."

"They're dead?" I ask. "Which ones died?"

"Oh, no, no. I mean they've retired. Or moved to different schools."

"Oh, good. I thought you meant they were dead."

"I understand how it sounded like that. Thankfully, they're all alive."

We sit in a brief awkward silence.

"Okay, I'll stay," I say. "Mrs. Destin is cool and, well, fuck it, you know? Why not? Might as well lean into this shit show."

"Carter!" Mom says.

"Sorry, I know. Pardon my language."

"It's really fine," Ms. Jones says, shaking her head as if she totally gets it. "You're processing a lot right now. Just try to keep things cleaner during class."

"Fuck yeah," I say, giving her a wink.

★ ★ ★

Once I've hugged Mom goodbye and am walking down the hall to my locker—#357, according to the Post-it Ms. Jones handed me—I'm immediately rethinking my decision. I wanted to end the conversation and get the hell out of that office, which may have led me to choose poorly.

Too late now, though. I'm in this.

I put my thick green hoodie away in the locker along with the books I won't need till later.

I could be wrong, but it feels like kids are staring at me.

Does literally everyone know about my situation?

Maybe Ms. Jones really *did* send out an email.

I generally hate being stared at. Unless it's because I just said something funny.

Even more unsettling than the staring, though, is that I don't recognize a single one of these kids. The entire school is populated by kids I don't know. Or kids I don't know that I know.

There is officially no way in hell this could be a prank.

I slam locker 357 shut and head toward homeroom. Head down, eyes forward.

Two girls walk by, both obviously trying not to stare at me, but then I feel the taller one glance my way for a moment. I glance back at her, then look away and keep walking.

I hear what sounds like a sob. When I look behind me, the tall girl is being comforted by her friend.

Was that my fault?

I hate this.

I walk into Mrs. Destin's classroom.

MAGGIE

I really thought I could change him.

So stupid, I know. The cliché of all clichés.

But I wanted to be the one to get him to seventeen.

To undo the curse or whatever. The Belle to his Beast.

Obviously, I didn't do it.

I knew it was hopeless when he didn't text this morning.

But still, some mentally damaged part of me thought I might come to school and just now, when I looked at him, he would be all, *It worked, Mags!*, and I would say, *Of course it did, Coco*, and we would high-five and make out right there in the hall as the music swelled—*"Tale as old as time, true as it can beeeeee"*—and the entire school would cheer and we would all live happily ever goddamn after.

But there's Carter, with those stupid little spikes in his hair, walking by me without a clue in the world.

He did actually stare at me for a second.

And, in that second, everything seemed possible. He looked vulnerable and adorable, and I wanted to hug him and tell him who I was and that we were going to figure this out together.

Then he kept walking.

At which point a vise squeezed my heart until it burst into a dozen bloody chunks that exploded a hole in my sternum and landed with a pitter-pat of thuds on the dingy hallway tile near my feet.

Now I am a dead person.

And suddenly it's crystal clear:

I cannot do this again.

I will not do this again.

Start from scratch? Do our whole relationship over?

No. No no no.

That sounds like fucking torture.

It must end.

"Yo, sorry, Maggie," Shana says, putting an arm around me as I let out a sob and collapse into a strange formation, like a broken tripod that won't fully close. "Totally sucks."

And for the briefest of moments, even though she's one of my closest friends, I want to grab Shana by the ears and scream, *"COULD YOU SAY ANYTHING MORE OBVIOUS RIGHT NOW?"*

But I don't.

Instead, I say, "I'm done."

Or I try to, anyway, but I can't even do that because I'm crying too hard.

Yesterday Carter knew me.

Today he does not.

And this pain right now—this brutal, kidney-wrenching pain—is why I can't do this again.

Why I can't talk to him.

Why I can't know him.

Why, starting now, I can't even *think* about him.

Because it's hopeless.

Like voluntarily putting my hand into a paper shredder.

Even Carter agreed. (The one from yesterday, not that zombie I just saw in the hall.)

(Is it offensive to talk about his condition that way? I'm sure it is. I'm a terrible person.)

(You're allowed to be a terrible person when your heart's in chunks on the floor.)

(I should make that into a T-shirt.)

(Or at least a mug.)

Point being: I know Carter would understand. We'll both move on.

Me knowingly, him . . . not so knowingly.

Mom will definitely be happy. She'd already been saying that continuing to date Carter would be "throwing away more time on someone who's just gonna forget you anyway."

I hated her saying that. But she's not wrong.

I spent the past five months with Carter, and he doesn't even remember it happened. So what was the point?

And where could we possibly go from here?

Am I going to be seventy years old, playing mah-jongg with my friends while my sixteen-year-old husband goes to high school?

Oh wait, that would be impossible because, at a certain point—probably somewhere in my early to mid-twenties—the very act of me flirting with Carter, once he has YET AGAIN forgotten who I am, will become definitively creepy and inappropriate.

So it ends now. We're done.

And I can enjoy some me time. I just got all my college applications out a few weeks ago, so bring on the BIG SENIOR-YEAR ENERGY. Time to hang out with my friends. Kiss new boys. Play with my *band*. (Which most of my friends are in, so the first and third items are pretty much the same thing. Makes me sound cooler if I say them separately, though.) Live my goddamn life!

Ugh, who am I kidding?

I can't be chill about all this. Not yet. It's too horrible.

The Carter Cohen I knew has died.

And there's no funeral to provide closure.

"Do you want to talk about it?" Shana asks, handing me a tissue, ostensibly to deal with the mascara swamp on my face. Of course I spent way more time than usual putting myself together this morning. So that, if the worst happened, at least I would make a good first impression.

"Yeah." I swipe the tissue down my cheeks. "I can't start this up again. With Carter. It's too much."

"So don't," Shana says. "You already knew this might be a possibility. He did too. Sure, you were weirdly cute together, but—"

Another sob bursts out of me. A couple of first-years flinch as they walk by, and one bumps into the other.

"Oh god," Shana says. "I am so sorry. That was the wrong thing to say. Redact that shit."

"Too soon."

"Of course, my dear. I think you just traumatized those kids."

"Sorry!" I shout, turning back in their direction. I blow my nose into the tissue, extra loud for dramatic/comedic effect. I can tell Shana is grossed out, but, uncharacteristically, she tries not to show it—a testament to how bad she's feeling for me.

"What if Carter . . ." I say. "What if he finds out we were together?"

"Not gonna happen." Shana puts an arm around me. "Ember and I are all over that. We'll make sure everyone keeps their big fat mouths shut. And you can just text his brother and his friends, tell them the deal."

"Yeah, okay," I say. "That's smart." I pull out my phone and go to Instagram since I don't actually have Carter's brother's number. I tap the word *Message* on his profile and try to compose something quickly without giving it too much thought.

Hi Lincoln. It's Maggie Spear. So obviously you know Carter looped again. Could you not tell him about me? When you talk? This is a weird message. Sorry. Hope you're doing ok.

And then I find the profile for Carter's current best friend, Bodhi, and send him a similar message (except with his I put *DO NOT TELL HIM ABOUT ME* in all caps because Bodhi's the kind of person who needs extra guidance).

"Okay, sent," I say, feeling relieved but also a little shady, like I've just done something illegal.

"Brilliant," Shana says as we approach Mr. Cha's homeroom. "Hey, so I have something actually."

"Oh?"

With Shana, a sentence like that could be referring to a billion things, from a pack of Trident she just bought to a party she's throwing in two days while her parents are away to a girl she hooked up with in a side room during a speech-and-debate tournament.

"We have our first gig. Angry Baby."

Angry Baby is our band (coming up with that name is one of my proudest life achievements), and I know how I'm supposed to react to this—with a *Squee!* and a *How did you . . . ?* and a *This is amaaaaazing*—but I'm not feeling any of that. It's more of a terror-nausea-why-are-you-telling-me-this-now-of-all-the-times-to-be-telling-me-this cocktail.

"You don't have to say anything," Shana says, swooping in before I can deliver a hard no. "Just listen to the details, store them in that beautiful brain of yours, and we'll talk more about it some other time. The gig is in February, a full *month and a half* away, at Bean-Age Dream—"

"Ugh, the coffeehouse?"

"Do you know another Bean-Age Dream? Yes, the coffeehouse, and my dad's friend Misty owns it, so don't make fun of the name like you always do. I agree it's an incomprehensible and stupid moniker for an establishment, but the actual place is pretty great, and my dad's friend is being kind enough to let us open for this other band without ever hearing us play—"

"Right," I say, dread oozing from my pores in the form of mean-girl snappiness, "because we've never for real performed anything and we're absolutely not ready!"

"We'll *be* ready," Shana says. "This will make us be ready."

"I think it will make us be embarrassed."

Shana laughs, shakes her head, playfully jostles my shoulder, and walks into Mr. Cha's class ahead of me. We're definitely going to end up doing the gig. That's just Shana's way.

But maybe there's something to it because, would you look at that: I just went a full thirty seconds without thinking about Carter.

A pathetic victory, but I'll take it.

I sit down at my desk and, as I'm putting my phone into my backpack, I see a new IG notification.

It's a message from Lincoln: *Totally get it. Won't mention you.*♡

I know it should be encouraging, but instead it just reminds me of the recently exploded hole in my chest. I wipe at my cheeks and hope Mr. Cha's morning lecture will be engaging enough to distract me for at least another thirty seconds.

CARTER

Today sucks. I hate it.

The school day is finally done. It felt like a week.

Like a long, no-good, terrible, very stupid week.

I knew I wasn't going to recognize anybody in my classes, or in the halls, or in the cafeteria, or anywhere at all, but knowing that and actually experiencing it are two totally different things. I mean, it seriously felt like I was a new kid, being introduced at the beginning of each class and everything. At a high school I've apparently been going to for, like, seven years.

I've always loved cracking people up in class, but that doesn't work nearly as well when no one knows who the hell you are. Or when they know exactly who you are and they're laughing *at* you more than *with* you.

Mrs. Destin was probably the best part of my day, mainly because she doesn't seem that different from how I remember her from yesterday. (Well, what I remember as yesterday, which was actually six freaking years ago.) She's still supercool and supportive and said I could always come to her to talk, which I guess we've done a lot in the past. She seemed slightly more tired than she was yesterday, but otherwise, she was very much herself. Her black hair wasn't even grayer. Maybe she dyes it.

The other repeat teachers are Mr. Davies for geometry and Ms. Hanif for US history—I've never had much of a relationship with either of them, so today felt pretty much like business as usual. As I was leaving Mr. Davies's class, though, he gave me a little nod and said in his awkward-ass way, "It's good to have you back, Carter."

It was confusing because, as far as I remember, I never left, never moved on to junior year before being forced to backtrack by this curse or spell or disease or whatever the hell it is.

Still, I give Mr. Davies credit for trying. "Yeah, thanks," I said.

Now I spot Mom's Prius in the after-school pickup line, and I more or less sprint into the front seat. Must get away from this place.

"You did it," Mom says. "How'd it go?"

"You know that feeling when the dentist is cleaning your teeth and they hit a nerve? And you get that surge of chills?"

"I do."

"It went like that."

"Well, all right, then," Mom says, shifting the car into Drive. "I'm really sorry, Carter."

She asks no further questions, which leads me to believe that maybe we've had this exact exchange in past years and her attempts to push for more information only made me more agitated than I already am.

I assume we're driving straight home, but then Mom pulls into the strip mall on Route 81 and parks in the lot.

"Are we . . . picking up dry cleaning or something?" I ask.

Mom shakes her head. "Usually now is when you want to see Manny. Do you want to see Manny?"

My stomach is wobbling like a spoonful of pudding as the door of Tech Haven slides open, and I walk inside on my own. I move past aisles of TVs and speakers and tablets, and then, there he is: my best friend, wearing the gray employee polo as he talks to a short woman about a charger he's holding.

He looks like a goddamn grown-up. It's creepy as hell.

"Totally up to you," Manny is saying, sporting this well-manicured beard, "but for my money, this one is the way to go. It charges faster than any of the other options, so you can get your phone up to one hundred percent within thirty minutes." He's talking like a real salesperson would. It's equal parts impressive and disturbing.

The woman decides to go for it and thanks him as she walks away with the charger, and that's when he sees me and breaks into a huge smile, almost like he was expecting me. "Hey, you looking for a charger too, my dude? New headphones perhaps?"

"Are they free?" I ask, smiling back.

"Nope."

"Then no, thank you."

Manny gives me a huge hug, and he feels stronger and taller than I remember.

"This is some messed-up shit, huh?" he says while we're still hugging.

"Worst prank of all time."

"Yeah, man. I hate it. Happy birthday, by the way."

It occurs to me that Manny, just like my parents and brother, has had to experience this insane thing happening to someone he loves. I've barely had time to process all this, but I definitely haven't thought of it as something that sucks for other people besides me.

"And you, like, work here?" I ask idiotically as we pull out of the hug, unsure what else to say.

"No," Manny says, smirking, "I just put on the shirt and pretend sometimes, so I can film some funny TikToks."

I assume he's kidding, but at this moment, I feel like I can't assume anything.

"Yeah, I work here," he confirms with a grin. "At least for right now. Back living with my folks since I graduated in May. Good ol' Dom and Gina."

"Dom and Gina are the best," I say.

Manny shrugs. "Sure, but I don't really need to *live* with them."

"Oh, yeah," I say, laughing, "your dad always takes the smelliest dumps."

Manny smiles a little but doesn't crack up the way I'm hoping. "Truth."

An awkward silence descends—it's been happening a lot today—and I scramble to find another subject.

"So you graduated from, like, college?" I ask. It feels unfathomable. Yesterday we were sitting side by side in Mrs. Destin's class, passing back and forth goofy drawings of dogs with boobs.

"Yep," Manny says. "I majored in business, but none of my full-time job applications have panned out yet. It'll happen."

I nod and look around, hating this gulf that's opened up between us. He's twenty-two years old, looking for work, and I'm a high school sophomore, looking for laughs with poop jokes.

"What, um . . ." I clear my throat. It's so dry. "What was college like?"

Manny shrugs. "It was cool. Chill. I mean, hard work. But dope too. Met lots of good people."

I nod, doing my best impression of someone who's able to relate in the slightest to what he just said.

"Immanuel." A tall white dude with glasses and a surprisingly low voice is standing fifteen feet away in a matching gray polo shirt. "Less chitchatting on the floor. Check in to see if those customers by the laptops need help."

"Absolutely," Manny says. "Will do, Tom."

"Immanuel?" I say once Tom has walked away. I realize Manny's name tag says that too, and it makes me smile. "They make you go by *Immanuel*?"

"Nah, they don't make me," Manny says. "It's what I go by now. Made a switch during my first year at school."

"Oh," I say. Embarrassment and FOMO heat up my neck and face.

"Aight, man, I need to get back to it," Manny—I'm not going to call him Immanuel, sorry, but I'm just not—says, patting me on the back, "but let's hang more soon, okay?"

"Yeah, perfect," I say. "I would love that. I *need* it, actually. Maybe you can come over and we can shoot around in the driveway. Or we can chill in the parking lot of Wade's Wings and—"

"That place closed, actually. And I don't really do much hanging in parking lots these days." Manny notices the depressed look on my face. "But shooting around sometime sounds good. Don't worry—you're gonna be okay, dude. You always bounce back after the first week. We met up in the summer a couple times, and you seemed really happy."

My brain spins as it tries to make sense of these information grenades. I *bounced back*? I was *happy*? Even though I saw my best friend only a couple times the whole summer? Are we, like, not even really friends anymore?

"Okay," I say.

Manny slaps my hand and gives me a quick hug before gliding

over to an older man standing near the laptops. "Can I help you with anything?" he asks with a confidence and charm that is so convincing, it really does feel like a well-rehearsed bit he's filming.

But it's not. It's real.

After some time has passed—maybe thirty seconds, maybe five minutes, possibly another six years—I realize it's more than a little weird that I'm just standing in the store staring at one of the employees. I take out my new big-ass phone and text Mom that I'm ready to get picked up, slowly moving toward the exit like a corpse floating in a lake.

CARTER

I have nobody.

That's all I can think as I stand near the curb in front of Tech Haven waiting for Mom to come get me. If Manny Alvarez, my best friend in the whole world since fourth grade, isn't really my friend anymore, then who the hell is?

This one kid, Caleb, who's a junior, introduced himself in the cafeteria today and said we were friends last year. So I guess him. But after I nodded and said, "Cool," I had no idea what to say next. Caleb was like, "You doing okay?" and I was like, "Not really," and he was like, "Sorry," and he said I could come sit with him and his crew if I wanted, but I didn't really want, so he slowly walked away, and the whole thing was awkward as hell.

Mom coasts toward the curb in her white Prius, and it's only once I'm in her car that I realize it's not Mom at all.

"Yo, bro," Lincoln says.

"Holy shit, you can drive?"

"Apparently." My younger/older brother smoothly pulls away from the curb, and even though he seems like a capable driver, it's supremely weird to see him behind the wheel. I grab on to the plastic handle bar above the window.

"So how's it going?" Lincoln asks. "I heard your first day sucked."

"Uh, yeah," I say, unable to take my eyes off this nineteen-year-old version of my brother. I've time-traveled into the future. And I'd like to go back now. "What're you doing here? I thought you were at college."

"Winter break, bitch," he says with a smile. "Had my last final this morning, then I knew I had to get home to see my big bro."

"Thanks," I say, looking away for the first time since getting in the car. "It's really good to see you."

"You don't have to be polite," Lincoln says. "I know it's weird as shit. How was Manny doing?"

"Old."

"Ha!" Hearing that Lincoln still has his classic guffaw is like being in a crowd of strangers and finally spotting the one person I know.

"It was good to see him and everything," I say, "but it didn't feel, like, the same."

"Well, yeah, CT, it wouldn't," Lincoln says, taking a left turn onto Wyncrest, which is in the opposite direction from our house. "Because he's in his twenties now. You've been living completely different lives for a while."

"Right," I say, staring out the window. "Pretty fucking depressing."

"It's definitely not the best," Lincoln says. "But you've made new friends. Connected with new . . . people. And you will again. I'm not gonna pretend it's a great situation or anything, but it will feel better than it does today. And I'm sorry you have to keep doing this."

"Yeah. Me too." I think about all the memories Lincoln has of me that I don't—whatever joyful moments we've had, hilarious ones, embarrassing ones, any stupid fights. I'm clueless about all of it. Who knows if we've even had fights, though. Knowing Lincoln, he probably feels too bad about my situation to ever argue with me.

"But guess what?" my brother says. "Whether you like it or not, no amount of looping is keeping me away from you. I don't care if I'm forty-five and people think you're my son, I'll still be here."

"That's so unsettling. A little vomit just came up into my mouth."

"Yeah, I felt gross as soon as I said it. Sorry. But you get my point."

Lincoln swerves into another parking lot.

"So we're not going home," I say.

"One thousand percent no." He steers us into a spot, and then I see it: the bright red lettering that forms the words *Cheesecake Factory*. "You need at least one good thing to happen today."

"Wait, Jon Polito and Eli Rosenthal are a couple?"

"For almost three years," Lincoln says. He nods as he sips his chocolate shake.

"That's . . . wow." We've been sitting in a booth chatting for almost an hour, our nachos and wings long since consumed, our round of milkshakes just arrived. Lincoln is bringing me up to speed on pretty much everyone we've ever known. It's been a relief to think about people who aren't me. Though I, of course, end up thinking about me anyway, as in: *I can't believe all this has happened and I have no memory of any of it.*

"Well, it makes sense, right?" Lincoln says. "Jon and Eli always did everything together anyway, it already kind of felt like they were in love."

"Yeah, I guess."

"Hey, Shaker Guy," a bald server says, pointing to me as he passes our table. "Back so soon, nice to see you again."

"Oh," I say. "Thanks?"

But he's already out of sight.

I turn to Lincoln. "I guess I was . . . just here?"

"Guess so," Lincoln says, shrugging and giving me a sheepish look. "Sorry, that must feel really disorienting."

"It's pretty insane, yeah. Like someone else has been driving my body around while I was asleep. Why am I Shaker Guy?"

"I have no idea."

"I wasn't here with you, was I?"

"No. Not me."

"Do you know who?"

"I . . . don't. Just got home, remember?"

"Should I ask the waiter?"

"I mean, you could." Lincoln takes a long sip of his shake. "In general, your therapist has advised us not to tell you much about what's happened in the previous years. That it can be too upsetting and confusing and it's better if you start fresh. Which I guess I get."

"Hm," I say. I really want to interrogate that bald server guy. *Who was I just here with? A friend? A group of friends? A girlfriend? ALONE?* But I can tell how uncomfortable that would make Lincoln, so I let it go. I take a deep slurp of my Oreo milkshake and move to another potentially uncomfortable topic. "What about you?"

"Me?" Lincoln asks, his eyebrows bouncing up.

"Yeah. How's your, like, romantic life?"

"Oh." My brother smiles and looks at the table, his face going tomato red. "It's good, actually. I've been hanging out with this guy Terrell. It's only been a month, but . . . I like him a lot."

"Yeah, bro!" I shout, loudly enough that it draws stares from several other tables. I reach across the table to punch his arm. "That's the best news. And you came out! I was thinking you must have, but I didn't want to assume, or—"

"Totally. Yeah. I came out at the end of middle school."

"Wow," I say, experiencing the same surge of FOMO I felt when Manny told me he was Immanuel now. Like, I wish I was there when Lincoln came out. I mean, I *was* there. But I wish I remembered it. "Did Mom and Dad handle it well?"

"Yeah, they were awesome. And not really surprised at all."

"Sweet. Did . . . I handle it well?"

"Yeah," Lincoln says with a grin. "You were cool too."

"Good," I say. I want to give Lincoln a hug, tell him I'm proud of him, but instead I punch his arm again. "So, back to this Terrell guy."

"Yeah, I don't know," Lincoln says, hands on his cheeks as if he's five years old. "He's a sophomore. And we're—okay, don't laugh at this, Carter, you have to promise."

"I mean, I can try to promise. But laughing can be hard to control sometimes."

"Nope." Lincoln smacks the table. "Not good enough. I really need you to promise not to laugh."

"Ohmigod, okay, now I'm nervous you're going to tell me that Terrell is a robot or something."

"He is not a robot. Do you promise?"

"Fine! Sure! I promise. GEEZ, DUDE."

"Okay. Excellent. Thank you." Lincoln smooths his forehead

curls down to the side. "So: Terrell and I are in the same a cappella group."

I want to laugh. I desperately want to. But I calmly say, "You? You're in an a cappella group?"

"Yes."

"Like one of those singing groups that isn't accompanied by any instruments?"

"Yes."

"Where the singers make instrument sounds with their voices?"

"Sometimes, yes."

"Which means you sing now?"

"I do."

"You're a singer."

"I am."

"Even though I've maybe heard you sing twice in my entire life? And both times you were so quiet it looked like you were lip-synching without a track?"

"Yes! Okay? Yes! I sing now, get over it!" Lincoln throws his used napkin at me. I catch it and hurl it back, but he dodges to the left, and it bounces off the shoulder of a thirtysomething guy behind him. Lincoln gasps and covers his mouth. The guy is looking at his phone, though, and doesn't even realize it happened.

We both crack up.

"Yo yo yo!" a tall guy Lincoln's age says, appearing next to our table. He has a ridiculously long brown beard that extends down to his neck. "What's so damn funny?"

"Ohmigod, hi!" Lincoln says, getting up from the table to give the tall guy a hug. "I didn't know you were back yet."

"Literally just got home a couple hours ago."

“Me too!”

“Yo, Carter, what’s good, man?” The tall guy extends a hand my way.

“It’s Prateek,” Lincoln says, clearly sensing I have no idea who we’re talking to.

“Holy crap,” I say. This hairy ogre of a man is the little pipsqueak who was over at our house all the time? WTF. Like, seriously.

“Oh shoot, it’s reboot day, isn’t it?” Prateek asks.

“’Fraid so,” Lincoln says.

“Sorry, Carter.” Prateek pats my shoulder, his beard lightly bouncing. “So what happens now with M—”

“Mom!” Lincoln shouts, cutting him off. “And Dad! What happens with Mom and Dad? Well, same thing that happens every year, I guess. We start over, try to make it work as best as we can. But it’s not easy. For them. For me. For all of us. But most of all, for Carter.”

“Truth,” Prateek says. “Anyway, speaking of moms, gotta go eat with mine.” He points to a woman standing twenty feet away, who waves. “But let’s hang soon.”

“Definitely,” Lincoln says, waving back as a hostess leads Prateek and his mom to a table. I can’t stop staring at Prateek.

“You all right?” Lincoln asks.

“He got huge,” I say. “What is he, like, in a jam band for sasquatches now? That was so disturbing. Aren’t you disturbed by that?”

“I’m . . . not. But it happened more gradually for me.”

“Right, yeah.” I stare forward into nothing as I aggressively sip the remnants of my milkshake, enjoying the abrasive slurping sound it makes once there’s nothing left.

“So much has changed,” I say.

“I know.”

"Like, everything."

"Yeah."

"Except me."

Lincoln scrunches up his mouth and blinks several times, like he's about to cry. "Look, CT." He reaches across the table and accidentally knocks over my empty milkshake glass. "Oops." He picks it back up, but I reach out and knock it over again. "We'll figure this out."

"How? I mean, that's a nice thought, but, like, how will we do that? Do we even know why this is happening?"

Lincoln stares at the table for a long moment. He wipes at his eyes with his fingers, clearly wishing he still had his napkin.

"Dad is looking into more doctors," he says finally. "He's not giving up. And Mom and I aren't either. I don't think you'll be stuck like this forever, Carter. I really don't."

"You said you were ready to be my forty-five-year-old dad," I say, wrestling with the knot in my throat.

"That was just a joke," Lincoln says with barely credible conviction.

"But it's possible this is my eternal reality, right? Everyone feeling bad for me, constantly explaining all the shit I don't remember, politely informing me that, sorry, they don't hang out in parking lots anymore. Does this even count as a life? What the fuck is the point?"

I pick up the milkshake glass and thunk it down loudly on the table right as our server is reaching out to clear it.

"Oh, so sorry," she says, flinching backward. "Are you done with that?"

"Not yet," I say.

I hold tight to my empty glass.

LINCOLN

THE FIRST LOOP

Watching you wake up on your seventeenth birthday fully believing that it was your sixteenth was an incredibly unpleasant experience.

The night before, you and I had gotten in a fight, and, as happened sometimes, I was so annoyed and pissed off that I was fully prepared to ignore/avoid you as much as possible that morning, birthday be damned.

So imagine my surprise when you acted as if that fight had never happened.

I thought you were gaslighting me, which only made me angrier.

But you had no idea what I was talking about and, it soon became clear, you thought Mom, Dad, and I were playing some weird prank where we were pretending it was your seventeenth birthday instead of your sixteenth.

You've always been desperate for us to be the kind of family who revels in pranking each other. But, alas, we are not. Dad tries sometimes, but mostly it's just you.

So it was kind of funny for a minute when you thought this was us finally pranking you. Then it got weird. Dad was confused, and Mom started getting angry, and she told you to stop joking around, and you said you would stop when *we* stopped. And then Mom said she didn't like your attitude, that you were probably tired from being out the night before, which confused you and pissed you off because you said you *weren't* out the night before.

That's when I realized you looked a little different. Like, younger somehow.

And eventually it became clear: You truly thought you were turning sixteen. And you didn't remember anything from the night before, or *any* of the nights from the past year. Mom started crying, and Dad did too. I didn't. I just felt, like, shocked.

It was a big, hot, scary mess.

And so was the rest of that year.

You saw so many doctors, got CAT scans, MRIs, psych evals, blood tests, along with tests that assessed hormone levels and adrenal levels and pituitary levels and all sorts of other levels I never even knew existed.

No one could figure out what the hell was going on.

I, meanwhile, was still fourteen, enduring the squall of eighth grade as I tried to figure myself out, which was made simultaneously easier and harder by the fact that you were taking up every bit of our parents' attention.

Also hard was that you were incredibly stressed out. I understood this, and I felt bad for you, but I hated that your main way of coping with that stress was to play pranks on me, or make a joke at my expense, or, I don't know, some variation on that. You were particularly obsessed with hiding my shoelaces and then pretending to be shocked that my sneakers didn't have any. I did not enjoy it.

By the time December rolled back around, I was in high school with you, and our family had more or less adapted to the situation, and we were all relieved that we could bid this horrible year adieu and move on.

Only then you woke up on your birthday, and you were sixteen. Again.

Nightmare.

But what was there to do but keep moving forward? Keep looking for a solution.

Keep trying to be the best younger brother to you that I could be.

Again. And again. And again.

And again.

MAGGIE

I'm always a sucker for winter break, but this year more than ever. Seriously, it couldn't get here soon enough.

Why, you ask? Well, it's simple.

School is where Carter is. Home is where Carter is not.

And these ten days of Not School will give me more time to Get Over This Shit.

I'm doing better. I really truly am. I went a whole four and a half minutes without thinking about Carter during a particularly spirited conversation about *The Scarlet Letter* in Ms. Karp's AP English class.

Wow. I'm bragging about four and a half minutes. That sounded more pathetic than I meant it to. So maybe I'm still a mess. A new cliché this time: the girl who can't stop thinking about the guy. Who she once loved but whose memory keeps getting erased every time he ages back a year.

I guess that's not really a cliché.

In spite of my best efforts, I passed Carter in the halls at least five times over the last school week of the year. As opposed to that first day, when he seemed clueless, he seemed more bristly and angry. Then the last time I saw him he was more hopeless and defeated, and I really, really wanted to give him a hug. Just an anonymous drive-by. No need to tell him who I was or to be overly flirty or anything. Just give him the hug and go.

But I didn't do it.

"Mind if I join you?" my sister, Vivian, asks from the top of the basement steps.

"I thought you'd never ask," I say, pausing the TV. I've been sitting on the couch down here, watching the latest Netflix show that everyone is obsessing over, a drama about the high-stakes world of circus performers. Well, watching is probably an overstatement. More like *letting the images move in front of my eyeballs while my brain spins on completely unrelated topics.*

But Vivian is home from school, and Vivian is coming downstairs holding that dish we love that has separate compartments for chips *and* salsa, and the compartments are *full*, and honestly, Vivian is exactly what I need right now.

Because Vivian is the best.

She's on winter break from her senior year at UPenn, where she's majoring in gender, sexuality, and women's studies and minoring in cinema and media studies, captaining an Ultimate Frisbee team, acting in avant-garde performance pieces, volunteering at a local soup kitchen, and dating a beautiful nonbinary junior named Brand.

Vivian's one of those people who's always had her shit together but is also very open about her insecurities and her anxiety and the SSRIs she's on, and not just because I'm her sister. She's like that with everyone, so it makes you feel less resentful and jealous of how good she is at everything.

"What're you watching?" she asks, gracefully sitting next to me and placing the chip dish onto the old coffee table from Dad's New York City days that he kindly left with us after the divorce.

"I don't really know. It's that circus show, *Three Rings.*"

"Overrated," Vivian sings, and somehow even this throwaway

joke sounds like something people would pay to listen to.

"Yeah, right? Like, is it *that* intense to work at a circus?"

"Even if it is, I don't think the dialogue at a real circus is that clunky."

I laugh and dip a chip, wanting to revel in this moment. Simple. Pure. Two sisters joking around about nothing. On a couch. With snacks.

"How did you even have time to watch this?" I ask, reaching for another chip. "Didn't it just come out a few weeks ago?"

"I would have it going on my phone while I was studying for finals," Vivian says with a shrug. "It was weirdly calming."

"Wow. And you were still able to pick up on the bad dialogue. Only Vivian Spear could pull that off."

"Well. Let's see how she does on her finals first and then we'll decide." She chomps down on a chip, and a little salsa gets on her chin. Her phone buzzes, so she pulls it out of her dress pocket and glances at it, frowns, and sighs.

"Everything okay?"

"Eh. Brand and I broke up, and they're not handling it well."

"What? You broke up? Why?"

Vivian raises her eyebrows and gives an exaggerated shrug. "It was getting a little too serious."

"So you're saying you dumped them."

Another shrug. "I don't want serious right now. I want fun."

"Vivvy! No!" I say, shoving her shoulder. "I liked Brand! I thought this time would be different. That maybe you'd make it past the eight-month mark."

"I thought that too," she says. "But I was wrong."

"Dang, sis. You're stone-cold."

"It is what it is. I gotta do me." She chucks her phone to the other side of the couch. "So what's going on with you?"

"With me?" I panic. I can't help it. "Nothing, why?"

"I dunno," Vivian says, "you just seem like you're in a little funk. And Mom confirmed this to be true. Since last week."

"Oh. Yeah. Well, it's not a big deal. I think it's just . . . senioritis, you know?"

"I don't think you're using that word correctly, but okay."

Here's the thing: If I'm gonna be honest, Vivian is another big reason why I can't be with Carter anymore. I mean, it's stupid to say that because she doesn't even know I was with him; she stayed in Philly last summer, so she was barely home during the time Carter and I were dating, which made it an easy fact to omit. But I irrationally worried Vivian would, like, silently judge me. Or worse, not-silently judge me.

I think I put too much weight on what Vivian thinks.

But . . . like she just said: *It is what it is!*

And it's a moot point now because Carter and I are donezo. Kinda wish I'd never told Mom I was dating him. Then I'd have only my own judgments to deal with instead of hers too. And it would make this transition to a Carterless life even easier.

"If this is about your love life," Vivian says, "you can totally—"

"It's not about my love life!" I try to sound chill, but instead it comes out more like the villain in a superhero movie right after they learn their evil plans have been foiled.

"Right, sure, okay," Vivian says, one calming hand in the air. "But if it *is*, you should know there are tons of people who would want to date you. You don't have to be single forever if you don't want to."

"What makes you think I've been single all this time?" I'm not sure why I said that, considering it points her in the exact direction I've been trying to avoid.

Maybe it's because she sounded a little smug when she said *single forever.*

"Oh," Vivian says, blinking away her surprise. "Are you not single?"

"No, I'm single right now, but I'm just saying you don't *know* my deal for sure."

"Geez, Mags. Fine. I guess I assumed you would *tell* me if you started hanging out with somebody."

"Oh." I feel a little bad that I snapped at her for no reason whatsoever. And that I never told her about Carter. "Of course I—"

"Girls, are you down there?" Mom is standing at the doorway to the basement.

"No," Vivian says. "You'll have to look elsewhere."

"Hilarious, Vivvy," Mom says, already walking downstairs to us, a jovial bounce in her step because it's Christmas Eve and she fricking loves Christmas.

"We'll help cook and set up," I say. "We're just being lazy."

"Oh, you're fine, you're fine," Mom says as if she wasn't stressing about this very thing as soon as we woke up. "I just wanted to say hello to my two favorite peeps."

"Nope," Vivian says.

"My favorite people." Mom seems happy in this almost unhinged way, and Vivian and I exchange a look. I'm grateful for Mom's timing, actually, as she's pushed Vivian and me past that tense moment. But her vibes are making me nervous. "What're you two up to down here?"

"I'm watching this circus show on Netflix," I say.

"Ooh, that sounds fun."

"In theory, yeah. Less so in practice. For example, one of the plotlines is this acrobat guy falls and breaks a bunch of bones because his partner is distracted during their act because the partner's wife is cheating on him with one of the ringmasters."

"Do circuses have multiple ringmasters?" Mom asks. Because that was definitely my point.

"That episode's actually really good," Vivian says.

"Yes," Mom says. "I see why that could be a very compelling show!" This is getting weird. Mom doesn't usually, um, what's the word . . . CARE about the details of random shows we stream.

"So," Vivian says, after a few seconds pass of us looking at Mom in silence.

"Oh yes." Mom rubs her hands together, then clasps her own fingers, then rubs them again. "So I also wanted to share some news. As you know, Ron and I went for our lake walk this morning."

"Indeed," I say.

"We do know this," Vivian confirms.

"Right, okay," Mom says, "so we went for our walk, and then—"

She stops speaking and puts a hand to her mouth. Vivian and I have no idea what's happening, but then I realize she's crying.

"Girls," Mom gasps, removing her hand. "We're getting married!"

"What?" I am stuck to the couch as Vivian responds the way I should be also, leaping up and shouting, "Ohmigod! Mom!" and giving her a huge hug and not letting go.

I will myself to a standing position and zombie-walk over to them. "This is so exciting," I force out as I wrap my arms around them.

My mom and Ron are getting married.

Fuck.

Ron is fine—he's sweet; he's good to her; he's nice to us; he's all the things. The problem is not Ron.

Mom and Dad have been divorced for almost seven years, so you'd think I'd have made peace with this. Dad's in Pennsylvania with his work, we're here in New Jersey, we see him many weekends, and that's what it is now.

But perhaps I have not made peace.

Because my mother marrying a man who is not my father feels like a butt splinter.

"This is so great, Mom," I say as we pull out of the hug.

"Is it okay?" She looks right into my eyes, as if she knows I'm the one who's going to be tough about this. "Is it? I know it might feel weird or strange or odd—"

"All those words mean the same thing, Mom."

"Ha!" she says, which is different from actually laughing at something. "You're right! But really, Mags, we want to do this in a way that works for everyone—"

"It works, Mom. It really does. I'm happy for you."

"Me too," Vivian says. "The best news."

"Oh, thank you, girls," Mom says, hugging us again. "I love you both so much."

And I really *am* happy for her, for the way she's glowing, for all the ways dorky Ron is a better fit for her than Dad ever was.

So why does celebrating this right now feel like dancing in quicksand?

It is possible I'm . . . jealous? Of my *mom*?

I mean, I obviously don't want to *marry* Carter, but it is kind of unfair. Mom and Ron are engaged, and Carter and I are . . . two people who don't interact because one of us has no idea the other one exists.

"Okay!" Mom says, accompanied by an emphatic clap. "Time for me to revert to being stressed again. I need you both upstairs, lots to do."

"Aye, aye," Vivian says, doing a cheesy salute.

"I'll meet you two up there in a minute," I say. "Just want to finish this episode."

"Oh, yes, of course, the ringmasters," Mom says as she heads up the stairs, which is both endearing and totally irritating.

"You sure you're good?" Vivian asks, putting a hand on my arm with a tenderness that makes me want to cry.

"I am," I say. "Really. Just want to . . . finish this."

She doesn't believe me, but she nods and follows Mom upstairs.

I sink down into the couch and stare at the high-def rainforest screensaver on the TV, thinking maybe I'll rewind to that scene with the broken-bones acrobat and watch it on a loop.

JANUARY.

CARTER

"Should I even go back tomorrow?" I ask before taking a bite of the curry salmon Dad made. Oh god, it's so delicious. As far as I can remember, he always sucked at cooking. Like, couldn't-even-scramble-an-egg sucked. But now suddenly he's Bobby Flay.

It's Sunday night before school picks back up after winter break, and I'm sitting at the dinner table with Mom, Dad, and Lincoln, feeling the Sunday-night scaries on steroids.

"Well, if you didn't go," Dad says, gesturing with his fork, "what would you do instead?"

"I dunno." I look to Lincoln. "More of what I've been doing the past week, I guess?"

That's mostly been playing Nintendo Switch with Lincoln—so many new games have come out, including a few we just got for Hanukkah—and pretending everything is normal.

"Right, but Lincoln will head back to school in two weeks, and then what?" Dad asks.

"You can still play the games with one player, Dad," I explain.

"You know what he means, Carter," Mom says.

"Here's the thing," I say, laying out my case like a TV lawyer. "That first week of school after my birthday was awful. Like, it really blew. And, I mean, I'll probably be right back here in a year, with no memory of any of this. So I can do school then. 'Cause what's the point of going right now? Maybe this can be a pass year.

A gap year! Isn't that what they call it?"

Mom and Dad look at each other, squirming in their seats because they know there's merit to what I'm saying. Lincoln chugs from his water glass.

"Look, Carter," Mom says. "You know I'd be the first to say you and Lincoln should both just stay here and never leave. I love this. I love being home with you boys. But it's not realistic."

"Right," Dad says, employing his stricter tone.

"Did you talk about any of this with Soren?" Mom asks.

"Kinda." I had my first appointment with my therapist a few days ago. He's a white guy with glasses and a mustache, younger than my parents but not by that much. Talking with him was fine but also annoying. Soren knew a ton about me even though, from my perspective, he's some random dude I just met. After I vented for a while about everything, how I wish this wasn't happening, how I want to find a way back to a life where I remember stuff and age like everyone else and people don't feel bad for me all the time, he said, "Thank you for that. Would you like to hear my take on all this?"

I wanted to say, *Not really,* but I nodded.

"So much of this is about acceptance," he said. "You shouldn't worry about trying to solve this or unstick yourself. You're only going to make yourself miserable, adding a layer of extra suffering onto an already-difficult situation. Instead, you can be present and look for the opportunities inherent in each day. Does that make sense?"

It did and it didn't. I was relieved when our time was up.

"Well, you should," Mom says. "Soren has been very helpful to you over the years. We understand that this can all feel pointless,

Carter, but . . . in past years, once you've gone to school for around a month, it starts to get better. You make friends, you find your people."

"And even though you've never been into doing extracurriculars—" Dad says.

"Got that right," I interrupt. "Not my thing."

"You joined yearbook this year," Dad continues, "and you were really into it. You take incredible photographs. Like, professional-level stuff. Did you know that?"

My brain flips around in that way I'm starting to get used to. "Of course I didn't know that," I say. "How would I? And what am I supposed to do with that information?"

"It's . . ." Dad is a little flustered. "You're supposed to . . . feel confident knowing there is a place for you at this school, even though it might not feel like that in this moment."

Mom looks at Dad, like, *Well said, honey*, and I'm tempted to overturn the table, watch with glee as all its contents smash against the floor.

"Okay," I say instead. "So I have a place. I make some friends. Then what? Because I don't remember those friends now! Who are they? *Where* are they? And being on yearbook—I mean, all right, I see the value of documenting experiences so I can at least show my future self and be like, *Bruh, look! You once watched a school football game!* But I'm not convinced that's enough to justify me going to school instead of playing video games with my brother who I really love and who has gotten much better at gaming since he was thirteen two weeks ago. The games are very competitive now, and that's really good for me because it pushes me to be better and—"

"It has been super fun," Lincoln agrees.

"Yes! See? It's been super fun, and I am a boy with a messed-up mystery disorder, and I deserve this!"

Mom and Dad have no response to this, so the next minute is filled with nothing but chewing and the gentle clatter of forks and knives on plates.

"We'll make you a deal," Mom says finally.

A spark of hope lights within me. A deal is good. A deal is promising.

"Yeah?"

"If you go to school for ten days straight—"

"Aw man!"

"Listen! If you go for ten days—two weeks—and you go with an open mind, and you still feel this way after that, you can take off the following two weeks for, you know, doing whatever it is you're dreaming of. All Nintendo Switch, all day. A couple of gap weeks. If you will."

"Gap weeks? That's not a thing."

"It could be," Mom says.

I don't like this deal. This is a bad deal.

"But," I stammer, "Lincoln won't even be here two weeks from now!"

"You can still play the games with one player, Carter," Mom says.

"Damn, Mom," Lincoln says, laughing. "Touché."

Even as I have to give Mom props for that one, I don't appreciate it right now, so I don't respond, instead taking another bite of Dad's salmon.

He really has become a sick cook.

★ ★ ★

I haven't officially taken Mom's deal yet.

Because for real: If I'm trapped in an endless loop, what is the goddamn point of going to school?

I bang around my bedroom like a maniac, opening drawers and slamming them shut until I find the one I need. As I wildly fumble for a pair of pajama pants, my hand collides with an object that's paper, not fabric.

I pull it out of the drawer and unfold it.

It's a note. In my handwriting.

> Hey Carter,
>
> Glad you found this! I'm not supposed to be writing to myself, but I am anyway. Don't tell anyone. Here's some extra stuff you should know:
>
> 1. If you haven't already, find Bodhi Chang. He's a junior. Close friend.

It's a list. I wrote myself a list. Soren was just saying at our appointment that I should have minimal exposure to past memories, which kinda makes me love this cheat sheet even more. Fuck you, Soren!

I read onward:

> 2. Lean on Lincoln. It's weird af that he's older than you, but he's actually really helpful.
> 3. But also: It sucks that he doesn't live here anymore. You probably already figured that out, or will soon, but it's like the balance is all messed up without him. Mom and Dad are weirder than usual.

4. We're pretty good at photography now. Dope, right? You'll have to relearn, but just, like, push through even when it feels hard. I did. And you're me. So. You can do this.
5. Not gonna sugarcoat it like I did in that video. This situation is very fucked. But it's not all bad. There's been a lot of good stuff in my life this year. And I bet it'll be the same for you.

The last item is in blue pen instead of black. The handwriting is messier too.

6. *Layla Banerjee could be the key.*

What?

Layla Banerjee? Who I've known since elementary school? What is she the key to? What does that even mean?

I lie back on my bed and read the list again.

And again.

Layla Banerjee. I can still picture her when we were six, sitting on the orange carpet at circle time. Wearing a blue dress with stars on it.

I pull out my phone and go to Instagram, signing on to the new profile I started on my new phone—part of the Soren starting-fresh protocol.

There are more Layla Banerjees in the world than I would've thought, but eventually I find her, the adult version of the girl I remember from just a month ago, when she was a fellow junior.

This will never stop being freaky.

I stare at her profile pic and scan her grid, and here's what I learn:

- Layla works for a tech company in California.
- She has a best friend named Nellie who she takes a lot of selfies with.
- She likes to run.
- She is passionate about helping dogs with no homes find homes.

Hm. Okay.

Not sure what to do with all that.

But the first item on my list feels highly achievable.

I can find this Bodhi Chang kid.

Though, if he's such a close friend, why hasn't he already found *me*?

Whatever. At least I have a reason to go to school tomorrow.

I'll take my mom's stupid deal.

CARTER

I can't find Bodhi Chang.

I'm not even convinced he's a real person.

It seems like something I would do, messing with myself by making up some random name and sending me on a pointless search for nobody. I can be a dick like that sometimes.

Otherwise, as predicted, school still sucks. Doesn't really matter how open my mind is, the facts remain the same: I'm stepping into a life that is technically mine but doesn't feel like it at all.

I asked a few people in my homeroom if they knew Bodhi, and all of them gave me that same pitying look and smile, like they wanted to be really nice to me since I'm the pathetic sick kid.

"He's a freshman, right?" asked the girl at the desk next to me who always wears jumpsuits.

"No, he's a junior. Supposedly." I hated Past Me right then.

"I don't think I know who that is," she said, shrugging apologetically as if now I might keel over and die from disappointment, falling onto my back with my legs in the air like a cockroach.

I did not die, but I did decide to retain my dignity and stop asking other students about Bodhi. Instead, I wait until four periods later, when I'm walking to the cafeteria and pass Mrs. Destin in the hallway.

"Hey, Mrs. D," I say, jumping into her path. "Is there a person at this school named Bodhi Chang?"

She smiles and laughs a little. "Indeed there is. You sat together in my class last year. Couldn't get the two of you to shut up, in fact."

"Oh, wow, he's real?"

"As far as I know," Mrs. Destin says. "There he goes now."

She points to a short Asian kid wearing a backward baseball cap walking in the opposite direction. He's in between two other kids, both taller than him.

He and I make eye contact, and after a flash of deer-in-headlights terror, Bodhi gives me a huge smile. "Carter! Yo! Walk with us."

Mrs. Destin releases me with a knowing nod, and I walk with Bodhi and his crew, away from the cafeteria.

"What's good, man?" Bodhi says, putting out a fist to dap.

"I mean, nothing?" I say as I touch my fist to his.

"You don't remember me, do you?"

"Dude, I don't remember anybody."

"Heh, I know," Bodhi says. "But I'm super memorable. Thought I might've cut through."

"I wish."

"Well, I'm Bodhi. And you probably don't remember these guys either." He gestures to his friends.

"No, them I remember," I say, completely serious. "Jake and Dino, right?"

"Uh," Bodhi says, trying to suppress a laugh as the friends give me the same pitying looks that Jumpsuit Girl gave me this morning. "Unfortunately that's incorrect, dude."

"I'm kidding," I say. "I don't know these people."

The three of them burst into laughter, I think mostly from relief.

"I'm Robbie," the kid with glasses and bangs says.

"I'm Amir," the tall, chubby kid says.

"Sweet, I'm Carter. As you know. Were we all friends?"

"Yeah, man!" Bodhi says. "For sure. We have good times."

Robbie and Amir nod, only a little awkwardly.

"Then, uh, no offense," I say, "but why didn't you introduce yourself during that last week of school? When I first, you know, forgot everything."

"I *knew* you were going to ask that!" Bodhi says. He puts his face into his hand and shakes his head. "I'm sorry about that, man, I really am. I chickened out! I didn't want to mess it up somehow. Or make you feel weird. But I'm happy you found me now! I figured we'd reconnect at yearbook anyway. You're coming today, right?"

Oh geez. Again with the goddamn yearbook.

"I didn't know there was a meeting," I say. "I mean, my parents were telling me I did that now, but—"

"You gotta come! Did they also tell you how sick a photographer you are?"

Robbie and Amir again nod awkwardly in support. The hall is nearly empty. Fifth period is gonna start any second now.

"They tried to," I say, "but—"

"Well, you are," Bodhi says. "Come to the meeting. We're in Ms. Himberton's room. One eighteen. At least let me show you some of your photos."

I don't know what to say to that. *He's* gonna show *me* my own photos? This is so stupid.

"Yeah, maybe," I say as the tone sounds for the new period.

"Not maybe!" Bodhi insists as Robbie and Amir disappear into a classroom. "Come see what a genius you are," he adds, in a whisper, pointing at me before following them inside.

I turn around and walk down the hall to lunch, my footsteps echoing in a way that sounds like they're making fun of me.

"Carter Cohen!" a woman shouts a few hours later as soon as I walk through the door to her classroom. She's a new teacher (to me at least), with short light purple hair, who seems like she's in her mid-twenties but is brimming with the energy and excitement of a teenager.

"You!" I shout back because I've forgotten what Bodhi said her name was. It gets a laugh from various kids in the room, including Bodhi, and, surprisingly, from the teacher too.

"So glad you're here," she says, "and even gladder to see that you still have your sense of humor. I'm Ms. Himberton. I supervise yearbook, and I have been thrilled by and grateful for your magical abilities with a camera over the past year."

"Oh," I say, surprised that even she has this opinion of my photography skills. "I don't actually, um . . . I don't really know how to use a camera."

"You'll learn," she says without missing a beat. "Now, since this is all weird for you, to say the least, Bodhi's said he's down to ease you in, tell you what we do, show you some of your past work."

"Word, bird," Bodhi says, gesturing for me to join him at the other side of the room near a laptop.

"That okay?" Ms. Himberton asks.

"Uh, sure, yeah," I say, walking toward Bodhi. "Thanks."

I'm relieved to hear Ms. Himberton pick back up with whatever she'd been saying before I walked in, the intense glare of the spotlight finally off me.

"Glad you made it," Bodhi says, putting an arm around my shoulders. "Otherwise I would've had to come to your house and drag you here at knifepoint."

"That's a fun image."

"Okay, let's get you up to speed, then." Bodhi clicks around on the laptop, opening different folders. "So, for starters, this is yearbook. Do you know what a yearbook is?"

I stare at him. "I lost years of memories, not basic concepts of existence."

"Well, I don't know!" Bodhi holds on to the backward bill of his cap. "This is my first time experiencing one of your loopbacks, I'm just trying to make this easy for you!"

"Okay, thank you," I say. "I know what a yearbook is."

"Great. And this thing is called a laptop."

"Yeah, I—"

"That was a joke," Bodhi says. "All right, so . . . here we go! Exhibit A." He turns the screen toward me. "Proof that you've done yearbook and, more important, proof that we're friends." It's the group photo for the yearbook committee—Bodhi and I are standing next to each other smiling.

"I mean, technically that just proves we were standing next to each other," I say.

"Dude!" Bodhi says. "I swear we're friends, I swear on my life. I swear on my dog's life!"

"I'm just messing with you, man."

"Oh, all right." Bodhi is back to clicking through folders. "That's fair. You deserve to have some fun. Ah, check this out! Here's one of your pics."

It's a tennis match, this kid's face contorted as his racket connects with the ball. You can feel the energy of the moment, see the sweat on the guy's forehead.

"I took that?"

"Yeah. It's unreal, right?"

I have memories of occasionally messing around with the camera on my phone, but I never produced anything like this. This picture is *legit*.

"Let me find another one," Bodhi says. "You're always really picky about what you show other people, so there aren't a ton. Oh, this is one. From Fall Fest."

It's a couple of Ridgedale High students behind a table, selling apple cider and hot chocolate. Yet somehow it's a gorgeous photo, the trees behind them in soft focus, an autumnal smear of orange, yellow, and red.

"This is so good," I say.

"I know, right? That's why we need you to join again." Bodhi continues his scroll.

"Yeah, but how do I even—"

"Oh, this is another one!" Bodhi stops on a picture of runners. "No, wait, never mind." He keeps scrolling.

"Was that not one I took?"

"I'm not really sure," Bodhi says. "I thought it was, but now I don't think so."

"Can you scroll back anyway? I want to see something."

"Um, maybe. I don't know if I can find it again."

"Just scroll back. It's right there."

"Yeah, oh, is it? I guess you're right." He's being very weird.

The pic is up on the screen again, what I can now see is a girls' cross-country meet. One girl is crossing the finish line with two others just behind her, friends and family cheering on the sideline. It's a cool action shot.

But that's not why I wanted to look at it.

When the photo initially blurred by, I thought I saw . . .

Yes. It's her.

The second girl in the photo—not the one crossing the finish line but the one right behind her—is the crying girl from my first day back at school. I've passed her in the hallway a few times since then. She even looked at me once, just for a second.

"Who is that?" I ask, pointing at the screen.

"Uh, who?"

"This girl my finger is literally touching."

"Oh, her. I think, um . . . Maggie something? Or maybe it's Lindsey. Yeah, I think it's . . . Lindsey. Or something."

"Why are you being weird?"

"Me? I'm not. This is how I always am. And also I don't really pay attention to the cross-country team. Boys or girls. They're not, like, on my radar. So that's why."

"Okay." I don't believe him, but at least now I know her name is Lindsey. Or Maggie. When she first walked by me, all I took in was that she was crying and tall, almost awkwardly so, but now I see she's also really pretty. Her dark brown hair is in a ponytail, and her cheeks are flushed, and her legs are long.

"Anyway," Bodhi says, scrolling onward and stopping at a new pic. "Check this out. My crowning achievement. I wrestled the Ridgedale Colt." It's a photo of him on the ground with his arms around someone wearing a horse costume.

"Nice," I say, and even though I wanted to look at Lindsey a moment longer, I let it go. Bodhi takes me through more photos, giving me glimpses of everything I've missed. Or didn't miss but can't remember. It's jarring every time I see myself in a photo, like I'm staring at someone else.

As we move further back through the years, I start to see some faces I remember. It's a relief. But then it gets kind of depressing. All of these people have moved on. Maybe their younger siblings are here, but not them. It's just me. Stuck here.

Forever.

"Yo," Bodhi says, obviously picking up on my vibes. "Let's forget about these." He closes the laptop. "I have an idea."

"You really think this is going to work?"

"I *know* it will," Bodhi says.

We skipped out of yearbook early, Bodhi explaining to Ms. Himberton that flipping through the past had been very triggering for me so he was going to take me outside to decompress. Which, honestly, was the truth.

But he left out the part about us driving to the liquor store.

We're in Toro, Dad's old Honda Accord—I drive to and from school now; it only feels a little bizarre—with Bodhi sitting shotgun.

"Look, dude," he says, "you're legally twenty-two. You've been on this earth for that many years, and your license confirms this fact, and that's just reality. So you'll be able to get us some liquid treats."

"That does make sense," I say, surprised it hadn't occurred to me yet.

"Also I know it's gonna work because we've done it before." Bodhi extends his hands like a magician after he's made something vanish. "Last year. When you were technically twenty-one. Heh heh."

"Oh. So, yeah. That's encouraging." I only have one memory of drinking: Manny and I snuck a couple of his dad's IPAs out of the fridge and each drank one really fast in the basement. It tasted okay, not amazing, and it made me feel silly and loose. And then vomity. "Have we, like, gotten drunk together?"

"We have," Bodhi says, grinning. "Once."

"Did I like it?"

"I think so. You were laughing your ass off."

"Hm." I can't say I'm in the mood to get drunk right *now*, but it's nice to have a friend to hang out with. Especially a funny friend like Bodhi. He kind of reminds me of Manny, actually. Young Manny, not the guy in the polo shirt selling chargers. And, though it's possible Bodhi is just using me to get alcohol, this is still better than most other options of what I could be doing at this moment.

We pull into the parking lot of Buy Rite. My hands are shaking as I put the car into Park and push the Off button. *You've done this before*, I remind myself. *And it worked out fine.*

The bell on the door jingles as we walk in, instantly drawing a stare from the short-haired, broad-shouldered woman behind the counter, who of course instantly realizes we are not of legal drinking age.

"Nice try, kids." She makes a shooing gesture with her hands. "Go buy yourselves some orange sodas at Burger King."

"Excuse me?" I pretend like I have no idea what she's talking about. "Oh, I see, you think we're . . . ? Ah, yes, people do make that mistake sometimes. I'm actually twenty-two. I just look very young for my age."

"Come on, buddy," the woman says. "Do I look like a complete idiot?"

"Not at all," I say, reaching into my pocket for my wallet with a still-trembling hand. "It's an honest mistake!"

"You look very smart and competent," Bodhi agrees. "A complete smart person."

"Here." I hand the woman my driver's license, which she begrudgingly takes, going through the motions of staring at it so she can get us to leave. "You'll note that my twenty-second birthday was last month."

"Happy belated birthday," she says, handing the ID back. "This is an impressive fake. Now get out."

"It's real, though!" I say. "It's totally real."

"And I presume you have a fake too?" she asks, pointing to Bodhi.

"Oh, no," he says. "I'm only sixteen."

"Ha!" the woman barks. "So only one of you has a fake. Brilliant plan."

"No," I say, "only one of us is twenty-two."

"So you're a twenty-two-year-old hanging out with a sixteen-year-old."

"We're brothers," Bodhi says, sounding genuinely offended.

The woman is about to bark again because obviously one of us is white and one of us is Asian, but Bodhi and I remain straight-faced, and she's forced to swallow the laugh back. It's not so impossible that we'd be related—either of us could be adopted.

"If you want to tell me what exactly about my ID seems fake," I say, still somehow maintaining my composure, "then fine. But I don't think you'll be able to. Because it's not fake. It's real."

"All right, let's see." The woman is completely fed up at this point. "What seems fake is that you're standing in front of me and you're obviously too young to drink, so leave now or I'll escort you out myself."

The threat holds weight, as this woman does look stronger than both me and Bodhi combined.

"This is looks-based discrimination," Bodhi says. "You realize that, right? We could sue you."

"Yeah, great," the woman says, cracking her knuckles. "I'm sure you could. Best of luck with that."

Bodhi and I look at each other and shrug. It's not happening.

So we drive five minutes farther down the road to Vespucci Liquors, where the tattooed dude behind the counter looks at my ID for approximately eight-tenths of a second before selling us two cases of hard cider and a bottle of Absolut vodka.

And there it is: the first official perk of being a repeat sixteen-year-old.

Score.

LINCOLN

THE THIRD LOOP

Your fourth time being sixteen (the third time you looped back) was arguably the weirdest for me.

It was the year I became older than my older brother.

Only by a little, though: I had just turned sixteen in October, so it meant you and I were almost exactly the same age, some supremely twisted version of fraternal twins.

By then, Mom, Dad, and I had gotten somewhat used to how this went:

You woke up, psyched for your sixteenth birthday, completely unaware that you'd been that age for a while now and that the world had continued spinning and evolving even though you hadn't.

We weren't going to be caught off guard like the previous year, when it hadn't even occurred to us that you might loop back *a second time*. No, this time we were prepared, even as we of course hoped that maybe the loop *was* finished, that it was a limited-time thing and you would triumphantly emerge from your bedroom crowing, "I'm seventeen! And I remember yesterday!"

That didn't happen.

Instead, I lay under the covers staring at the ceiling, a hard knot of dread in my stomach as I heard you whistle your way to the bathroom and start the shower. I waited to take my turn until I heard you leave the bathroom and shut your bedroom door, like you were the horror movie ghoul I was desperately trying to avoid.

I wanted to put off the Moment of Realization, followed by our parents' Faux-Calm Explanation, for as long as possible. I knew nothing could match the awfulness of that first loop day, when we had no idea what the hell was happening, but the previous year's wasn't really much better. Your birthday had quickly become my least favorite day of the year.

"Yo, Link," you said upon my entrance to the kitchen, chunks of brown sugar cinnamon Pop-Tart crumbing from your mouth onto the table.

"Happy birthday, CT." My voice was actually shaking because I truly didn't want to be doing this again. Mom and Dad weren't even downstairs yet; they were obviously dreading it too.

"Did you . . . get a haircut or something?" you asked, your expressive eyebrows pressing downward.

"Um," I said, listening for our parents' footsteps on the stairs so I wouldn't have to explain this on my own.

"You look, like . . . different."

"Yeah," I said, opening up the fridge, mainly as a way to hide. "I do look different."

"Well, it looks good! Actually makes you look older."

I wanted to crawl into the fridge, curl into a ball, and wedge myself between the orange juice and the milk. I could reemerge later that day. Or next week.

"Hey, bud," Dad said, finally appearing in his assistant principal uniform—button-down, tie, and khakis—with Mom right behind him. "Happy b-day."

"Whaddup, Dad!" you said. "Your firstborn is sixteen today!

Glad you didn't forget. That's what happens in the movie *Sixteen Candles.* It's old. You probably haven't even heard of it, Lincoln."

You were technically right—I wouldn't have heard of it, if you hadn't said the exact same thing on your previous three birthdays.

Mom and Dad exchanged a look, which I knew meant, *Okay, here we go.* Mom gave me a nod. I nodded back. It was as if we were all about to get on a roller coaster. In a way, we'd been on one from the moment you first regressed, and here we were approaching another big drop. Another big loop.

"Carter," Mom said, taking a seat at the round table. "There's something we need to talk to you about."

"Oh boy." You flipped the last nub of Pop-Tart onto your tongue. "Are we doing the birds and the bees talk again? Are there details you think I'm still not aware of?"

"It's not the birds and the bees talk," Dad said, sitting on your other side and gesturing for me to sit too.

I slowly lowered into a chair, even though I wanted to sprint out of the room. Out of the state.

"You really do look older," you said to me, a note of disgust in your voice. "It's weirding me out a little."

"That's actually a great segue." Dad folded his hands on the table as if he were discussing plans for a funeral. "Lincoln looks older because . . . he *is* older."

You narrowed your eyes and scanned them over the three of us.

"Lincoln is your age," Mom said. She gestured for me to speak, as if that was going to somehow solve this.

"Yeah," I said. "I'm sixteen."

"You—" Mom tried to speak, but her voice got too wobbly to continue.

"You have a condition, Carter," Dad said. "You can't age past sixteen. This is your third loop, your fourth time having this birthday."

You burst into laughter. You actually threw your head back before slapping the table. "You guys decided to celebrate me turning sixteen with a time-loop prank? Giving Lincoln a new haircut and making *him* look sixteen? That's so bad it might actually be good."

"It really isn't a prank," Dad said.

"Ha!"

As you can imagine, things went on like that for a while.

We were both late for school.

Our parents had already prepared for the next part, following the playbook they'd crafted the year before with our principal Mr. Nguyen: You would return to Ms. Destin's sophomore homeroom in order to have one familiar element in your school life. Lucky for me, I was not in that homeroom. You and I had only one class together that year—geometry—and thank god, because otherwise *both* of us may not have made it to age seventeen.

I'd known for a while that I was a better student than you, and I'd known for a while that our parents knew it too. They'd made it annoyingly clear with comments to you about applying yourself like your brother does, about not being so afraid of failure that you didn't try at all.

I remember the first time that happened. I was in third grade and you were in sixth. I came home with a hundred on a math test, and Mom and Dad were so psyched.

"See?" Mom said to you. "You could do this too, Carter—you study, you do the work, you get a hundred. It's not hard."

I was stupidly proud in that moment. Here, finally, was something I did better than you. In my mind, you were untouchable in so many ways—first and foremost by, like, being a charming, funny person who had a fearless ease when interacting with others. I could never even begin to fathom how to do that. So I actually thought *you* might be excited about my score too.

"Wow," you said, sarcasm tendrils creeping like vines into your words. "Way to go, Linky." Then you flicked my ear really hard and laughed.

So, now, being in the same grade, doing the same work, even sharing the same car—Dad's old Toyota Corolla, the one you named Rex—I knew it wouldn't go well.

And it didn't. You gave up trying in school very early in that loop, instead choosing to channel your energy into being a perpetually annoying brother.

"Cool if I drive?" I asked one night in May when we went together to pick up dinner from this nearby Thai place.

"Nah, sorry," you said, holding out the key and unlocking the car. "Older brother gets dibs."

"Right," I said. "But, I mean, technically, I *am* older now."

"Dude. Are you seriously gonna play that card? I have a condition."

"Okay, fine," I said, even though I didn't see what the big deal was if I drove the seven minutes to Lucky Thai.

"You drive like a grandma anyway," you said as we got into the car. "No offense."

I knew it was true—I was and am an overly cautious driver—but it still felt dickish to call it out like that. And I did take offense.

I silently stared out the window as we pulled out of the

driveway, thinking maybe we could avoid talking.

"Do you have a crush on Teddy Landerham?" you asked, this grin in your voice.

Apparently talking was unavoidable.

"Why?" I asked. "I don't even know if he's gay."

"I know, I know. It just seems like you guys have a good connection. When you're talking at lunch."

"Oh." My neck heated up, secretly thrilled that you had picked up on this. I *did* have a crush on Teddy Landerham, but it was too risky to straight up tell you that. Secret-keeping had never been your thing. "Maybe. He's cool, but . . . I don't know."

"I could ask him out for you if you want." You took your eyes off the road to wiggle your eyebrows at me.

"That won't be necessary. Ever."

"I gotta say," you said, "it's kind of amazing being twins with you. Getting to observe you up close in your natural habitat."

"Yeah, it's fun," I lied. It wasn't a complete lie—we'd had some great moments together that year. Mostly, though, I felt that becoming the same age had been a very bad thing for our relationship. The dynamic was all off, and you didn't even seem to realize.

"Whoa," you said. "It just occurred to me: If we figure out how to cure this thing and get me to seventeen, we'll be twins forever."

"Oh yeah," I said, gripping the handle above the window. That could not happen. I could not allow that to happen. "I know I say this all the time, but I really am sorry you're going through this."

"Hey, thanks, Link," you said. "It does suck very much. But, you know, not your fault."

"Yeah. Well."

I watched Scoops 'n' Sprinkles move in and out of my view, which meant we were just two minutes from the Thai place.

"Does feel like I should try to make lemonade out of lemons, though, right?" you said. "Like, since I'm kind of famous for my condition, I should probably use that to make bank as an influencer or something, right?"

"You did that last year, actually. It didn't go great."

"For real? What happened?"

"You know, what you'd expect. You got tons of followers, and then there was a backlash. People saying you were lying about your condition, that you were just pretending to be sixteen over and over again for attention. And you got super anxious keeping track of what everyone was saying, and you could never be apart from your phone, so Mom and Dad had to confiscate it, and you were so pissed, et cetera et cetera."

"Oh god. That sounds horrible."

"It was."

You were silent for a few seconds. "Maybe," you finally said, "you were just jealous of all my followers."

You poked your fingers into my rib cage, which made me laugh against my will because, as you know well, I'm very ticklish.

"Definitely not," I said, pressing myself against the car door as I continued laughing. "And stop."

"I don't know if I can." You tickled me even more intensely. "This is my responsibility as your brother."

"Seriously, CT. Fucking stop!"

"All right, all right, geez—"

"STOP! STOP!"

Distracted by your moronic tickle attack, you drove straight through a red light. A car was coming at us from the left, but you slammed on the gas just in time to fly past it and instead crash into a streetlight approximately fifty feet from our destination.

The air bags came out, we both experienced some minor whiplash, and the front of Rex was demolished. The people at the auto repair shop told Mom and Dad it could be fixed, but it was going to be so expensive that they decided to just buy us another used car instead.

And that pretty much sums up the third loop.

MAGGIE

Shana and I are walking out of school through the main entrance, deep in a heated discussion about the set list for our first gig—she wants to open with "No, Thank You," which I think is a horrible idea—when I see Carter. He's hanging out with Bodhi, Robbie, and Amir near the big tree. They're doing what they do: talking loudly, laughing even loudly-er, and radiating the overly confident, obviously insecure energy of peacocking teenage boys. I knew it was only a matter of time before Carter found his way back to Bodhi.

It definitely makes it easier to stay away. These first weeks back to school have felt infinitely better than those tragic days before the holidays. The distraction of Mom's engagement to Ron turned out to be really helpful, both because it meant Mom was in the Best Mood of All Time and because it gave me something to bitch about that wasn't Carter. Plus, Vivian being home generally makes everything better. So I came into January on good footing, and every time I've passed Carter in the hall has felt slightly less eventful than the time before; I don't even look over anymore.

It's impossible not to notice him right now, though. He is King Bonehead, doing over-the-top impressions of teachers and intentionally bad parkour moves off the tree trunk as he gets huge laughs from the hyenas. He is a funny person, but this obnoxious brand of comedy has always felt cheap to me.

Shana takes Carter in, I know she does, but she continues with our conversation, subtly shifting our path to the parking lot so we won't pass as close to him. "Starting with a ballad is a bomb move," she says. "You pull in the audience, make them lean forward to take in our tender melody, then hit 'em hard the next song with some *rawk*. Blow their faces off. And blow their minds too."

"Yeah, no, I get all that," I say, fighting to concentrate solely on her. "But I worry an opening like that will just put everybody to sleep—"

I stop speaking because Carter is waving at me.

At least that's what it looks like.

"Lindsey!" he says, looking straight at me as he leaps and grabs a tree branch, kicking his legs in random directions. "Right?"

My heart pounds. Fast.

Shana gasps. I'm frozen, my heart the only part of me in motion. It's thumping like I just finished a race.

Carter grins as he hangs from the branch like he's the subject of an inspirational cat poster. "Anyway, whoever you are, how's it goin'?"

I nod like a bobblehead and mutter a nonsense response: "Uh, yes."

"Keep walking," Shana hisses in my ear as she gives my torso a gentle shove. "Just keep walking."

Carter loses his grip on the branch and falls on his ass, which gets a monster laugh from the hyenas—actually just Robbie and Amir, Bodhi is looking at his phone—and helps thaw me out enough so I remember how to walk.

Or speed-walk, as the case may be, since Shana is pushing me along like a shopping cart at a Black Friday sale.

"What was that?" Shana asks once we've made it safely into her car and are pulling away from the school. "Why is he waving at you? Have you been waving at him?"

"Of course not!" I sputter. "I've been avoiding him!"

"Oh Christ. Someone told him about you."

I think about Bodhi looking at his phone. That twerp. He said he wouldn't say anything!

"Well," Shana says, taking the ramp onto Route 51, "he clearly doesn't know all that much, considering he thought your name was Lindsey. So you just need to play it cool. Cooler than cool. Ice-cool."

"You mean ice-*cold*."

"Sure, if that phrasing is more helpful for you. Whatever you need to do to avoid falling for him again."

She's right. Of course she's right.

But the freakiest part of Carter waving and shouting at me was how *exciting* it was.

My heart didn't just pound; it leaped out of my chest and landed on the pavement, pulsing blood squirts onto my white Nikes.

Minutes later, I'm still not okay. My brain is sideways, my hands are unsteady, and, even if you paid me a hundred dollars, I wouldn't be able to focus enough to return to whatever conversation we were having.

The car stops. We've pulled into a spot in the Costco parking lot.

"Okay, so I have something," Shana says.

"Oh boy."

"No, it's good. You'll approve. It's directly related to you needing to be ice-cool."

"Ice-cold," I say.

"Right. So my family's going skiing this weekend."

"We hate skiing."

"That's right, we do," Shana agrees. "With a passion. Which is why I convinced them I should stay home."

"I see."

"Do you?"

"You want us to . . . do band practice at your place?" I ask. "And we can be loud as hell?"

"No. I mean, yes, that too. Good idea. But the reason we are parked here at this moment in time is because I just decided there will be a party. We need a party."

"Oh no, Shane. Do we?"

"WE DO. So we are going to stock up on some supplies. In bulk. And we are going to forget about swinging-from-a-tree-branch boy and *live* our freaking lives."

"The October party got so nuts, though."

Shana gives me a deadpan stare. "Like you know anything about that party. You were making out with tree-branch boy the whole time."

The grin appears on my face before I can wipe it away. Carter and I snuck into Shana's younger brother's room and pretty much spent the whole party in there, messing around beneath Adem's *Stranger Things* poster. Damn you, make-out memories.

"Sorry I brought that up," Shana says. "But actually, here's something else I have for you: Marigold wants to set you up with this guy she knows."

"Marigold?"

She's a weird girl who graduated last year. Shana's stayed in touch with her much more than I have.

"Why are we trusting Marigold's judgment? Have you seen the people she dates?"

"I have." Shana laughs. "But she's much better at matchmaking for other people than she is for herself. She was the one who introduced me to Bella!"

"You and Bella lasted two months."

"Yeah, but that first month was—" Shana nods a few times and smiles. "And that's what *you* need, Mags. Doesn't have to be a long-term fit. Just someone who's hot enough and interesting enough to sweep you off your feet for a minute. Take your mind off . . . other folks."

"I'll think about it." I step out of the car as a way to end the conversation.

"He's apparently super attractive and has his shit together," Shana says, also out of the car and following me toward the Costco entrance. "Marigold met him at school."

"Fine," I say with a sigh. "What'd you say his name was again?"

"I didn't. It's Chord."

"Great. I will consider the possibility of being set up with Chord. He sounds like a real catch." I'm only saying this to be nice. I can't imagine being with anyone right now.

"Yay! Marigold says he's free to come to the party Saturday."

"What? I thought you *just* decided to have the party now."

Shana shrugs and smiles. We cross the threshold of Costco and she makes a beeline toward the frozen appetizer aisle. I should've been on to her instantly. But I know she's looking out for me. And she's probably right. This is what I need.

Ice-cold, I think as I watch Shana awkwardly grab a box of 128 mozzarella sticks out of the freezer. *Ice-cold*.

CARTER

"Yo, dude, you are the fricking *man,*" this long-haired sophomore Everett says as I hand him the three boxes of vape juice he requested.

"They didn't have Strawberry Peach Banana Bash, so I just got you the Raspberry Dragon Melon. Hope that's all right."

"Oh yeah, absolutely," Everett says. "I love dragons."

I look around the school parking lot to make sure that standing behind my car is properly concealing us from any administrative authority figures hanging around after school. "Though, I feel like it's also my responsibility to inform you that vaping is actually quite destructive for your health. But, ya know, it's your call."

Everett cracks up as he unscrews the top of his vape pen and opens one of the new boxes. "You're fricking funny, dude."

So Mom and Dad were right—I kept an open mind, and school has become a lot more interesting. I've found my purpose.

And that purpose is to be the fricking man.

Once Bodhi opened my eyes to the power of my state ID (when shown to the right people) (a.k.a. NOT the scary lady at Buy Rite), everything changed. In the span of three short weeks, I've somehow—well, it's because Bodhi told everybody—become the go-to guy at Ridgedale High for all your illicit needs. You want beer? I'm on it. Hard cider? Sure! Vodka? No problem. Weed gummies? You betcha! Or, in the case of this giggling skater boy taking a deep pull from his newly replenished magenta vape pen: Here, have some fruity smoke juice!

My condition means I have a special talent. Or, at least, something I can do that few others can. Which means other kids actually, like, *need* me.

It's a good feeling.

Bodhi and I have turned it into a quasi business. Depending on the request, people will pay an extra $5, or $10, even $20, so that we can procure items that their age would otherwise prevent them from procuring. Or sometimes the payment is just giving us a can of whatever they're drinking, and that's fine too.

I've discovered that alcohol can be fun.

I'm not out of control with it or anything, but after that first successful mission at Vespucci Liquors, Bodhi and I sat in his bedroom downing hard ciders, and I was able to forget about the shitty reality of my existence. We just drank and laughed and watched stupid videos of people puking after eating ghost peppers.

Since Lincoln's back at college, I'm extra grateful for Bodhi. Without him, I don't know what I'd be doing. Probably sitting around like a lonely, depressed piece of human furniture. Instead, I've got Bodhi, and Robbie and Amir, and we act like idiots together.

And earn some spending money by taking advantage of my special gift.

"You're so lucky, bruh," Everett says after a poorly aimed exhale that slams me in the face with a sickly sweet stream of air.

"Why's that?"

"'Cause you get to be sixteen forever. But with all the legal powers of being an adult. That's, like, sick as hell."

"It's—" I'm about to launch into a rant about why the reality of what I'm experiencing is much closer to the traditional definition of the word *sick* than the one he means. But it's clearly not what he wants to hear. And in some ways, I can see how he's right. "Totally sick as hell."

"So jealous, man."

As I get in the car and start driving home, I listen to a voice memo Bodhi just sent.

"Heyyyy," he says. "Got a new request through Amir. It's pretty dope. Some senior needs us to be the keg hookup for her party Saturday. She's willing to pay us fifty smackers! We'd just have to get two kegs, which I think they sell at Vespucci? So it should be easy. Or, if not there, they'll definitely have them at the brewery. That dude with the lazy eye loves us. And here's the best part: If we do it, we're *totally welcome at the party.* I bet we'll be some of the only juniors. Oh shoot, you're a sophomore again. So that's even cooler! You'll for sure be the only sophomore. I'm so hype. Let me know if you're in."

I nod and smile, as if Bodhi can see me or something. A party sounds nice.

I cue up "Old Town Road" on my phone and reroute the car toward Vespucci Liquors.

MAGGIE

I can't fall asleep.

Even though I've been steadfast in my determination to avoid Carter since he waved at me a few days ago, he always seems to worm his way into my brain every night as I'm lying in bed.

Lindsey! Right?

It's actually Maggie! I shout back at him in my mind. *Let's make out once more and then never see each other again, 'kay?*

Luckily, every time I'm in one of these missing-Carter moments, I have a surefire antidote for eliminating the feeling: I remind myself of our last night together. The night before he forgot me.

It was less than two months ago, but it feels like another lifetime.

We ate at the Cheesecake Factory. We considered going somewhere fancier, like this Italian place Vincenzo's that makes all their pasta fresh, but we decided a more casual dinner was the more optimistic choice—if we made less of a big deal of our evening, then maybe it would, in fact, turn out to be not that big a deal. Maybe the next day Carter would wake up seventeen, and we would still be a couple.

But as I took bites of my Thai chicken salad, it was hard not to think about the distinct possibility that Carter would forget me by the morning, along with every experience we'd had together.

We didn't talk about that, though.

Instead, we discussed stupid stuff. Meaningless stuff. Carter wondered aloud about who invented the saltshaker. I told him it was Edna Shaker, which I knew because I'm related to her, that she's like fifteen generations back on my dad's side. Carter laughed and said he was so honored to know me. We then proceeded to share this made-up fact with our server, a nice bald dude named Rich, who seemed genuinely astounded.

Like I said, stupid stuff.

After dinner, we got into Toro—Carter's car—so Carter could drive us to his house. Where we were maybe going to have sex for the first time.

I say maybe because we'd gone back and forth about the question of sex a lot. Like, on my end, I felt like it might not be wise to do this incredibly special thing together if Carter was going to forget about it soon after.

Part of me was thinking we should wait until Carter turned seventeen.

But the rest of me knew that might never happen, so why wait?

We'd never really landed on a decision.

And we both knew that night might be our last chance.

"I'm gonna play something for you," I said as soon as we pulled out of the parking lot. I knew I would lose my nerve if I didn't do it right away.

I plugged my phone into Toro's sound system and scrolled to the track.

I took a deep breath, like I was about to dive underwater, and pushed Play.

As the voice memo recording began, me plunking away at

piano keys, messing up, needing to start again, I curled up in an awkward ball in the front seat.

"Oh god," I said. "I meant to edit that out."

Carter didn't seem to mind. The girl on the track who sounded like me started to sing, and I felt even more self-conscious. This amateur recording featuring my amateur trembling voice singing my amateur, overly sincere lyrics about the person sitting next to me. I had to close my eyes and disassociate until the song ended.

We sat in silence for a moment.

"You wrote a song about me," Carter said quietly.

"I did," I said.

"Thank you." I couldn't tell how he felt about it. He was just staring straight ahead as he drove.

"Was that okay?" I'd made a mistake. I should never have played it for him.

"Of course," he said. "It was really . . . It was really great."

"But . . . ?"

"But nothing. You're an incredible musician, Mags. You sounded so good. And I love the song. I think it just made me feel . . . like, a little sad. About tomorrow."

I nodded, and then came the tears, as if they'd been patiently waiting in the wings for their cue. "I'm sad too, Coco."

"You're so great," he said, glancing at me for the first time since the song ended.

"So are you," I said. And then I knew the time had come. It was now or never. "I really think . . . I mean, I *know*, that . . . I love you, Carter."

"Oh," he said. He froze again behind the wheel, and my insides froze too.

"Yeah." I worried he was about to break up with me.

"Well," he said, what felt like three hours later. "I think . . . I feel that too. For you."

"Like . . . love?" I asked.

"Yeah. Like. Yeah. I love you. Too."

OHMIGOD HE SAID IT BACK TO ME.

I'd been waiting weeks for Carter to say those words. For all the clichéd reasons people want to hear them, yes, but also for another one:

I thought Carter might have just unstuck himself.

And I was so relieved and overjoyed that I lost myself a bit.

"This is amazing," I said, my eyes still glassy, my hand on the back of his neck.

"Is it?" Carter turned us onto his block. "I probably won't even know who you are tomorrow."

"You might, though. I think you really might."

"I love the optimism, Mags, but there's no reason to think this time I will—"

"You said *I love you*, Carter! And you meant it." The words spilled out of my mouth like loose change off a dresser.

"Wait," he said, pulling the car over to the curb in front of his house. "So what? What does that have to do with me making it to seventeen tomorrow?"

My mind couldn't scramble fast enough to come up with a legitimate-sounding excuse. "Well," I said, "I have this theory. But it's not—"

"You have a *theory*?" Carter seemed very annoyed. "You mean about how to fix me? And you didn't think I might want to know?"

"No, I couldn't tell you because . . . Because then maybe it wouldn't work right. Like, you saying those words would have to happen on its own! Not because I told you about it. You know?"

"Not really!" Carter ran his hands through his hair. "What in the actual fuck, Maggie? You think if I said *I love you* it would break the spell or something? Like my life is a Disney movie? Why would you even think that?"

I couldn't tell him why I thought that. Or I could, but I didn't want to. "It's . . . I don't know. I learned some stuff from Lincoln."

"You were talking to *Lincoln* about this?"

"Only a little!"

"Jesus, Maggie."

"The night before you first looped, you dumped some girl, okay? Apparently she said 'I love you' and you—you didn't say it back. Your response was, 'Oh wow. That's really awkward because I actually want to break up.'"

Carter pressed his index fingers against his closed eyelids and groaned. "And you think that caused all this?"

"I don't know," I said, suddenly questioning everything. "Maybe that's insane."

"So you've just been waiting for me to . . . Did you even mean those words when you said them? Or was this just all part of the plan?"

"Of course I did!" I shouted. He needed to know how much I cared. "I love you, Carter. I really love you. I just felt scared to say it. And I didn't want . . ."

"Me to say it just because you did? 'Cause then the magical spell wouldn't break?"

I grimaced and shrugged.

"Who was I dating?" Carter asked.

"What?"

"Who was the girl I broke up with?"

I was prepared for this question, on the off chance I messed up—LIKE I JUST DID—and it needed to be answered. "Layla Banerjee."

"*Layla Banerjee?* I've known her since kindergarten. We were dating?"

"Apparently," I said.

Carter shook his head and exhaled. "How could you know all this and not tell me any of it? I feel kinda . . . I don't know. It's hard to think that this is love if you were lying to me about all of this."

"No, please don't think that. I'm sorry." I wanted to throw up. What was supposed to be a Magical Night Together was rapidly turning into a devastating one. "I messed up. I thought I was doing the right thing." I put my hand on Carter's cheek and looked into his eyes, a streetlight shining on us through the windshield.

He seemed so disappointed.

I turned toward the window and sobbed.

"It's okay," Carter said. "Don't . . . I don't want you to feel sad about this. If what you're saying is right, then . . . then I'll be seventeen tomorrow, and we can figure all this out."

"And if I'm wrong . . . ?" I asked, staring out into the night, the dark shadows draped on his family's front lawn.

"Then we're screwed either way, I guess. On the bright side, I won't remember we had this argument."

His joke wasn't funny. It was excruciating.

"So what?" I asked, turning back to Carter. "Are we even gonna keep hanging out tonight? Or we're just gonna be mad at each other and then that'll be it? We see if you still know me in the morning?"

"I dunno," Carter said, tapping the steering wheel with his hand. "I guess we could still hang out. You mean, like . . . to have sex?"

"Oh wow. Doesn't get more romantic than that."

"Well, maybe having sex is part of breaking the spell, right? So we probably should."

It was like a smack in the face. "No," I said.

"But it could be true, right?" Carter asked. "Not that I would have any idea. Just my whole fucking life we're talking about."

"I said I was sorry! I made a mistake. I should've told you sooner."

"Yeah, you should've."

I saw tears forming in Carter's eyes, and I wished he would just let them fall. Instead, he turned and looked out his window.

I looked out mine.

We sat like that for a while. I'm not sure how long.

Eventually I felt Carter's hand clumsily grab for mine.

I grabbed back, and we looked at each other.

"I'm pretty scared," he said, and somehow this demolished my heart eighty times more than when we'd been yelling at each other.

"I am too."

We kept sitting there in his car. And then he kissed me. And I kissed him back.

We made out for a while.

Gently. Quietly. Sadly.

We didn't have sex.

Carter drove me home around nine thirty.

"I really do love you," I said.

He just nodded back at me, his mouth wobbling somewhere

in between a smile and a frown.

We shared one last long kiss over the gearshift.

Neither of us said goodbye.

I walked into my house. I cried.

He drove away.

And the next morning, Carter was a sixteen-year-old boy walking down the school hallway with no idea who I was.

So *that's* what I'm thinking about now as I lie here in bed, duvet tangled around my legs, battling the urge to kiss that tree-hanger who seemed to only sort of know who I am.

I cannot go back to that pain.

Must move forward.

I will go to Shana's party tomorrow night. I will meet this Chord guy.

I will have some good, old-fashioned Carter-free fun.

I will. I will.

I will.

I must.

CARTER

"Oh glorious day," Bodhi says as we pull up to the curb in front of a large yellow house. "I can't believe we're gonna get to go to this. Amir says the parties here are epic. That's what he heard, I mean. He's never been. *You* have, though."

"Seriously?" I say. "I've been to a party here?"

"Well. Maybe," Bodhi says. "I, um, don't know for sure. Probably not, actually. I think I'm thinking of someone else."

"Hmm, all right. Because that wasn't shady or anything."

"No, I just—I got confused. Let's go, they're probably waiting for us!" Bodhi throws open his door and bounds out of the car. I get out too and meet him at the trunk, pop it open.

"Just look at those beauties," Bodhi says, staring at the two kegs we just picked up from Vespucci Liquors, gleaming even under a rapidly darkening sky.

"Hi!" a voice calls. There's a girl standing on the front porch, pretty and solid, with long black hair and glittery eye shadow, wearing a light blue sweater. She looks vaguely familiar, but I'm not sure why. "You need help bringing those in? You're Amir's people, righ— Oh, come on." The girl suddenly drops the facade of politeness. "Bodhi? *You're* the hookup?"

"Uh, well, yeah. I mean, me and . . ." He points to me. "Shana, this is my friend Carter."

Shana puts her face in her hands and sighs. "Good to meet you,

Carter," she says with a forced smile, like she's reading the lines of a play she doesn't want to be in. "Bodhi, would you mind coming over here to speak to me? Privately?"

"What's going on right now?" I ask.

"Nothing, nothing, don't worry about it," Bodhi says, gently closing the trunk before hard-patting my shoulder like he's smacking a mosquito to death. "I got this, baby."

As he walks across the front lawn to Shana, I'm suddenly able to place her: She's Lindsey's friend. I mean, *Maggie's* friend. After I randomly waved at the runner girl earlier in the week, I decided to consult the yearbook. Her actual name is Maggie Spear. Shana is the one Maggie's always walking with in the hallway.

And I'm willing to bet that whatever Shana is ripping into Bodhi about right now, it involves Maggie. I wish I could hear what they're saying. Shana's doing most of the talking—big, dramatic gestures accompanied by a sharp, hushed whisper that keeps me from hearing any of the words. She sounds more like a sprinkler system than a person.

"I didn't!" Bodhi says. "I really didn't!"

She does some more aggressive whispering, and Bodhi responds, his voice quieter but still loud enough to understand.

"Well, if we go, the kegs go too."

More whisper attacks.

And then Bodhi is nodding. "I know. Of course. *Of course.* It won't be a problem, dude, I promise."

Shana says a few more things and points to him and makes the universal gesture for slit throat across her own neck before stomping inside and slamming the front door shut behind her.

Bodhi trots back across the lawn like a happy puppy, as if he hasn't just spent 180 seconds in a super intense conversation that ended with his life being threatened. "Okay, we can roll the kegs around the house to the backyard and then—"

"What was that about?"

"Huh?" Bodhi asks. "Oh, you mean the—with her over there? Nothing big, she just, uh, didn't want us at the party because . . . we're not seniors. But I convinced her it's okay. So we're good!"

"That's seriously the reason she flipped out at you? Because we're not seniors?"

"Well," Bodhi says, clearly thinking really hard even though he's trying to make it seem like he's not, "yeah. Ageism is rampant, I guess. Pretty messed up when you think about it."

"This is about Maggie, isn't it?" I ask. "Maggie Spear?"

Bodhi coughs twice. "Muggy? Who's Muggy?"

It's so obvious he's lying I want to laugh in his face.

"Really," Bodhi says. "Muggy Sphere? Who is that?"

"Dude, come on! *Maggie. Spear.* The cross-country girl who was in that photo I took. The one I waved to earlier this week. You thought her name was Lindsey?"

"Ohhhh," Bodhi says. "*That* Maggie. I thought you said Muggy Sphere."

"Yeah, okay. So obviously I have some history with this girl or something, and— Is she gonna be at the party? Is that the problem?"

Bodhi's eyes go wide for a split second. Then he regains his composure and his mask of skepticism. "Bruh, how the hell should I know if Maggie Steer—"

"Spear."

"If Maggie Sphere is gonna be at this party? Yes, I vaguely knew that was her in the picture because I know who people are at our school. Because I'm on yearbook. So it's my job to identify fellow students, get it? But it's not my job to track my classmates in their social life to parties and shit—"

"I know it's not your job to track people! I'm just asking if that's what Shana was over there hissing at you about. Should I not be here or something?"

"Well, yes, because you're a soph—"

"Right, right, because I'm a sophomore. Okay. Fine. Should we take these kegs to the backyard?"

"Definitely," Bodhi says.

I open the trunk back up.

"Oh, last thing." Bodhi puts an arm around my shoulders. "Shana doesn't want us staying here before the party officially starts."

"Doesn't it start in, like, twenty minutes?"

"Something like that. But she thinks, like . . . if *we're* there when people first arrive, they'll see we're not seniors and think it's not a cool party and leave. I respect that."

"You mean if we're here when *Maggie* arrives, she'll see me and—"

"Look, it's not my rule!" Bodhi shouts. "It's Shana's! And it's her house! So the alternative is skipping the party, which I know you wouldn't want."

"I mean, honestly, I'd be fine to not go to this."

"WE HAVE TO GO!" Bodhi's hands clutch his baseball-capped head in a panic. "We've worked so hard to get here, and I am not giving this up! And you aren't either!"

"Okay, okay," I say. "Calm down." I nod at a guy across the street who's glaring at us from his mailbox. He death-stares a second longer before grabbing his mail and walking up his driveway. "So we'll drop off these kegs and go hang out somewhere else for a while. It's all right. Everything's totally all right."

Bodhi takes a few deep breaths with his eyes closed before giving me a hug. "Thanks, man. This party really means a lot to me."

"Yeah. I'm getting that."

We work together to heave the kegs out of the trunk one at a time and roll them on their side into Shana's backyard.

They're incredibly heavy.

MAGGIE

"Come," Shana says, pulling me by the arm, "we need to check on the snack table."

"Do we, though?"

We're an hour into the party, and the bass is bumping, and the beer is sloshing, and the rooms are filling up, and it's seeming like it's going to be even more insane than the October one.

But Shana's being a weirdo. She's all jumpy and anxious—this is the fourth random task she's brought me along for out of nowhere. "Mags, let's go see who just walked in." "Should we make a new playlist?" "Oh shoot, come with me. Need to make sure the bathroom is clean."

I'm sorry, but mid-party toilet tidying is not something we've ever done before, nor do I think it's necessary. If you're looking for an immaculate bathroom, maybe don't go to a high school house party.

"Yup," I say once we've arrived at the snack table. "They're still snacks."

"Yeah, but—" Shana puts down her red Solo cup so she can slightly re-angle the bowl of tortilla chips, shift over the salsa a few millimeters, and grab a paper towel from the kitchen to wipe clean some smudges and crumbs before adjusting the gigantic basket of now-cold mozzarella sticks.

"Are you okay?" I ask, taking a sip of gross-tasting beer from my cup.

"Yeah, why?" She swaps the positions of the chips and salsa.

"Because you seem to have lost your mind. Why do we keep bouncing from room to room like lunatics? These snacks do not need us. Are you even having fun?"

"Me?" Shana asks, finally looking up from her frenzy of reorganization. "Of course! Do I not seem like it? Woooo!! Party time!!" Shana throws her arms in the air and accidentally knocks the entire basket of mozzarella sticks to the ground. "Dammit."

"Is one of your exes here or something?" I ask as we kneel on the ground, picking up gelatinous sticks of breaded cheese. "Bella? Meagan? Phineas? You can tell me."

"No, no, none of my exes are here. Especially not Phineas. Blech. I just want things to look good. That's all."

I'm considering the slight emphasis she placed on the word *my* when there's a roar of laughter and hooting from behind us in the family room, the very room we left minutes ago. I step toward the noise like a moth to flame, and as Shana shouts, "No, Mags! Wait!" the puzzle pieces slide into place—she hasn't needed my help, she needs me to switch locations, like I'm one of the bowls on that goddamn snack table—until, with a horrifying click, I understand exactly who it is I'm going to see inside this impromptu ring of chanting, cheering, intoxicated peers.

Not Shana's ex.

My ex.

There's Carter, doing the worm in the middle of the room, undulating his body across the Demirs' family room rug as everyone shouts his name and says he's funny as hell. His routine doesn't end there, transitioning into some kind of handstand thing, where he kicks his legs into the air like a donkey, followed by a roll onto his back, crunching his legs in and trying to spin around like a turtle.

I've seen him do moves like these before, back when I found them hilarious and charming, but now I just find them gross. Carter's eating up every bit of attention, and he's obviously drunk, which I hate, and of course twerpy Bodhi is here too, leading the cheer squad along with those hyenas Amir and Robbie and WHY ARE THEY AT THIS PARTY?

"I'm sorry, Mags," Shana says, appearing at my shoulder. "I'm so sorry. He's not supposed to be here."

"So you thought you'd just keep migrating me through the party all night every time he got close?"

"I didn't know what else to do!"

"Why is he even here?"

"Well," Shana says, her face tightening like she's preparing for me to scream at her, "it turns out Carter was our beer hookup."

"WHAT?"

"I didn't know! Really! This guy Amir was the hookup—he found me by my locker and said he heard I needed kegs and that he could take care of it, and I said, 'Sweet,' and that was it. But it turns out he was working with Carter!"

"Why are you surprised by this? We've seen Amir and Carter together multiple times in the past two weeks!"

"We have?"

"Yes!"

"That's interesting." Shana brushes a hand through her hair, what she always does when she's nervous. "I guess whenever we see Carter, I'm too focused on getting you to a new location to actually notice who he's with."

The crowd flips out as Carter starts twerking. Good god.

"This is my guy!" football captain Chris Colasurdo shouts.

"This is bad," Shana says. "And I apologize. I'm gonna have to murder Bodhi. I told him he was only allowed to be here if he made sure Carter was never in the same room as you."

"How is that even remotely realistic? This house doesn't have enough rooms."

"I know! But we really needed the kegs. Want me to tell Carter to leave? I will. I'll tell him he has to leave."

"No, no," I say, my fiery indignation simmering down into resignation. "If you tell him to leave, it just makes a big thing of it, and everyone will wonder what happened, and *he'll* wonder what happened, and it's not worth it. I'll go."

"You can't go!" Shana says. "I need you here!"

"Shana." I take her hand. "You're such a good friend. And I appreciate the anxiety spiral you've sent yourself down to protect me. But this isn't your fault."

"It sort of is."

Now Carter is bringing other people into the dance circle, doing a flirty tango thing with Tatiana Robinson that I wish I could unsee.

"It sort of is, yes, but my point is I love you, and we're both going to have more fun if I get the hell out of—"

"Paging Dr. Demir," a voice interrupts from behind us. "Paging Dr. Spear. You're both needed in the emergency room, stat."

There's only one person who would greet us in such a bizarre way.

"Marigold!" Shana shouts, giving our old friend a huge hug. I definitely wouldn't have recognized her based on appearance—her shoulder-length light brown hair is gone, replaced by a closely shaven scalp with a light blue faux-hawk spiking up from the top.

It's kind of insane but also feels more *her* than any of her previous looks.

"What's up, kiddo?" Marigold says. She turns from Shana and wraps me in a hug. "Oh, my sweet Maggot, how have you been?"

"I'm okay," I say. "Still hate that nickname."

"Sorry about that." She leans in closer to whisper into my ear. "But I come bearing a gift."

I notice the tall, very attractive guy standing behind Marigold on the threshold of the kitchen. In all the Carter chaos, I completely forgot about the setup guy.

But, seeing as I must leave the premises, this timing is not ideal.

"Shana, Maggie," Marigold says, raising her voice to be heard over the music and the still-ongoing dance circle, "this is my compatriot, Chord Ramirez. He is a stellar human being."

"Hey," he says, leaning in to shake our hands, which is when I realize that, besides being superhot and a few inches taller than me and dressed in a fuchsia button-down shirt made of a fabric so nice that it shimmers, Chord also smells very good. Like a very manly tea.

"Hi," I say. Behind him, Shana nods at me with her eyebrows way up, like, *Wow, yes, you need to make out with this guy. Stat!*

"Wild party, huh?" Chord asks with a dash of irony, gesturing over to the crowd now jumping up and down to the music, randomly chucking a big couch pillow back and forth in the air like a beach ball.

"That's one word for it," I say.

"I haven't been to a high school rager in so long," Marigold says. "They're so cute!"

"Condescending much?" Shana asks.

"No, I really mean it! Look at them bouncing around over

there like adorable schoolchildren."

"Maggie, right?" Chord says, giving my arm a gentle touch just below the shoulder that sends a small chill ricocheting down my vertebrae.

"Yes," I say. "Me Maggie."

"Would you mind showing me where the beverages are at?"

This is too much. Yes, Chord is a good-looking man-boy with a thin layer of stubble that I would be intrigued to run my hand over, but Carter is fifteen feet away and drunk in the other room, and none of this feels right. "Actually, I'm about to head—"

Shana's eyes go wide as she mouths a silent *WHAT?*

I see her point.

I don't know if I've ever *stood* next to a guy as put-together as Chord, let alone *kissed* one.

"To the place where the beverages are!" I say, finishing the sentence with way too much gusto. "As I, too, am in need of another." I take a few giant gulps from my beer. It is a mild torture that ends with me coughing for fifteen seconds after some of the beer goes down the wrong pipe.

"You all right?" Chord asks with genuine concern.

"I am," I say once I can speak again. "I am all right, Chord Ramirez."

I lead him through the kitchen to the back door. As we step outside onto the patio where the kegs are, there's a loud thud from the family room behind us. This is followed by a chorus of *Oh!*

"Well, that didn't sound good," Chord says.

"No, sir," I say, handing him a red Solo cup and trying to pretend we're on a small island far away from everything and everyone happening inside Shana's house. "It most certainly did not."

CARTER

"Come on," Bodhi says, pushing me toward the kitchen.

"What? Why?"

"Because. We need to hit up the keg again!"

"I actually don't." My red plastic cup is still halfway full.

"Okay, fine. But *I* need to hit up the keg again! And I want some company!"

After killing time before the party by walking around a series of nearby streets and cul-de-sacs in the dead of winter like a couple of creepers, we finally entered the house around seven thirty. The beats were going, and there were already at least twenty people there, but none of them was Maggie Spear. Not like I was looking *that* hard for her, but after seeing that girl Shana flip out on Bodhi, it was hard not to feel like *Something is going on here, so, uh, what the hell is it?*

We got our first beers from the keg, me and Bodhi both pouring mostly foam until a girl with headphones around her neck showed us the right way to do it. Amir and Robbie arrived not long after we did, seeming every bit as psyched to be there as Bodhi was, eyes wide like little kids in Magic Kingdom, hoping to catch a glimpse of Elsa.

"That's Eric Rogers," Amir quietly pointed out with awe as we stood in a hallway, people-watching, awkwardly bouncing to the music, and sipping our beers. "He's the student council VP."

"Check it," Robbie said, flicking his bangs toward the other room. "Janessa Suher. She's the point guard on the basketball team."

It's been twenty or so minutes of that until now, when Bodhi is suddenly desperate to get back to the keg even though I can see his cup, like mine, still has liquid in it.

"YO!"

We're stopped on our way through the kitchen to the patio by this muscular, vaguely Captain America–looking dude. Except he has a wider face.

"You wanna know what's in this?" he asks with a smile, shaking a flask in the air.

"Uh, alcohol?" I say.

"That's what I was gonna guess too!" Bodhi agrees. "I think it's alcohol."

"It's the vodka you got me!" the guy says.

I *knew* I recognized him. I've been getting stuff for so many people the past couple weeks, it's hard to keep everyone straight.

"Oh, sweet," I say.

"Really appreciate it, man. Grey Goose is the *shit*! Here, have a swig! As a token of my gratitude."

I stare at the flask he's holding in my face. I've never actually had vodka before. At least not that I remember.

"I'll take one if he doesn't want it," Bodhi says.

"No, I want it." I take a chug from the flask, and OHMIGOD vodka tastes insane. It's like I just swallowed gasoline and now it's lit a fire in my stomach. "Thanks," I say in a raspy voice.

"Good, right?" Wide-Faced Captain America says.

"Can I still get some too?" Bodhi asks.

"Nah, sorry," the guy says, screwing the cap back on his flask.

"Shit's expensive. Thanks again, Carter. Guess this always-sixteen thing is finally giving you some sweet perks. I'm gonna tell everybody you're here, they're gonna be pumped."

He pats me on the back and walks away.

"Oh, dude, my dude," Bodhi says, completely giddy as we head out into the cold winter air of the patio. "Do you even know who that was?"

"I mean, kinda. His name is Chris, I think?"

"You *think*? That's not just any Chris. That's Chris Colasurdo, the goddamn quarterback of the goddamn football team. And he's pumped to see *you*! This is dreams! This is a movie! This is movie dreams!"

"Cool," I say, all nonchalant, even as I feel this rush of validation, like maybe there's hope for me to be known as more than that kid with the messed-up age regression disorder. Maybe I can be that kid who brings joy into everyone's lives.

"Carter!" this cute girl at the keg says as she pours herself a beer. "So great that you're here!"

"So great that *you're* here!" I say, vaguely remembering that maybe I bought her some . . . hard lemonade?

"And great that I'm here too!" Bodhi says.

"I'm Lizzy." The girl waves the hand that's not holding the tap. "You got my friend Tatiana those edibles. They were clutch. Thank you."

"Hey," I say with an aw-shucks shrug. "It's what I do."

"Who do you think got this keg you're currently extracting from?" Bodhi asks.

"Whaaaat?" Lizzy says. "That's dope. Seriously. Cheers to *that*." She clinks her full plastic cup against mine and then Bodhi's as she walks back inside. "See you in there."

"You know we will!" Bodhi shouts, giddier than ever as he starts pouring more beer into his cup. "Dude, she was getting mad flirty with you!"

"Come on." I realize I'm starting to shiver because we've been standing outside all this time without our coats on. "She wasn't flirting. She's just happy I helped her get high."

"I dunno," Bodhi says. "I think she was, and that means other seniors will likely be flirting too, and I want to be there when it happens so I can ride the hell out of your coattails."

"You really found a way to make that expression sound inappropriate," I say. We both start laughing, and Bodhi fills my cup to the top, and I take a large sip, and a new song starts playing inside, and I don't recognize it—which, let's face it, is unsurprising, seeing as there's a six-year gap in my musical awareness—but I like it. I want to be back in the house, moving to the sound of those bouncing synths.

I step back into the kitchen, apparently before Bodhi is ready, as he darts ahead of me, shouting, "Wait! Let me lead the way, just to . . ."

"Just to what?"

"To make sure you get a proper entrance!"

Bodhi is a strange person, but meeting him has undeniably made my life better. And if he has a weird thing about needing to be the line leader, I can live with that.

"Turn!" Bodhi says, spinning around to literally grab me by the shoulders and redirect me just as we're about to pass a snack table that features an unsettlingly massive pile of mozzarella sticks.

"I know this may be surprising," I say as I shrug his hands off, "but being stuck at age sixteen does not mean I don't know how to turn while walking."

"Ha ha ha!" Bodhi laughs in this obviously fake way as he slides behind me and nudges me toward the family room, which has gotten packed in the time we were gone. "Sorry, it's just a fun game I like to play. It's called steer your friend!"

"I don't like that game."

"Most people don't!" Bodhi shouts, and then we're crossing the threshold into the family room. Chris Colasurdo is shouting my name, and everyone's eyes shift in my direction. A wave of raucous cheer rises up and splashes down on us, and it's because of *me*.

That rad song is still playing, and I start bouncing my head. Chris hands me his flask again, and even though I don't want any more gasoline juice, I take a swig because it seems like the right thing to do. There's another eruption of joyful noise, and the vodka doesn't burn as much this time, and now I'm moving my arms, and people are *loving* it.

They're all drifting to the sides, as if giving me room to show off my stuff, so I guess I gotta show off my stuff! I ask Bodhi to hold my beer, but first I take another chug, which gets another reaction, and look, Robbie and Amir are here too, and if I don't do something soon, people are gonna get bored of me, so here goes nothing.

I crouch low and take a flying leap into the air, like I'm about to dive into an empty swimming pool, but instead I put out both hands and catch myself, controlling my body and swooping my torso up while my legs ripple like a mermaid fin.

The worm, baby.

I taught it to myself when I was twelve, obsessively practicing in my room until I got it perfect, for vague reasons and motivations unbeknownst to me until right now.

This is why I learned how to do the worm.

Everyone in the room freaks out. They completely lose their minds.

So I do it some more.

And some more.

They are chanting my name. Someone says I'm funny as hell.

I need to bring out some other moves.

But the worm is the only move I have.

I try something else, kicking my legs into the air like I'm a skateboarder at the top of a half-pipe. It gets chuckles, not the ecstatic roar I was seeking, so I transition gracefully into a move I've seen but never attempted—I get onto my back and hug my knees to my chest, then try to spin myself around like I'm an upside-down turtle balanced on its shell. It makes people crack up, but I think you need to be on an actual dance floor and not a rug to get the proper spin momentum. It probably also helps if you're an actual turtle.

I spring to my feet, ready to improvise some more Dance Magic, when Robbie leans over to tell Amir something, thereby opening up a gap in the crowd that reveals to me, at the very edge of the room, on the threshold to the kitchen:

Maggie Spear.

She's here. I *knew* she had to be!

Man, I love being right.

She looks very pretty. Her eyelids, like Shana's, are literally sparking with glitter. Her lips are sparkling too. She's wearing a blue cardigan over a T-shirt with a rip near her stomach, and the overwhelming feeling I have is that she's infinitely cooler than I'll ever be.

She and Shana are arguing about something.

Then Robbie goes back to where he'd been standing, and Maggie disappears.

I feel this quick, sharp burst of . . . sadness? Or maybe just disappointment. Either way, it weirds me the hell out, seeing as I don't even know Maggie. Or at least I *don't know* what I know about her.

I also don't know how much time just went by, but everyone's still looking at me, so I break into this old-school move Uncle Jed did at my bar mitzvah during the hora, squatting and holding my arms like a genie and kicking my legs out one at a time.

It gets the wrong kind of laughs. People are confused.

In a panic, I hop onto this cabinet unit thing, put my hands on the wall, and start twerking, my butt moving forward and back at lightning speed as the room absolutely erupts.

"This is my guy!" Chris Colasurdo shouts.

"Mine too, baby!" Bodhi shouts.

If I turn my head from this higher vantage point, I can see Maggie again. I'm hoping she might be watching my glorious twerk display, but she's still deep in it with Shana.

Nothing will top twerking, so I leap off the cabinet to get other people involved. The first person I see is Cute Lizzy from the Keg. I dance up next to her, and she laughs. Then I recognize her also-cute friend as Tatiana Who I Procured Edibles For. I shimmy my shoulders in her direction. She smirks and shimmies back at me, and I start walking her into the dance circle. Tatiana trips and says "Whoa!" and falls into me. I catch her and suavely transition us into some kind of bizarre tango, one hand on her back, the other interlocking with hers, extended out to the side. For reasons unknown, I sing "La laaaa!" as we march around the room like that. Tatiana cracks up into my shoulder.

Other kids join the dance circle. Chris Colasurdo passes me the flask again and tells me to kill it, and I'm thinking that probably means I'm about to drink Chris Colasurdo's backwash, but I drink it anyway, and it's definitely not backwash, or at least not *all* backwash, unless Chris Colasurdo has burning demon saliva. I don't like this song as much as the last one, but I'm dancing anyway, and Robbie passes me a beer. I drink the beer, and the room is gently spinning, but in a nice way, and then the seas part again.

And there's Maggie.

She's only like twenty steps away, so I'm going to talk to her. Just straight-up ask if we ever knew each other.

But oh! She's shaking the hand of some superhot guy. He looks like an adult. Like my dad. No, not that old. Maybe like my older cousin Ben. But still. He's *very* adulty. With very defined cheekbones. And glowing adult skin.

I stop walking.

I'm intimidated. But I *shouldn't* be. Because technically I'm probably the same age as that guy! I am *technically* adulty!

But my skin doesn't glow like that.

Something large and soft collides with my head. It appears to be a beige couch pillow.

"Yo, keep it going!" Amir shouts with a confusing amount of urgency. It takes me a full five seconds to understand that he wants me to pick up the couch pillow and throw it into the air again. Which I do.

Somehow I drift with the crowd to the other side of the family room, so I again can't see Maggie. Why do I care? I'm not really sure, but I peel myself from the blob of people and climb back up onto the twerking cabinet.

I spot Maggie Spear again. Glowy Adult Dude has his hand on the small of her back as they walk toward the kitchen. I take a step to follow them and walk straight into a big white speaker. I lose my balance and topple off the side of the cabinet. So does the speaker. Everyone in the room goes "Ohhhhhhhh!"

I'm on my side on the rug. So is the speaker. Somehow it's still blasting music.

"Oh no, my dude!" Bodhi says, concerned but laughing, one of many people leaning over me. "You wiped out, you okay?"

"I know Maggie's here," I say, inexplicably choosing to express that rather than the twenty-five other options, for example that my knee is throbbing and the palms of my hands feel raw and rug-burned.

"Okay," Bodhi says with a shrug. "Can I help you get up?"

"Guys, seriously!" Shana says, pushing through the crowd. "That speaker is like my dad's baby, you can't do shit like—"

She sees that it's me. I smile big and wave, lifting up onto my elbow.

"Oh god. Carter."

"It's a-me!"

"Bodhi!" Shana shoves him in the chest so hard that it sends him backward. A couple of dudes splash their beers in their efforts to dodge him. "Did I not tell you I would slit your goddamn throat if you messed this up?"

"You did, you did," Bodhi says, looking genuinely terrified.

"But I made sure they were never in the same room!"

"I KNEW IT!" I shout like the detective in the final twenty minutes of a whodunit, leaping up from the floor and then wincing from the screeching pain in my knee. The room is spinning more than ever, like we're on some rickety ride at a state fair. "It was evident from the start that the problem wasn't that we weren't seniors! I just had to put the final pieces together!"

"Congrats," Shana says. She takes a deep breath. "Look, it's fine. Maggie wasn't even inside to see this. So. It's all good. Just be cool. Okay? Everyone be cool. And pick up my dad's speaker so he doesn't slit *all* of our throats."

"Why do you keep saying that about throats?" Lizzy asks. "It's so intense."

"On it, Shay!" Chris Colasurdo says. He lifts the speaker with one hand and tucks it into the crook of his neck, then trips over the same wrinkle in the rug that Tatiana did and drops the speaker to the floor. "Aw shit, sorry!"

Miraculously, the audio equipment never hits the ground.

Janessa Suher has bounded across the room with arms extended, catching the sleek dinosaur egg like it's a loose ball.

"YO!" The room explodes, louder than any of the reactions I got for my dance moves.

"That was insane!"

"Did anybody film that?"

"Chris, she saved you from getting your throat slit!"

Soon the walls echo with a chant of Janessa's name, and I join in too because it really was spectacular, but also I'm feeling a little empty inside, and my knee is still in pain. Bodhi passes me a new beer, and I drink it fast because maybe it will make me feel better, and it sort of does. Then everything starts to blur.

I'm wandering from the family room to the kitchen, and different people keep asking me to purchase things for them, like not *right now* but sometime soon, and I say sure, and it makes them happy, and I think *I should keep a list of all that in my phone*, but I don't, and Bodhi and I are laughing about something, and I'm wandering some more, and I don't even know what I'm looking for, but *of course* I know *who* I'm looking for, but she's not in the backyard anymore, and then Tatiana is talking to me, I think flirting with me actually, and she's really hot, but I don't even know what's happening, and then we're in a new room with lots of books in it, and we're kissing, and then I tell her I have to pee, because I *do* have to pee, and so I do, and it feels like four straight minutes of pee, I'm not even kidding, and when I'm walking out of the bathroom, I look to my left, and I see the back of Maggie's cardigan, she's so stylish, and I'm so glad I finally found her, so I walk over to say something, but I realize she's no longer talking to Glowy Adult Guy, she's MAKING OUT with Glowy Adult Guy, and I make a surprised monkey noise, which I wish I could take back, how embarrassing, what even was that, and I walk the other way, and I'm struck by the overwhelming feeling that I don't belong here, that if I wasn't a freak with an authentically old driver's license I *wouldn't* be here, and no one would care that I existed, and that's hard to face, but it's the truth, and I need to get out of here, so I do.

MAGGIE

I might be imagining Chord Ramirez. It's the only explanation.

He is charming; he is composed; he is a delight to stare at; he has a *life plan*.

And he seems to be very into talking to me.

Like seriously: Where did this guy come from?

It's not that I have zero self-esteem; I'm just not used to being hit on in this way by someone of this caliber. I guess I haven't been single for a while, and during that time, I changed and evolved as a person. And also got older. So now guys like Chord—guys who are in their first year of community college, while also working a part-time job at the front desk of an urgent care clinic, with an eye on transferring to a state school after their second year, to be followed by medical school and the ultimate goal of becoming a doctor, ideally a cardiologist but possibly a gastroenterologist—are guys interested in chatting me up at a party.

It's blowing my mind a little bit. Or a lot bit.

We've been talking in Shana's backyard, and it's kind of freezing, but thankfully I wore my cardigan, which I've wrapped around myself so that the patch of belly skin exposed by the stupid rip in my T-shirt doesn't get frostbite.

"Should we go back inside?" Chord asks, like the gentleman he is.

"Oh, maybe," I say.

But then I remember that Drunk Carter's pinballing around in there. Another chant is happening, probably of his name.

"How about in five minutes? I kind of like the fresh air. And the stars and everything."

"Don't have to ask me twice," Chord says. He sips from his beer and looks up at the sky. "If it's a choice between whatever's happening in there and the chill vibes out here, it's an easy call."

"You mean chill-y vibes," I say, which is so bad and dorky, I feel my face instantly turn red. It's just shadowy enough out here, though, that he probably can't tell.

"Ha," Chord says, the ultimate courtesy laugh. "Right."

I'm so embarrassed, I can't speak again for fear that another clunker will unexpectedly emerge.

"Plus," Chord says, pointing deeper into Shana's backyard, "I'm really hoping to try out that killer swing set. You interested?"

I forgot that was back here. Shana's parents haven't taken the swing set down because her dad is insanely nostalgic. I remember competing with Shana to see who could climb across the top of the monkey bars fastest.

I also remember sitting with Carter on those swings in October. We held hands. We talked. We made out. We migrated to Shana's brother's empty bedroom. Where we did other stuff.

So Drunk Carter is inside the house, and Ghost Carter is out here.

"No swing set for me right now," I say. "Worried it might make me barf."

"Fair enough," Chord says. "Maybe instead we can find a baseball bat to balance our heads on and spin around as fast as we can, see who can stay upright longer."

"Um," I say.

"That was a joke. Obviously. Didn't you ever do that as a kid?"

"Put my head on a baseball bat and spin around? Absolutely not."

"Wow! It's, like, a known kids' activity."

"Sure it is," I say, happy that the power dynamic has shifted and I can be the one questioning *his* subpar joke.

"It's real!" He's arguing in this very cute way that makes me want to kiss him.

I can't believe I just had that thought.

MORE PROGRESS.

"All right," Chord says, putting his cup down on the ground so he can rub his hands together, "now I'm the one feeling those chilly vibes, so I vote we go inside."

I kinda feel like he's pretending to be cold because he can see how much I'm shivering, and I both appreciate that and find it annoying. Because I'm scared to go back inside.

"Your vote has been tallied," I say, "and the official results are in: One hundred percent of the constituents of the backyard have voted YES on the proposal to go into the house."

"Wooo!" Chord shouts, throwing his hands in the air, with such surprising enthusiasm it makes me flinch. "Democracy in action!"

"Congrats to all of us."

As we go back through the kitchen, I involuntarily flinch again, worried what I'm going to see, but it's just Shana and Marigold and a couple of others having a lively conversation by the now demolished snack table. Shana immediately takes my hand and leads the three of us into the family room, which is now blessedly Carterless and way less rowdy. A Harry Styles song comes on, and this is when I learn there is something Chord can't do: dance.

He moves his arms up and down, his hands in fists like he's slowly milking a cow, as he shifts his body side to side way off the beat of the music. It's definitely a surprise, but, on him, it's endearing.

"He's great, right?" Marigold says directly into my ear as we all dance. I'm going to assume she's talking about him as a human and not as a dancer.

"Yeah!" I say into her ear. "I feel like I made him up."

"You *should* feel him up!" she shouts.

Rather than go through the trouble of correcting her, I give her a thumbs-up, and she giggles.

Chord takes my hand, and we awkwardly move back and forth before he lifts his arm to spin me under it. Supremely charming. And, since he's a few inches taller than me, it makes me feel kind of short, which never happens, so I don't care if he's a good dancer. Because I love this.

(Carter is an inch shorter than me. In case you're wondering. Five-foot eight to my five-foot nine.)

And then suddenly I have to pee. Very much.

Or maybe I've had to for a while but just wasn't paying attention.

"Be right back," I say to everyone but mainly Chord. "I must urinate!" Probably didn't need that extra sentence.

"Well, okay!" Chord says with a grin. "Have fun with that."

I nod and walk away fast to outrun the embarrassment.

"Does the music sound a little staticky?" I hear Marigold ask behind me. "Like it's fuzzy or something?"

"Oh Jesus no," Shana says, "really?"

"Yeah, I might be hearing that too," Chord says.

"GODDAMMIT."

As desperately as I have to pee, I can't help but do a quick scan of the party on my way to the bathroom. I pretend I'm doing it to make sure everybody's staying in line and not messing up the house too much.

But of course I'm looking for him.

I peek into the dining room, where there's a surprisingly restrained game of beer pong happening, Eric Rogers and Kelly Hsu against Lizzy King and Bodhi the Twerp, with a handful of fans cheering on the sidelines. No Carter. Bodhi sees me, and it's clear he's terrified. I like that.

When I get to the bathroom, the door is closed, and I hear someone in there. Damn. I stand there trying not to think about my bladder. I notice the light's on in the office down the hall, which Shana and I specifically marked with "STAY OUT" Post-its—her parents would lose it if anything in there got messed up. I walk down to look inside, hearing annoying giggles.

I'm ready to shoo the laughers out of there like an irate chef broom-prodding mice out of the kitchen, but instead I find myself frozen, watching as Carter sloppily exchanges spit with Tatiana Robinson.

Oh god.

Down the hall, someone exits the bathroom, and it snaps me out of my stupor. I scurry away before Carter or Tatiana sees me (now *I'm* the mouse), trying desperately to erase the part of my brain that holds on to images as I slip into the bathroom and lock the door behind me.

He was kissing someone who wasn't me.

I hated that.

I have to pee so bad.

Once I sit and finally let my bladder flow free, I'm able to think more clearly. Well, slightly more clearly.

Here's what I think:

FUCK YOU, CARTER.

But then, a new thought:

Carter can kiss whoever he wants.

Because Carter doesn't know who I am.

And he certainly doesn't know we were in love.

We *were* in love, right?

I keep waiting for all this to feel less fucked-up.

Maybe I was *supposed* to see Carter kissing Tatiana, though.

Maybe it's a little nudge from the universe, encouraging me to move on.

I mean, wasn't I just thirty minutes ago thinking I wanted to kiss Chord?

And wasn't there a tiny part of me that felt bad about that?

So, yeah, this is a *good thing*. I don't have to feel bad at all. I can go find Chord and exchange some spit of my own, can't I?

I flush the toilet, wash my hands, and look into the mirror.

I look pretty. And powerful.

"Maggie Spear. Version two point oh. GO."

I open the door. Chord is standing right there, like I've summoned him.

"I realized I had to go too," he says almost sheepishly.

"Oh cool!" I say, which is a very weird response. But it's only because I'm thinking *Kiss him. Kiss him now.* "Actually . . ." I lean toward him, and I have to angle my head up a bit, which is new in a good way, but then I see this surprised look in his eyes. "Oh shoot. I should ask if—I mean, can I kiss you? Is that okay?"

"Yeah," Chord says, a smile breaking across his face like a sunrise. "It's definitely okay. But let's move so we're not right next to the bathroom?"

"I support this proposal, and it has passed."

"We're two for two," Chord says with a laugh.

He takes my hand, and we walk a few steps, or maybe more, like fifteen, until we're next to a wall near the threshold of the kitchen, where there's a picture hanging of Shana and her family on a beach somewhere. After an awkward pause, two long seconds, he leans down toward me, and our mouths are touching.

It's good, I think.

It's odd.

But it's nice.

I don't really know what it is.

I'm glad it's happening, though. His kisses are gentle but hungry, and I try to match mine to them. He tastes like beer. So do I, I guess. Maybe I'm tasting myself. I put my hand on his face. Man, that stubble feels even better than I hoped it would.

I am kissing someone who is not Carter.

Hell yes. Amen. Hallelujah.

This is how it feels to move on.

And I—

There's a birdlike yelp from behind us, cutting through the chaos of the party to pierce my eardrums. I want to ignore it—there's no reason *not* to—but it had a subtle, wounded quality that leaves me unsettled.

"What was that?" I say, pulling my head away to look behind us.

I find myself staring at the back of that green, ratty hoodie I know so well as a figure staggers away from us.

Carter.

Was that sound his response to me making out with someone else?

Why would he care? Does he *care*?

And why is he walking out the front door, leaving it wide open behind him, obviously still wasted?

Does he think he's going to drive home like that?

Oh shit.

That's probably exactly what he thinks.

Dammit, Carter.

"You okay?" Chord asks.

"I am," I say. "But just lemme . . . I, um—I know that guy who— That guy who is very drunk, and I'm worried he's gonna . . ."

"Yeah, of course, you should go after him. Might be saving his life. Want me to come?"

"No!" I say it so forcefully Chord takes a step backward. "Sorry. That's really sweet. But I got this. I'll be right back."

"All good. I still really have to pee anyway, so this works out well."

I nod and smile and run.

MAGGIE

I'm out the front door just in time to see Carter stumble across the sidewalk two houses down and hold up his key to unlock Toro. I charge toward him like it's the final sprint of a 5K.

"No!" I shout across two lawns, the same tone of voice you would use to reprimand a dog.

"Huh?" Carter looks up, genuine terror in his eyes.

"That's not happening." I slow down as I reach him and rip the key out of his hand.

"Hey, I need that!" Carter says.

"Too bad."

"You're stealing my car?!"

"No, idiot. I'm preventing you from driving it."

"Oh." Carter takes me in, a small grin growing on his face, and this is already way more interaction than we should be having. "Because you want me to stay at the party?"

"What? No!" I need to keep this straightforward. Efficient. To the point. I pull out my phone. "You're drunk, okay? You can't drive right now. So I'm getting you a Lyft home."

"What thinks you make I'm drunk?" Carter asks, wobbling back and forth like a large piece of seaweed.

"I'm not going to dignify that with a response."

"Okay. Whatever you say. I'm glad you care, Maggie." I can tell he's just saying my name to see how I'll react.

"It's not that I care," I say. "I just don't like death."

He's unnervingly silent, staring at me as I stare at the app scanning for nearby drivers. It's still quite cold out, and neither of us is wearing a coat.

"I saw you kissing that handsome adult," Carter says, flicking his eyebrows up and down really fast. I can't keep myself from laughing, goddammit, which makes him grin even bigger than before.

"Please stop talking," I say.

"What? It's what I saw!"

"Roberta will be here in four minutes to drive you home," I say, keeping my eyes on my phone in order to get myself through this.

"Roberta."

"Yes."

"That's kind of like the name Robert," Carter says. "I never realized that. Did you? Like a female Robert."

"I guess."

"I could do that with my name. Cartera. That's beautiful, isn't it? Look at Cartera on the balance beam! She's magnificent."

I laugh again. Jesus. "And why is she on a balance beam exactly?"

"She loves gymnastics, I guess. I don't know." Carter holds on to the side of the car, exhaling a huge puff of white breath and buzzing his lips together like a horse. "I might do a puke. Make a puke. Puke a puke."

"Oh god," I say. "Three minutes till Roberta. Wait, no. Four again. No, okay, it's back to three."

"So what's our deal?"

I freeze. This is my cue to run. I must leave here. I've done my part. He can wait for Roberta without me. "What do you mean?"

"What do you mean what do I mean? It feels like we have some kind of history. Like, when you looked at me on the first day of my reboot, and then I thought I saw you crying."

I stare at my phone. Roberta is still three minutes away, her little car icon stopped at the traffic light on Donner Hill Road. *MOVE, LITTLE CAR, MOVE!!!*

"Yeah, I was crying," I say finally. "Because I felt bad for you. But not because . . . any other reason."

"You wanna know what I think?" Carter says, grinning more than ever, holding on to the side of his car to stay upright.

"Not really."

"I think you're *lying.*"

I have no idea what to say, so I just shrug. "Roberta's here in two minutes."

"Then again, very possible I'm wrong and embarrassing myself. As you are aware, I don't actually know anything. Unless it happened more than six years ago. Then I'm *solid*. Hey, is Taylor Swift still a thing?"

"Well. She's a woman, not a thing. And yes, she's like the most popular person on the planet. Some of her new stuff was playing at the party."

"I *thought* that was her! Wow! That's impressive. Staying famous for so long. That's, like, a lot of famous. How do you even do that?"

"I know. I think if you work with really good producers, they help you— GAH! I don't want to be having a conversation with you!"

"Nevertheless, you are. Hard to stop, right?" He flicks his eyebrows at me again.

"I can stop. I'm stopping right now. And Roberta's only a minute away. So stopping is easy."

"We have good chemistry," Carter says, and my brain thuds onto the street with a dull squish. "Don't you think we have good chemistry? Yet another reason why I think you're lying to—" He interrupts his own sentence to buzz his lips some more.

"Look," I say after I've had a moment to pick up my brain and reinsert it into my skull, "we don't have chemistry. And we don't have history. And we—"

"How about precalc? Do we have precalc?"

"No! We don't have any of those. And we won't! Because I'm into Chord now. I just met him, and he's very mature, and his name is a musical term, and I like that. A lot!"

"Cord? That's not a musical term, it's a wire."

"No, it has an *h* in it. Like when you play a—"

Roberta finally pulls up in her blue car, god bless her, and hilariously enough, it is a Honda Accord, just like Carter's car, Toro.

"ACCORD!" Carter shouts, staring at it. "Like when you play ACCORD! That is a freaky-ass coincidence. Her car finished your sentence." He's not wrong. "Also freaky because it looks just like my car." His jaw drops. "Maybe *I'm* Roberta! Am I Roberta? That would be a cool twist."

"You are not Roberta." I pull open the door to the back seat. "You need to get in and go home."

"But we're having so much fuuuuuuuun."

"Gosh, I know," I deadpan, even as a small part of me is cringing in shame because I really *am* having fun.

"How will Roberta even know where to take me?"

"I already gave her your address. That's how the app works."

"Aha!" Carter throws a triumphant finger into the air. "You know where I live! Because of our history!"

He should not be this cogent when he's this drunk! "Just get in the damn vehicle." I shoo him into the car with the back of my hands because using my palms seems too intimate and therefore risky. "I have a Chord to make out with."

"Okay, but make sure it doesn't get tangled around your neck. That could be dangerous."

I shut the door and walk around to the driver's side, where I hand Carter's key to Roberta and tell her to give it to him when he leaves the car. I'm impressed that her bob cut looks exactly like it does in her thumbnail, and I almost tell her that before realizing it's more of an observation than a compliment. Roberta probably doesn't need that.

I don't look back as they drive away, but I do whisper a silent prayer that Carter won't puke in Roberta's Accord. Then I walk back toward the house, wrapping my cardigan tighter around me as I process a confusing mix of joy, shame, and the distinct feeling that I just did something I absolutely shouldn't have.

CARTER

Ooh baby, do I feel like a steaming pile of fecal matter or what?

I do indeed.

I shift around in bed, and an electric current of pain extends from my knee up through my thigh. Ouch. I grit my teeth and suck in air through the sides of my mouth.

My head is thumping, like someone jammed a dart into my skull just above my right eyebrow. The palms of my hands are raw, and I sort of feel like I could throw up.

"Well, seems like you had an eventful night." The blinds rise with a dramatic zip, and the sun pours in, revealing Mom standing there. "I'm sorry I woke you, but it's almost noon."

"That's okay," I say. "I'm okay."

"Very convincing." Mom takes a glass of water off my dresser and hands it to me, followed by two Advil.

"Thanks." I sit up, pop the capsules into my mouth, and slowly chug the entire glass. I don't remember much of last night's party. That's a feeling I've gotten used to. I know I drank a fair amount of that beer I bought, and I think I . . . danced?

"Someone dropped you off last night," Mom says. "You left your car at the party. That was smart. Thank you."

"Oh." I have no memory of this. But now that she's said it, it does ring a bell, like the answer to an impossible trivia question that sounds more familiar than you were expecting. *Of* course *amino acids are the building blocks of protein! I totally knew that!* "No prob. It didn't, um, seem safe to drive."

"I know you can't really remember your past sixteens," Mom says, "but I do feel like you're learning. Somehow. Is that possible?"

"Maybe," I say, though I have this feeling she's giving me more credit than I deserve.

Then it comes to me, like a gentle smack in the face:

Maggie. Maggie Spear.

She of the blue cardigan and sparkly eyelids.

She was the one who put me in the car.

With the driver who had a female man's name.

Johna? Michaela? Steva?

"I like to think you're learning," Mom says, kissing my head, and it's one of those moments that jolts me into her point of view, how she has this son who repeats the same stupid shit every year and never evolves. And she and Dad have to somehow, in spite of that, keep supporting and loving me and being patient with me. "Come downstairs and eat something."

"I think you're right," I say. "I think I am learning."

"That would be—" Mom's eyes get glassy like she's about to cry. "That would be really wonderful." She covers her face with her hand, and here come the tears.

"Do you want to, like, sit?" I ask, patting the foot of my bed. "I'm . . . I'm really sorry about all this."

"No, Carter," Mom says, accepting my offer and plopping down onto the bed. "*I'm* sorry! I don't want this for you. You know that, right?"

"Yeah, of course I know that. You don't have to apologize,

Mom. It's not your fault. You and Dad should be, like, empty nesters or whatever by now."

Mom puts both arms around me and sobs over my shoulder. "Carter, we want you here as long as you need to be here." She pulls back and looks into my eyes. "Every mom has moments where they wish their kid would freeze in time. Not like this, though. I never would have— I really don't want this for you."

She says it with so much intensity, it's like she's trying to convince me.

"I know, Mom. I really do."

Her tears are nearly contagious, but I stifle the sob in my chest before it emerges.

"Have the doctors," I say, "like Dr. Reedy and whoever else . . . Have they ever said they think I'll get to seventeen? Do they have hope?"

"Honestly, Carter," Mom says as she grabs a tissue from my nightstand and blows her nose, "I generally believe in doctors. But when it comes to this? And a condition they've never seen before? They say a lot of fancy things, and they try to seem confident, but it's become clear to me none of it means all that much. Because they don't have a fucking clue what's going on with you."

"Whoa, Mom. Language."

"As you know, sometimes cursing is necessary. And cathartic."

"Fuck yeah I do."

Mom laughs. "And, to answer your question, sweetie: *I* have hope. And so does Dad. Which is why he just set up an appointment for you with an Ayurvedic doctor for early next week."

"Okay. Do you think that's the answer?"

Mom shrugs. "Worth a fucking try, right?"

I lean in and hug her again. "Thanks, Mom."

"Love you, Carter."

"Love you." I move my leg, and the pain isn't nearly as bad. The Advil must be kicking in. "Hey, Mom?"

"Yeah?"

"Have we . . . had this conversation before?"

She pauses a moment, and I can tell she's not sure if being completely honest will mess with my head too much. "We've had a version of it," she says. "But not exactly like this. This is the best one yet."

"Sure it is," I say, laughing.

"Now get your butt out of bed so you can start your Sunday."

"On it," I say, and somehow, Mom has made my first hangover feel about a hundred times better than it did ten minutes ago.

Roberta.

That was the driver's name.

I wonder what I said to Maggie Spear. Hope I didn't embarrass myself.

I should message her to say thanks.

I pick up my phone and see a string of texts from Bodhi:

Yo heard you got a car home, sorry didn't get to say bye

I was too busy DOMINATING BEER PONG w Lizzy

And then we DOMINATED EACH OTHER'S MOUTHS

(we made out hardcore is what I mean by that)

IOU for getting us into the party, it really was a movie

I text back: *YOU AND LIZZY! YEAHHHHHH*

I'm happy for him. I almost mention Maggie, but I don't need to have another useless exchange about Muggy Sphere.

I check to see if Maggie's name is in my contacts so I can text her, but of course it's not. I have literally nine contacts, and three of them are my family members. I found Maggie on Instagram after I saw her in that yearbook photo, but her account was private and I felt weird trying to follow her. I push the button now.

I go to Bodhi's profile, and he's got just one pic up in his stories, a selfie of him and Lizzy screaming into the camera lens.

I go to Lizzy's story, and she's got several photos up, along with a video of me being ridiculous. Seems I did the worm. And a bunch of other weird shit.

There's a photo with Lizzy and Shana, so I go to Shana's profile and *JACKPOT*: There's a pic of her, Maggie, and this girl with a ridge of blue hair traversing the center of her head like a lawn-dividing shrub.

I stare at Maggie. She's so pretty. Her smirking face sparks a memory.

She was laughing last night.

At something I said. Who knows what.

And also:

"We don't have a history!"

She said that to me.

But I don't think I believed her.

I find the name of one of my nine contacts and push on the camera icon next to his number.

"Well, hello there," my younger-older brother says moments later, sitting in his tidy dorm room with his earbuds in.

"Howdy-ho," I say.

"Still in bed, huh?" Lincoln asks.

"Well, yeah. But . . . I'm getting up in a second. Went to a party last night."

"Ooh. How did that go?"

"It's, uh, hard to say for sure. Fine, I think? I just watched a video of myself twerking."

"Yikes." Lincoln laughs. "Way to go, CT."

"I know you're making fun of me, but I'll take it. What're you up to?"

"Oh, you know. Pretending to get work done, watching TikTok instead. My roommate's here too. This is Leo." Lincoln flips the camera toward a white guy with glasses and shoulder-length hair parted down the middle, sitting on his twin bed and restringing an acoustic guitar.

"Hey," Leo says, giving a barely perceptible nod.

"He's very focused on his instrument," Lincoln says, overly enunciating each word to be funny as he turns the camera back to himself.

"Fuck you," Leo says off camera.

"So, look, I was wondering if you could tell me about Maggie Spear," I say, cutting right to the point of my call.

"Sure, what about her?" Lincoln says without missing a beat, none of the awkward stammering I've gotten used to from Bodhi.

"Just, like . . . Did she and I ever hook up or anything?"

"Wait, Maggie Spear who goes to your school?" Lincoln looks convincingly confused in a way that instantly deflates the entire story I've constructed in my head. "Not that I'm aware of. Why do you think you hooked up with her?"

"Well, I don't. I mean, maybe it wasn't a hookup. But just— The first day I was back at school, on my birthday, I saw her sobbing in the hall as she looked at me. And then I showed up at this party her friend was throwing, and her friend didn't want me there. She was trying to keep me and Maggie in separate rooms."

"Huh," Lincoln says, brushing curls away from his eyes. "You and Maggie definitely knew each other at school, I think. So I get why she'd be bummed to see you go through this. But I'm not sure you were super close or anything."

"Okay," I say.

There was a tiny skip in his voice when he said *I think*. Maybe I imagined it. The tiniest millisecond of hesitation.

Maybe I'm just desperate to believe I'm somehow connected to Maggie because I might have a crush on her based on the exactly one conversation we've had, in which the only sentence I can remember her uttering is the one where she insisted we have never been romantically involved.

"Yeah," Lincoln says. "If it makes you feel any better, I hear she's annoying."

"What? Annoying how?"

"I don't know. Just, like, annoying."

"Who said that?"

"People. Who I know from Ridgedale."

"People. Huh. Okay."

Lincoln shrugs. "Yeah. Anyway, I should get back to work. I have lots to read and an a cappella rehearsal in an hour."

For the billionth time, I'm completely in awe of how mature he seems. The Lincoln I remember was this shy little dweeb. Quietly hilarious and bighearted, but a definitive dweeb. The guy on my screen, though, is like . . . cool. A confident college kid. Comfortable in his own skin. I'm proud of him, but I also want to smash the screen and scream so loud it makes my throat ragged.

"Cool," I say. "Thanks for taking a minute to talk, Link."

"Always. Love you, brother. Byeeeeeeeee."

"Love you." We hang up, and I punch my pillow three times so hard I briefly see spots. I know I'm supposed to shower and head downstairs, but I go back onto Instagram. I pull up Shana's profile again in the hope of seeing more Maggie pictures. Maybe there's nothing between us, maybe I've constructed this narrative out of thin air and Maggie's just a friend I kind of know.

But I cannot deny that I want to keep looking at her.

There's a photo of her from September wearing a paper tiara, arms in the air, melty ice cream sundae in front of her. Underneath it, Shana has written: *happy 17 to the funniest and most beautiful bad-choice-maker I know.* Setting aside the fact that rubbing a seventeenth birthday in my face like this seems incredibly rude, I have to wonder: Is it possible I'm one of Maggie's bad choices?

I go back to Shana's grid. The most recent post is black-and-white with text overlaying it; I thought it was a random meme, but I see it's actually a poster for a gig Shana's band is playing. They're called Angry Baby. And there, sitting on some steps with Shana and another bandmate, all of them glaring at the camera, is Maggie. She's in the band. I didn't even know she played an instrument. Maybe she doesn't. Maybe she's the singer. Either way, it's pretty hot.

The gig is next Thursday at a place called Bean-Age Dream, opening for a musician named Linda Schweitzer.

Maggie can continue to dodge me and say we have no history

and hang out in a different room than me at parties, but she can't tell me not to come see her band.

I mean, every concert needs an audience.

Right?

LINCOLN

THE FOURTH LOOP

A couple of months into your fifth time being sixteen, I made the mistake of telling you about the breakup that had happened the night before you first looped. That, plus a new desperation inspired by my being a full year and grade ahead of you—the creeping sense that you were being left behind—meant you were dead set on finding a way to reverse your situation.

"So you're saying I was a dick, right?" you asked, going over the facts of the breakup as you drove us home from school in our new old car, Toro. "A jerk?"

"I mean," I said, "I think you just didn't want to be in the relationship anymore, but yeah, the timing was unfortunate. She was like, 'I love you,' and you were like, 'No, thanks.'"

"And then the next day, here we are." You shook your head and gritted your teeth. "Loop Town. Loop City. Loop-de-loop."

"Well," I said, squirming in my seat. "I don't actually think that's what—"

"I should try to reverse it, right?" you asked, as if you'd just stumbled upon the idea for an app that would reshape society as we know it. "Unloop myself! By being the kind of boyfriend who is *not* a jerky dick!"

I tried to talk you down, but you were unflappably obsessed. In March, you started dating this senior girl, Nina Chen. She was really cool—played volleyball, obsessed with horror movies—but

I felt worried that you were just going through the motions more than anything else, determined to be the Best Boyfriend Ever. You wrote Nina notes, brought her tulips at school, took her out to eat at that Italian place Vincenzo's that serves homemade pasta. Alas, Nina eventually saw through it, could feel that you weren't really in it, and dumped you in July. I was relieved.

But you more or less gave up after that, descending into a funk that was exceedingly unpleasant to be around. Come December, on the night before your birthday, you rallied whatever enthusiasm and drive you had left and attempted to break the cycle by pulling an all-nighter. "If I never sleep," you said, again with the fervor of an overworked scientist fumbling madly for an epiphany, "there's no way to send me back to sixteen, right?" Except there was because, around 6:00 a.m., you closed your eyes for a moment, which turned into five minutes of sleep.

When your eyelids rose, you hopped out of bed, excited for your sixteenth birthday.

And I was officially two years older than my older brother.

FEBRUARY.

MAGGIE

"Hey, Magpie," my father says in the voicemail he left three minutes ago when I ignored his call. "I'm sorry I can't be there tonight for your big debut."

"Put the phone away!" Shana shouts. "That's not helping us get in the zone."

"Yeah, it really isn't," my friend and bandmate Ember agrees, their eyes closed, in some kind of meditative state. They play the drums, wear a faux leather jacket, and have short pink magical-fairy hair. They're definitely too cool for our band.

"I know, I know," I say. "Just wanted to hear what my dad said."

The three of us are standing near the dumpster behind Bean-Age Dream, minutes away from our first-ever set, an odor best described as *dead mouse latte* permeating the air. We're all nervous af.

I figured Dad wasn't going to make it from Pennsylvania, but it's still a bummer. He's an amazing father, but he's not always so . . . parental. I listen to the rest of his excuse, something about not being able to get out of some fancy catering job. Though Dad is a very talented artist—some of his multimedia pieces have sold for thousands of dollars—he's always grabbing various odd jobs to supplement that. Currently, his main ones are teaching after-school kids' art classes, managing projects for a landscaping business owned by his old college buddy Bernie, and working as a captain for a catering company, which I assume means he helps lead all the servers or something.

Do I wish he could skip this random catering gig and come see my show?

Yes. Of course. But I know this is just Dad's way.

There's a buzz during the end of his voicemail, and I look down to see a text from Chord: *Good luck tonight! You're gonna kill.*

"Okay, it's gone," I say, flicking the phone into my bag like a hot potato. "My dad's not gonna make it. Chord is here, though. Which is both sweet and nauseating. So much pressure. I wasn't even gonna tell him about it, but he saw on Instagram."

"It's *good* he's here," Shana says. "Because you're gonna sound fucking hot. And look fucking hot too. Playing that piano. *Stroking* those keys. *Caressing* those ivories."

"Oh, geez, too much," I say.

"It's just the truth. The undeniable truth."

"Teela's out there too," Ember says, finally opening their eyes. "So."

"That doesn't count," I say. "You and Teela have been dating for like a *year.*"

"Yeah, but that makes it worse in a way." Ember pops a square of gum into their mouth and starts frantically chewing. "Because it means Teela is totally comfortable being herself with me. And herself is a very critical person. If our band sucks, she will let me know."

"True. I don't think Chord will let me know. He'll just run away. And then ghost me forever."

"Hm." Ember holds out their plastic container of Ice Breakers Cubes. "Did you want a piece of this?"

"Okay." I deposit the gum into my mouth and try to focus on nothing but the explosion of minty freshness, even though my brain has somehow found its way to Carter again. It was probably the thing Ember said about Teela being herself because they've been dating so long. Carter and I dated five months and twenty-four days (not that I was counting or anything) and I felt very comfortable being myself around him.

I miss that.

Still, it was a mistake to help him at the party. Not entirely, because he really was in no shape to drive, and that could have been disastrous. But talking to him again felt like a form of torture. Like trying on a perfectly fitting pair of jeans you know you'll never be able to afford.

I know Carter was too wasted to remember our interaction Saturday night, but he clearly remembers *something.* Every time I passed him in the hall at school this week, he seemed like he wanted to talk to me; I've started taking longer routes to class to make sure we don't cross paths. It's exhausting. But the alternative is about eight thousand times worse. I don't want jeans that suddenly stop fitting in a year and then I have to teach them how to fit all over again.

"Can we please stop talking about the opinions of these people who are not *us*?" Shana asks. "*We* know how hard we've been working on these songs and how fucking great we are. So let us focus on *process* and not *outcome.* And also on our hotness."

"I'm not sure we should play the song," I say, suddenly seized by such intense panic my gum falls out of my mouth and lands on my Chuck Taylors.

"Which song?" Ember asks.

"You know," I say, "the one about the—"

The back door of Bean-Age Dream swings open, and Misty, the gray-haired woman in her fifties who owns the place, pops her head out. "You three ready to roll?"

Shana, Ember, and I look at each other.

I violently shake my head.

CARTER

Bodhi is talking to me, but I'm not really hearing the words.

I'm sipping my hot chocolate and staring at the empty stage—it's nothing fancy, probably just a foot or two off the ground, with a piano, acoustic guitar, and drums set up and ready to go. I wonder which instrument Maggie's going to play. I bet the drums. She seems pretty intense, like she could really whack the shit out of those cymbals.

"Are you keeping those sunglasses on the whole time?" Bodhi asks. "Probably gonna be hard to see."

"Oh." I wore them along with my Knicks cap when we came in so I could be as inconspicuous as possible. It's been all too apparent this week that Maggie wants nothing to do with me, so I don't really want to be spotted. "No." I pull off the sunglasses.

Bodhi and I have planted ourselves at a table in the very back. It's not that big a place, but this spot gives us the best chance of getting lost in the shadows.

"Anyway, what do you think about that?" Bodhi asks. "Like, with Lizzy. Should I text her again or wait some more?"

"Uh," I say, having taken in none of the context for this question. "Probably makes sense to—"

"All right, folks," a woman with gray hair in a dark blue blazer says, leaning over slightly into the microphone near the guitar. "We are *very* excited to be hosting the debut of a new band. They're called . . ." She squints down at her phone. "Angry Baby! Isn't that a killer name? I just love it. So let's give these three a warm hand! Angry . . ." She looks down at her phone again. "Baby!"

Shana emerges first from a door next to the stage, followed by an Asian kid with short pink hair, and then Maggie, who's wearing jeans, dark blue Converse, and a light green, short-sleeved button-down that looks so good on her, it makes my chest go floaty. Shana goes to the guitar and confidently flips the strap over her head. I assume the pink-haired bandmate is headed to the piano, but instead they sit down on a stool behind the drums while Maggie slides slowly onto the piano bench.

Wow. She plays piano. And, from the way the microphone is set up right next to it, sings too.

There's complete silence as Maggie arranges her fingers on the keys. They're shaking in a way that makes me nervous for her.

She begins, her hands plunking out gentle chords as the other two musicians watch. After thirty seconds and a few bungled piano notes, Maggie opens her mouth and starts to sing.

Her voice comes out thin and quiet, even with the microphone. It's hard to make out the lyrics until she gets to the chorus where she repeats the words *No, thank you* a couple times. With a resonant strum, Shana announces herself on guitar, followed moments later by the drummer, who comes in with this cool shuffle sound.

As if buoyed by the arrival of her bandmates, Maggie's voice gets slightly more powerful, her fingers more decisive. Her singing has a ghostly quality, and there's also, like, an honesty to it. Like I could just listen to her for hours and believe every word.

I start to get lost in the song. I wasn't expecting the music to be this . . . good. I look over at Bodhi. He's got his phone under the table, texting. Annoying. When the song ends, I join the crowd in applauding, though not too loudly, as I'm still trying to stay under the radar.

"Whoa," Maggie says into the mic, blinking into the crowd. "Thank you."

"You mean, *NO*, thank you," Shana says, which gets a laugh.

"As you heard, this is our first-ever show," Maggie says. "And we are all very afraid."

"Don't be afraid, you're killing it!" some dude shouts from the other side of the room. Maggie smiles and blushes. I glance over, and, wouldn't you know it, it's Glowy Adult Guy from the party.

So they're some kind of thing now.

I hate Glowy Adult Guy.

No, wait: *Cord*.

Maggie said his name is Cord.

That's even worse. He looks every bit as handsome and adultified as he did at Shana's house, and he's sitting with three other similarly adult-looking people. *College* people.

I should've been the one to shout something to Maggie. Definitely would have said something more original than Cord.

We're afraid of how talented you are!!!

Yeah. That's what I would've said.

I'm not sure why I've deemed this Cord guy my rival, seeing as all signs point to him being in an actual relationship with Maggie, unlike my imaginary, grasping-on-to-shreds-of-evidence relationship with her. I just don't trust him.

When I shake out of my Cord-loathing spiral, they're deep into a more upbeat song, Maggie pounding on the keys. She and Shana are singing in a harmony that *almost* works. I think Shana's a little off-key. The drummer is absolutely wailing away. It's drowning out Maggie and Shana a bit, but it's still pretty sick. Cord cheers and whoops when the song ends. He's even *more* vocal after their next two songs.

"I think that dude had too many espressos," Bodhi says.

"Right?" I say, greatly appreciating that I'm not the only one who thinks Cord sucks. "Like, tone it *down*, man."

"Yeah. Someone should tell him the show is happening onstage, so we don't need him putting on another from his seat."

"Seriously!" I notice Maggie and Shana having some kind of quiet argument before the next song starts.

"Their band is pretty good, though," Bodhi says. "Sorta messy, but I would totally stream these songs."

"I know!" I'm again deeply gratified to have my own feelings validated. "I didn't know what to expect, but this is genuinely killer music."

I whisper the last three words because a new song has started. It's another quiet one, Maggie alone on the piano. She plucks out a gentle melody and sings, her voice wavering a little. She seems less nervous, though, and more sad.

"That look in his eyes," she sings. "Like he doesn't understand. Breaks my heart, so I take his hand."

Probably wrote this song for Cord. He seems very dense, like he doesn't understand things. Also like he's a jerk who cheers too much. But that's unrelated to the lyrics.

"He's the boy who got stuck," Maggie continues, her voice the slightest bit hesitant, her eyes cast down at the stage. "He's shit out of luck. 'Cause no one gives a fuck, about the boy who got stuck."

There's a jolt in my stomach.

Is it narcissistic to think this song might be about . . . me?

The guitar and drums come in on the next verse, and I'm listening to the words like a spy trying to decode foreign intel. The lyrics are all pretty vague, but they *could*, in theory, apply to my situation. I am a boy who got stuck!

"And he's funny," Maggie sings, "makes me laugh like wow. But will he know that five months from now?"

It's me. It has to be about me.

I look to Bodhi for confirmation. He nods and whispers, "This song slaps hard."

I want to scream *I THINK IT'S ABOUT ME!* but I just nod and whisper back, "Totally."

The song builds into a huge repeating chorus, including a three-part harmony that really does slap, and my throat tightens. Am I seriously about to cry right now? That's insane. And embarrassing. I down the rest of my hot chocolate.

The song ends, and as Maggie holds out the final chord, her eyes land right on me. I freeze. She's surprised.

But maybe it just *seems* like she's looking at me. Maybe she was so deep in the song that she forgot there was an audience, and that's why she looks stunned.

Either way, her eyes flit away within seconds. The crowd of about forty people roars louder than ever. Maggie, Shana, and the drummer are all glowing as they walk awkwardly to the front of the stage and take a sort-of bow. Cord starts shouting "Bravo!" and Maggie's possibly seen me already anyway, so screw it: I fling my hat onto the table and scream, trying to outcheer his ass.

MAGGIE

I can't believe he came to my freaking show.

I also can't believe we *had* a freaking show.

And that it went well.

Like really well.

I want to bask in that, but I can't help but be the teensiest bit distracted by the fact that, just before we were about to start "Stuck," I spotted The Boy himself in the back of the room. FREAKING CARTER. AT MY SHOW.

I don't know why I hadn't noticed him and Bodhi sooner; Carter doesn't usually wear baseball caps, so that's one thing. Also I was intentionally avoiding looking into the audience as to not add to my already considerable nerves.

But he came. To see me.

WHY DID I TALK TO HIM SO MUCH AT SHANA'S PARTY?

So stupid. I should've just silently pulled him away from his car when he was trying to leave, then waited for Roberta to get there without saying a word. Or I should've acted like a huge asshole, like making fun of his clothes or his hair or something. Or his face. Instead, he's, like, *intrigued* by me.

And probably even more after hearing the GODDAMN SONG I WROTE ABOUT HIM.

Maybe I should also blame Chord.

Sweet Chord, loudly whooping it up after each song. It was endearing at first, but then it started to feel like a little much. He was more boisterous than ever after we finished "My Big Ego," which is what drew my attention into the audience, where I happened to notice two dudes talking and looking in Chord's direction, also seeming to be observing the too-much-ness. For a brief moment, I felt defensive of Chord, but that was soon replaced by the horrifying realization that the people I was staring at were Carter and Bodhi.

"Psst!" I whispered across the piano to Shana and Ember. "Let's just end our set there."

"What?" Shana said. "Why?"

"Just because! I can't do this last song."

"But we're destroying! And this is probably our best one. We have to do it. We owe it to this audience."

"Yeah, we gotta do it," Ember said.

"I really don't want to, though."

"Fine, then I'll just start it myself on guitar," Shana said, raising her pick in the air.

"Argh," I grunted. "Forget it!" And I began to play, feeling like I was walking the plank, soon to be chomped into bits by a crocodile.

But I somehow got through it.

On the final note, I couldn't help myself: I had to look at Carter, see if he understood the song was about him.

He did. He definitely did.

And the shocking thing was, he looked sort of devastated.

Goddammit. Should have ended the set early like I wanted to.

But now I'm standing up and moving to the front of the stage with Shana and Ember, and everyone is flipping out for us—Chord and his whole table are standing—and Shana starts a bow, so Ember and I follow her lead, which feels ridiculous, because it's a concert, not a school play, but once we do it, it feels kind of good.

We did a show. And it didn't suck.

There's a startlingly loud scream of approval from the back of the room, and I see that it's Carter. I involuntarily smile even bigger—damn you, Carter Cohen—before looking away.

The applause dies down, and the coffeehouse puts on some indie-folk transition music so Linda Schweitzer can get set up, and Shana, Ember, and I hug and hop our way off the small stage.

"Ohmigod, that was so good," I say.

"We fucking rule!" Ember shouts into our faces.

"Seriously," Shana says. "That went even better than I thought it would."

"What. A. Show," a nerdy voice says from behind us. It's Ron, standing with Mom, the two of them beaming.

"That was so wonderful!" Mom says. "I had no idea you could play music like that, Mags."

"Not to mention *write* music like that," Ron adds.

"Uh, yeah," I say. I'm annoyed that Ron is here and Dad isn't, but still, this warmth spreads through my chest. "Thanks."

"Really, though," Mom says. "I knew Vivvy could sing, but it turns out you can too!"

I've been waiting so long for her to say something like that. I shrug and smile.

"Wish she could've seen this," Mom says. "I know she'll be so proud."

"Yeah," Ron says. "I leaned over to your mother in the middle of the set and said, 'When can we get the album?' And I really meant it!"

"Well, guess we'll have to make one," I say. It's hard to be annoyed by Ron's presence when he says something like that.

"I have to ask," Mom says, leaning in closer and speaking in a hushed voice. "I saw who was sitting in the back of the room. Did you invite him? Are you getting back together?"

"Mom, no," I say, my mouth going completely dry. "I didn't invite him. I don't . . . I don't know why he's here, but don't worry, it's not— It's just not."

"Okay, fine, fine. And look, you can date whoever you want to, of course, I just think it's a tricky road to—"

"Mom!" I shout-whisper. "Not here, okay? Everything is fine. We're not dating. Or even talking. Be chill!"

"I'm chill," Mom says, shrugging and looking to Ron for confirmation. He nods, as if to remind her of something else entirely. "Oh, right! On another note, sweetie, Ron and I had an idea that we want to talk to you about later."

"Oh?"

"A *big* idea," Ron says, raising his eyebrows and dork-smiling.

"Ah, what the heck, we'll just ask you now," Mom says. "We want Angry Baby to be the entertainment at our wedding this summer. We'll pay you and everything."

"Wait, what?" Ember leans toward us from where they were talking to their older brother, Lee, pulling in Shana by the arm from a separate conversation with her mom.

"We want you three to play our wedding," Mom repeats.

"What do ya say?" Ron asks with a wink (which unfortunately

nudges him back into annoying territory).

"Oh hell yes!" Shana says, looking at me and Ember like we just won the lottery.

"We are so in!" Ember says.

I wish they would've consulted with me first, as I'm not sure exactly how I feel about this. But it is another gig, one that actually pays money. And Mom and Ron loving our set so deeply that they want us to perform at their wedding is incredibly meaningful.

"Sure, yeah!" I agree.

"Woo!" Mom gives Ron a cute but overwhelmingly corny high five. "This is the best!"

"We really lucked out, my dear," Ron says.

"This is such an honor," Shana says, taking Mom's hand. "We won't let you down, Laurel, we promise."

"Oh, I know that," Mom says.

"Hey." A hand taps me lightly on the back, and there's Chord behind me, grinning so big his shiny white teeth temporarily imprint dots onto my retina.

"Oh, hey," I say.

"That was so damn good."

We hug, and he smells fantastic, like pine tree and coffee, and he asks me why I never told him I was a total rock star, and I say I guess I forgot, and this feels like a dream. How is all of it actually happening? Mom is looking over at us, and I can tell the shallow part of her is impressed that this super attractive guy is hugging her daughter. It leaves me simultaneously proud and furious. Like it's such a surprise someone like him would be attracted to *me.*

Chord introduces me to his friends, whose names I don't have a chance in hell of remembering, and they're all very sweet. I try my best to be sweet back to them. As cool as this is, it's a lot to take in.

I excuse myself to the bathroom so I can take a moment to decompress. I'm almost there, nodding and smiling at some random people who tell me it was an incredible set, when Carter appears in front of the bathroom door.

An ambush.

"Hi," he says, adjusting the bill of his Knicks cap. "And sorry. That I'm here. I get that you don't want to interact with me for . . . reasons. Which remain mysterious. But I just wanted to say that was ridiculously awesome."

"Um. Okay. Thank you."

"And also, like . . . Was that song about me?"

Shit.

"Which one?" I ask, like an asshole.

"Come on."

"Oh, the last one, you mean? About the stuck boy? That's actually based on . . ." I try to think fast. "A *New Yorker* article I read. About this kid who survived an earthquake. In Morocco." This feels like an offensive lie. I dunno, I'm scrambling here!

Carter narrows his eyes. "Interesting. I tried reading *The New Yorker* once. It overwhelmed me."

I laugh without meaning to. It just pops out. "You always hate when I bring up *The New Yorker*," I mutter.

"I *always* hate that?"

"Uh."

"So we do completely know each other!"

"Dammit." I shuffle to the side to get around him, but he grabs my hand before I can.

Oh.

His fingers. Brushing the back of my hand.

I pull away.

"Sorry," Carter continues. "I just— I could use someone in my life right now who knows me. And knows that I hate *The New Yorker.*"

This is not good. Vulnerable Carter is my kryptonite. I can't look directly into his eyes. I might start making out with him. In the same room as Chord. In the same room as my *mom*.

But if I don't cut this off now, he's just going to keep trying. Finding me at school. Coming to more of our shows.

"I can't be in your life, Carter, okay?" I say, eyes trained somewhere to the right of his Nikes. "You're right. We know each other. We dated. Last year. But we can't do it again. I really can't! I thought maybe I could save you, but—"

"Save me? Like, get me unstuck?"

"Yes, but it didn't—"

"How were you going to do that?"

"Just by . . . It doesn't matter, it didn't work!" In my peripheral vision, I can see Chord staring over this way, deciding whether or not to intervene. I hope he doesn't. Against my better judgment, I look into Carter's eyes. "If I tell you everything I know, will you please stop?"

"Stop what?" Carter asks, desperation in his voice that reminds me of our last night together in his car. "I just want to know what you know! Please."

"I mean, I don't really know anything. It's just, like, a theory."

"So tell me the theory!"

I put my hand on a small table nearby to steady myself. The

triumphant vibes from the set are a distant memory. I can't believe we have to have this conversation again.

"Okay," I say. "The night before you first started looping, like five years ago or whatever, you and your girlfriend broke up. Well, she said I love you, and you didn't say it back. And you said you wanted to break up. And then . . . The next day . . ."

"Ohmigod," Carter says, taking a step backward. "That's why I'm stuck in this hell? Because I dumped my girlfriend? Who was she?"

"I'm . . . I'm not sure."

Carter gives me a skeptical look and twitches his head like *What?* "Then how do you even know for sure that that happened?"

"It's complicated," I say, desperately wishing there was a teleportation app on my phone.

"Everything all right here?" Chord asks, putting a hand on my back as he steps up next to me.

He'll suffice, I guess.

"Yeah, totally," I say. "We were—"

"Wait, was it Layla Banerjee?" Carter asks, ignoring Chord completely. "Was that who I dumped?"

I feel the color spill from my face, splashing a Jackson Pollock onto the floor. "Why would— How do you—? Who told you that?"

"So it *was* Layla!" Carter says, one finger pointing in the air like he's just had the idea for a new invention. "She *is* the key!"

"Maybe you should give Maggie a little space." Chord puts his arm in front of me like he's a tollbooth.

"Seriously, how do you know about Layla?" I ask Carter. Did

he *remember* what I told him that last night in December? (Mental note: That would make a great lyric.)

"Let's just say a little friend told me," Carter says, stepping closer in spite of the tall, muscular fellow blocking his path. "A little friend named *ME*! Ha!"

He left a message for himself about Layla. Not great.

"All right, all right," Chord says, putting an arm around me and directing us away from Carter. "Maggie, you want to come with me over here?"

I definitely want to exit this conversation, but I could use that decompression time in the bathroom more than ever. Explaining that to Chord, though, seems like more hassle than it's worth.

"Um, sure," I say.

"So was that everything?" Carter asks.

I look back at him. "Yeah," I lie. "That's everything. I'm sorry, Coco. I mean Carter."

The crowd cheers as Linda Schweitzer takes the stage. Chord takes my hand, and we hunch over and run to his table, where his friends shift around to make a spot for me.

I feel weird that I didn't even say bye to Carter, but when I glance back over toward where we were standing, he's already gone.

CARTER

"You seem agitated," Soren says.

It's the day after the concert. Friday. I freaked out at Bodhi as I drove him home last night. I asked him why he never told me that Maggie and I had dated. He said he was really sorry but Maggie had asked him not to mention it. I said that sucked. He agreed. Then he pulled a bag of Takis out of his coat pocket and asked me if I wanted one. I did.

Today in school I aggressively ignored Maggie the two times I passed her in the hall. That'll show her.

And now I'm at my 4:00 p.m. therapy session with Soren. Very well-timed, actually.

"I am agitated," I say, sitting forward in the red cushiony chair in his office, holding the random-ass rooster-wearing-glasses tchotchke that is always sitting on the small table next to me. "Turns out Maggie and I dated last loop. Did you know that?"

"I did," Soren says, nodding with his eyes closed, which, when combined with his glasses and annoying hipster mustache, makes him look smug as hell.

"And you didn't think that might be valuable information for me to take in?"

"I'm sorry, Carter," Soren says, not seeming to mean it at all. "We've gone over my approach before. I won't bring up anything from a past loop until *you* do. Otherwise, it—"

"Gets too confusing for me, yeah, yeah. But I *did* bring up Maggie! I said she seemed to be avoiding me, but I had the feeling we'd had some kind of relationship."

"That's right. And we discussed that."

"But you didn't say"—I hold up the rooster as a stand-in for Soren—"'Uh, yes, Carter, you're absolutely right. She was your girlfriend.'"

"You didn't explicitly ask," Soren says.

"Ohmigod, dude!" I put the rooster down and slide it all the way to the edge of the table. "Do you understand that not telling me shit like this is *also* very confusing?"

"I do, Carter, and again, I'm sorry. Would you like to ask me questions now?"

"I WOULD."

He offers another smug nod.

"What did I tell you last loop about Maggie?" I ask. "When did we start dating? Did I really like her?"

"You first told me about her in the fall, September I think, but I believe you'd started dating in June. You said you didn't want to mention it at first because it didn't even seem like a big deal. But then you did. Mention it."

"So I must have really liked her."

"I think so."

"Did I say that?"

"More or less."

"Well, did I or didn't I?"

Soren clasps his fingers together. "Something I've learned about you, Carter, is that, understandably, you have a hard time letting people in. Maybe because you know you're going to forget them. Which is incredibly difficult."

"That's . . . I let people in all the time! I mean, I'm not even two months into this, and I've got close friends like Bodhi and Amir and Robbie. And so many kids in school know me. I hang with, like, everyone."

"Of course. Yes. That's admirable. It's just my observation that it's hard for you to let people into the most vulnerable parts of yourself. You're not alone in that. It's hard for lots of folks, even those without your condition."

"Yeah," I say, gnawing at one of my fingernails. "How did Maggie and I meet? School?"

"As I recall, you worked at the same ice cream place. Scoops and . . ."

"Scoops 'n' Sprinkles? I worked there?"

"Apparently."

"That's rad. I bet I got a lot of free ice cream."

"Probably."

We sit in silence for a few moments as I imagine making myself a big-ass sundae with as many toppings as I want.

"I can be vulnerable, you know," I say. "You should have seen me at the concert last night."

"Oh?"

"After the show, I went right up to Maggie and told her that I could tell one of her songs was about me."

"Oh wow. Was it?"

"Yeah, it totally was."

"Good for you."

"Then she said that we did date but she couldn't be in my life again."

"That must have been hard to hear."

"I don't know. Maybe. At first I was just glad to be right about the dating thing. Like, my instincts are good, you know? Even if my memory isn't."

"Absolutely."

"But then, yeah. Kind of a bummer. I mean, what do I do now?"

"Well." Soren shifts his crossed right leg down to the ground and crosses the left one over his knee instead. "I think you listen to her. If she says she can't do it, then you need to respect that."

"Yeah. Of course. Totally."

"How does that feel?"

"Bad!"

"Good. I'm glad to hear you being honest about that."

"Am I not always honest about my feelings?"

"In the past, not always, no. For the reasons outlined earlier."

"Hmm." I stare down at the Soren Rooster and resist the urge to flick it off the table. "Hey, have I ever mentioned Layla Banerjee?"

"No, I don't believe so," Soren says.

"Maggie said the night before I started looping, I broke up with this girl Layla. She said I love you, and I didn't say it back."

"Ah, yes. I knew you'd broken up with someone the night before the condition started, but I didn't know that was her name."

"Okay, yeah! So I've been thinking. Like, you're saying I have trouble being vulnerable, so maybe I have to reach out to Layla and apologize. Maybe that's part of my healing or whatever."

Soren gives me a pleased nod, this time with eyes open, which makes it a little less smug. "I think that's a great idea."

CARTER

And so:

Maggie Spear and I are over.

I mean, we never even really started.

But I hereby release her from any obligation to me, Carter Cohen.

I will stop bothering her. I will stop going to her shows. I will take the hint and get on with my stupid stuck life. That's what a mature seventeen-year-old would do, right?

I will be the change I want to see!

It's kind of freeing in a way.

And now at least I have someone else to focus on.

As I drive up to the curb in front of our house, my mind tabs over to Layla Banerjee. The person who, whether she knows it or not, may be the key.

The key to what, I'm not exactly sure. Unsticking me?

Could it be as simple as an apology? A *vulnerable* apology?

I hope so.

I breeze into the kitchen, where Dad is chopping away at zucchini, already deep into cooking dinner. "Smells good!"

"Thanks," Dad says, pulling off an impressive spin move to cascade the zucchini chunks from the cutting board into a sizzling pan. "How was therapy?"

"Good! I think . . . Yeah."

I don't want to get into all the details, nor do I want to bring up Maggie to my parents. I probably didn't share that much with them, so it'll be more annoying than helpful. They might have opinions I don't like.

"All right, great. I don't want to pry, of course, but if you ever want to share more . . ."

"Thanks, Dad, yeah. There weren't like any major epiphanies or anything. But it was helpful to talk with him."

"I'm glad." Dad holds the pan above the flame and gently shakes the contents around. This guy could seriously have his own cooking show. "Hey, and you've been taking the herbal medicine, right? From the Ayurvedic doctor?"

"Oh, yeah." I forgot to the past two days, but I don't want to tell Dad that. The appointment happened earlier this week. The doctor was warm and smart and wise, and talked about everything in the body and mind being interconnected, but I wasn't really sold that she'd be able to cure me. Dad seemed so hopeful about it, though. "It's good. I mean, I can't really feel if it's, like, gonna help me turn seventeen. But who knows, right?"

"As long as you're taking it. And doing the pranayama breathing exercises too."

"Definitely." Nope. I suck.

"Hello!" Mom says, taking off her long camel coat as she walks into the room. "My boys in the kitchen, what a lovely sight to come home to." She kisses Dad and wraps an arm around me.

"Hey, Mom," I say.

"Carter had a good therapy session," Dad said. "And he feels like the herbal medicine might be working."

"Oh! That's great news!" I can't fully read Mom's expression.

But it seems possible she's just as skeptical about the effectiveness of any of this as I am.

"Yeah!" I can't maintain this faux-hopefulness for much longer. "I'm just gonna drop my stuff in my room and do one thing before dinner."

"Go for it," Mom says, giving me one final squeeze before releasing me.

Once I'm in my bedroom, it's Layla time. I pull out my phone, dive onto my bed, and head to Instagram.

Layla has a story up, a reshare of a dog rescue looking for a family to adopt a fuzzy little creature named Peaches, who is looking directly into the camera in a way that's unexpectedly moving. Maybe I should adopt Peaches. Maybe that would fix everything.

I scroll through Layla's grid again. She's definitely attractive. But nothing on here makes it seem like we'd be a perfect match or anything—I'm not actually a dog person, and I prefer captions that have jokes in them—so I get why I might've wanted to end it. Still, I need to apologize for being a heartless sixteen-year-old.

And show her—and the universe—that I have what it takes to be seventeen.

I begin crafting a message.

Layla! Whaddup! You are looking so good, girl!

No. Delete.

Layla! Yo. Do you remember me? Because of my condition, I only just found out we dated. Fun! But then I also found out I broke up with you like a real jerkhole. Less fun!

That's not right, either. Delete.

It's hard to write a message when you're hoping it will, like, singlehandedly solve your life.

Ten minutes and approximately eighty-five drafts later, I compose something I'm happy with:

Layla! Hi! Carter Cohen here. How are you? I hope great. As I'm sure you know, I've had this weird disorder since our junior year, where I keep regressing back to age sixteen and forgetting everything that happened the previous year. It's fairly horrible! But I recently learned that you and I were a thing that year before this happened. And I heard the way I ended things was, shall we say, NOT SO NICE. *I have no memory of this (how convenient, right??) but hearing about it made me feel bummed. So I was hoping we could talk at some point if you're down. Hope all else is good for you. Your life seems pretty cool!*

I press Send.

You hold my fate in your hands, Layla Banerjee.

I hope you respond.

I stare at my message for a while, trying to will those three *I'm typing* dots into existence below it.

They don't appear. But a thought does instead, something that's been bothering me since Maggie told me we'd dated.

I call Lincoln.

"Hello, brother," he says, the world moving behind him as he walks. "Mind if we make this a call instead of a FaceTime?"

"Sure, sure." We switch to audio only. I hear loud voices in the background. Laughter. Singing. "Is this not an okay time?"

"Yeah, yeah, I can talk a sec. Just leaving a cappella."

"Noice! Is Terrell with you?"

"He is."

"Tell him I said hey."

"Carter says hey," he says. "Terrell says hey back. So what's up?"

"I know that Maggie and I dated. Despite the fact that you

pretended Maggie and I never dated."

There's a pause on Lincoln's end of the line, filled with two guys harmonizing a lyric of some song I don't recognize.

"I'm sorry I lied to you, CT," my brother says finally. "Maggie didn't want me to tell you. I was trying to protect her. And you too."

"I guess I get it," I say. "It just feels freaky."

"No kidding. I despised having to do that."

I scroll over to Insta to see if Layla's written back. She hasn't.

"So is that why you told me Maggie was annoying?" I ask.

Lincoln laughs. "Yeah, I'm sorry. She told me to say that. Like, I had texted with her asking what I should do if you started asking me about her because I didn't want to lie to you. And she said, 'Just say you've heard I'm really annoying!' So I panicked and did that."

"That's actually hilarious."

"It is," Lincoln agrees. "But I'm sorry. I never really know how to handle those conversations. What the right thing to do is."

I lie back in bed, staring at the off-white ceiling. "Anyway," I say, "Maggie doesn't want to be with me again. Because it's too hard to start over."

"Ah, sorry."

"It's not a big deal. I mean, I don't even know her. We've talked like twice."

"Right. But, I get that it might feel shitty."

"You sound like my therapist."

"I try."

"Can I ask you something else?"

"Depends on how uncomfortable it makes me."

"From your perspective, did I like Maggie a lot?"

Lincoln's end goes silent again except for a voice saying, "What if we did it like this?" followed by a bunch of guys roaring with laughter.

"I think you did," he says eventually. "But there will be others, CT. I promise."

"Yeah." I pop up from the bed. Need to walk around. "Maggie told me how this all started, the breakup the night before my first loop."

"Oh wow. Well, I definitely want to talk about that, but I actually gotta go. We're at this bar on campus. It's my turn to demolish Terrell in darts."

"Ha!" I hear Terrell say. "Sure you will."

"All right." I want to ask Lincoln to just stay on with me a couple of minutes longer. But I don't. "We'll talk some other time, then. Have fun."

"You too, bro. Later."

The silence after he hangs up feels unbearable.

My throat feels tight.

I go back to Instagram.

Next to my message to Layla, a word has appeared:

Seen.

LINCOLN

THE SIXTH LOOP

Your sixth time being sixteen has hit differently than all the rest, mainly because for the first time, I haven't been there to see most of it happen.

Which, if I'm going to be real, has been a relief.

I've had stretches where I'm able to completely forget it's even happening. I can pretend I'm just a normal college kid with a normal family living my normal life.

Throwing normal darts with my normal boyfriend in a normal bar.

But then I have a conversation with you like the one we just had, and I remember: I'm not normal at all. I'm just as stuck as you are. Forever doomed to repeat these same conversations over and over and over again. When I lie to you, it feels horrible. When I tell you the truth, it feels horrible.

Because the reality is that, no matter what I say or do, I'm leaving my older brother behind. And it's the worst fucking feeling in the world. I will keep evolving and changing, and you just . . . won't.

Worse still, it's my fault.

I've gotten better at not thinking about that fight we had the night before this all began. The fight that almost immediately followed your breakup. I asked you if you were okay, and . . . you weren't. I wish I'd never asked. But there's no point in thinking about it now. Four months into the First Loop, I worked up the nerve to tell you what happened. And you flipped out. Rightfully so.

So I've never gone there again.

It's just something I have to live with. This terrible situation is my fault.

And no matter how shitty it is for me, how depressing it is to be forever reliving these same conversations, it's about a billion times worse for you.

Which, if I'm going to be real, doesn't make me feel better at all.

I throw another dart and miss the board entirely.

CARTER

"Man, this is the most delicious," Bodhi says after taking a swig from his bottle of hard lemonade.

"It's freaking scrumptious," Robbie agrees.

Bodhi, Robbie, Amir, and I are hanging out in the woods in Robbie's backyard, one of our go-to after-school activities on days when Bodhi and I don't have yearbook. Well, usually we hang out inside, but since I picked up a six-pack of hard cider, we're back here. The trees obscure us from view in case Robbie's parents get home early from work.

"You realize this is considered, like, kind of an immature thing to drink, right?" Amir asks as he takes a swig from his hard lemonade. "We should probably start getting IPAs or something."

"Yeah, yeah," Bodhi says. "I know it's not the coolest position to take, but I gotta be real: I think beer tastes pretty bad, dude."

"You are a child," Amir says.

Bodhi shrugs. "I can live with that." He raises his bottle in the air. "Being a child was dope!"

"Are you even drinking, Carter?" Robbie asks.

"Uh, I will," I say, fiddling with some buttons on my fancy digital camera as if I know what I'm doing. I snap a pic of Robbie with the sun setting behind him through the branches.

I look at it on the small digital screen. It's actually kind of good. Not ready to be shown to other humans who aren't me, who might rightfully call it out as unpolished or trying too hard. But I do like it.

"Though I actually might pass," I say, "because someone's gotta drive two out of three of you losers home."

"So proud of you," Bodhi says in a jokingly sincere voice. "So responsible. So thoughtful. At this rate you'll turn seventeen for sure."

"Yeah. Maybe." I snap another pic, this one of Bodhi and Amir.

"Hey," Bodhi asks, "did that Layla lady hit you back yet?"

"Nope," I say. It's been more than three weeks since I messaged Layla Banerjee, and my hope of her being any kind of key has pretty much fizzled out. I searched for her on other platforms, but the only place I found her was LinkedIn. So I sent her the same message there.

No response. Is it possible she's *still* mad at me five years after I dumped her? Or maybe she's weirded out. Or maybe she didn't look carefully at the message and thinks it was from some rando.

Whatever the reason is, I can't apologize to her if she doesn't respond. Not the way I want to, anyway. So I've tried to put Layla out of my mind, into the same locked box where I'm keeping Maggie.

I didn't mean for that to sound so creepy. The box is figurative. Like, in my head. I haven't put any of my exes into boxes! Is what I'm saying.

"Yo," Robbie says. "Do you think this really happened because you dumped someone? Because if it did, I might be seriously at risk. I dumped Lina in September after eight months, and I didn't even tell her like you did. I just stopped replying to her texts."

"You mean you ghosted her," Amir says.

"It sounds more messed up when you say it like that."

"It *is* messed up," Bodhi says.

"What? I didn't want to be with her anymore!" Robbie says. "And I knew she'd get really upset if I told her that."

"Wow," Amir says, gesturing to the unopened bottle of hard lemonade next to my feet. I hand it to him. "Just wow."

"Do you think I'm gonna get what Carter has?" Robbie asks. "I really don't want to."

"Don't worry, Robbie," I say, framing his panic and taking a pic. "I think you would have gotten it by now."

"Okay, yeah," Robbie says. "'Cause yours happened the next day, right? Yeah."

"I've dumped a ton of people, and I keep aging," Amir says. "They usually deserve it, though. Like Patrick. He didn't take my food allergies seriously at all. He'd eat hummus, like, right in front of me."

"Such a dick," Bodhi says, taking a final swig of his bottle before flinging it deeper into the woods, where it lands unseen with a somehow gentle shattering noise.

"Bruh!" Robbie says. "This is my backyard, man! My parents might find that."

"Oh, shoot," Bodhi says. "I just thought it would be cool to throw it."

"It wasn't!"

"Kinda was," Amir says, taking a final swig of the bottle I'd passed him and chucking it in the same direction as Bodhi's.

"BRUH!" Robbie says.

"Don't worry," Amir says, giggling, "mine didn't make a sound."

"Didn't throw it hard enough," Bodhi says. He pulls out his

phone and checks a text, then smiles goofily. I snap a pic.

"Must be Lizzy," Amir says, looking to Robbie.

"So what if it is," Bodhi says without looking up.

"Are you guys official yet?" Robbie asks.

"We're not concerned with labels," Bodhi says.

"So no," Amir says.

"Yo, actually, Carter." Bodhi finally lifts his eyes, aiming them toward me. "Lizzy says Tatiana has a crush on you. Would you ever be down to hang out with us? Like a double date?"

"Uh. Maybe."

"You know you made out with Tatiana at that party, right?"

"Yes," I say. "This is, like, the eighth time you've told me that. I still don't remember it, but . . ."

"Well, let me know if you'd be down," Bodhi says. "Tatiana is mad cute."

"Yeah. I will." Tatiana Robinson *is* super cute. And I know I should be excited to hang out with her.

But, try as I might, I still haven't been able to fully steer my brain away from Maggie. I have stretches when she's completely out of my thoughts, but then I have other stretches, like right now, when I'm fixated on that moment after her concert when I grabbed her hand. My fingers on her skin, my heart whooshing around like an extreme weather event.

There was something there. I know Maggie felt it too. And I get why she doesn't want to associate with me, I really do. Like, why would you want to relive a relationship knowing it's just going to end in more pain?

But then I think maybe you *should* relive it. Because maybe the good outweighs the pain. And maybe a genuine connection is profound, no matter what the freaky circumstances surrounding it are.

"You're serious?" Amir is asking Robbie when I stop fuguing out about Maggie.

"Yeah I'm serious!" Robbie says. "Go pick it up! You too, Bodhi! Get your damn bottle shards."

"All right, fine!" Bodhi says, stepping deeper into the woods.

I stay back and photograph the three of them arguing as they venture through the crisscross of trunks and branches, the sun ahead of them in its last moments before setting. It's sort of gorgeous.

As a reward for taking this artful photo, I pull out my phone and go to Chord Ramirez's Instagram profile.

Since Maggie is private, Chord's story and grid provide my best opportunity for getting a pulse on her love life. Much to my chagrin, it immediately delivers. There's a selfie on the grid from yesterday of Maggie kissing Chord on one of his well-defined cheeks as he smiles at the camera, gray winter sky behind them.

The caption: *Lucky guy*

Ugh. Someone fetch me my puke bowl.

I immediately post a comment:

Blech get a room

I can't do that. Why did I do that?

I delete it.

Chord will probably still be able to see what I said in his notifications, which is not ideal.

But whatever, he should know that was a heinous photo/caption combination! I would hate it even if I had never met him or Maggie. People understand how to use the internet now even less than they did six years ago.

Still. I don't love that I did that.

I keep pretending that I'm fine with everything, with this stupid spiral life, but I am not.

I need to be trying harder to get myself out of this loop. I go to Layla Banerjee's profile and dash off a new message:

Really need to talk with you. To apologize. PLEASE.

I hit Send right as Robbie, Amir, and Bodhi stumble back, giggling from their bottle retrieval mission.

"I'm down to hang with Tatiana," I tell Bodhi. "I'm definitely down."

MARCH.

MAGGIE

When I pull into the parking lot of the Divine Diner in Pennsylvania, I immediately see Dad's old blue Prius, and it's like a warm blanket around my shoulders. He got that car when I was six, and somehow it's still running. Or running enough to get him where he needs to go anyway. I'm sure there are at least three warning lights he's been ignoring for weeks.

I deliberately left a smidge later than usual this morning because I was tired of always getting here before him. He and I do a monthly Sunday brunch with Vivian, and it's always one of my favorite days, an escape from whatever's going on. Even though everything that's going on right now is pretty good—Chord and I are still dating, and I've been highly successful in my effort to avoid Carter in the month since the concert. He's been avoiding me too, so that helps. I'm moving forward.

Vivian can't come this morning because of some paper she's writing or some film she's editing or some play she's rehearsing or some Ultimate Frisbee she's throwing, I can't remember. I'm honestly a little glad, though, as I love getting alone time with Dad.

"Hey, darling," the blond woman in her fifties standing at the front podium says, chewing gum as always. "He's back at your usual booth."

"Thanks! How're you?"

"Oh, you know. Can't complain."

We have this exchange every time. I fucking love it.

As I approach Dad, his mug of coffee is already in front of him, and his head is down in his phone. His bald spot is looking bigger than ever. Vivvy and I tell him he should just shave his head, but he said he's holding on as long as he can, hopefully till his nineties.

"These kids today," I say, once I'm in earshot. "So addicted to their screens."

"Oh!" Dad says, not acknowledging my bad joke. He holds up the phone and presses a button. "Greetings, Maggie," an alien voice says. "We are so pleased to see you."

"No, Dad," I say as I laugh. "I do not approve of this."

"Wait, wait." He swipes his finger across the screen and holds up the phone again. "Greetings, Maggie," a dignified British man says. "We are so pleased to see you."

"That's a little better." I slide into the booth across from him. "Though I'd still prefer to actually speak to each other. With our normal voices."

Dad quickly types into his phone and holds it up again.

"Okay, sweetie," a monster's voice growls. "We can do that."

"Thanks, weirdo," I say. "You and your apps."

"They're so amazing, though, Mags!" Dad says in his actual voice. "When I was a kid, you'd have to buy goofy contraptions like this individually. Now you can get 'em all on this one machine, it's unbelievable."

"You sure Apple isn't paying you to go around saying this stuff?"

"Shhh." Dad dramatically puts a finger to his lips before bending down under the table. I assume it's part of the bit until he reappears with some kind of painting on a square of cardboard. "For you, my love."

"Whoa. Dad." It's a mixed-media piece, with paint and newspaper scraps and what appears to be melted crayon, combining to form the image of a very familiar cartoon beaver. "This is beautiful."

"Just some new techniques I'm messing around with," he says. "Thought Billy needed a comeback."

"Damn right he did." Billy Beaver is this character Dad first came up with when I was little, inspired by my obsessions with Daniel Tiger and Peppa Pig. Billy was meant to be a more countercultural cartoon buddy, featured in silly art pieces for me and Vivian, usually imparting some lesson like *Always question authority* or *Don't assume something is good just because it's mainstream!* (He might need to talk to Dad about his iPhone addiction.) In this latest work, Billy Beaver is standing on a riverbank gnawing on a chunk of wood represented by shreds of newspaper.

"I assume that was *damn* spelled *D-A-M*," Dad says.

"Naturally. What's the message of this one?"

"Oh, I don't know." Dad pats the table like it's a pair of bongos. "Try new things even when you feel old and past your prime?"

I hate hearing him say that. "Come on, Dad, you're still in your prime. You might live another fifty years!"

"Eh, fair enough." He pages through the menu, though he's going to order the same thing he always does: an omelet with Swiss cheese and mushrooms. "I was thinking: Why didn't I make the beaver female, you know? Like, I had two daughters. Why didn't I make it Becky Beaver? Or Bonnie Beaver?"

"Uh . . . Maybe because it instantly feels ninety times more inappropriate once you do that?"

"Ha! That's a good point." There may be nothing better in the world than Dad laughing at one of my jokes. "You're funny." Okay, maybe him saying that.

"I try," I say, definitely blushing. "Seriously, though, I love this. Thanks, Dad. Long live Billy Beaver."

Dad and I each put our hands together, as if in prayer, and solemnly bow our heads. When we're done, Dad is giving me a little grin. I grin back.

"Taking a while for Doreen to get here," he says, looking around. "I bet she thinks we're still waiting on Viv. You know what you want? Any deviation from the norm?"

"No deviation, sir. How about you?"

"'Course not."

Dad flags down Doreen, who's blond like the woman who stands in front, but at least ten years older. I order my spinach feta scramble, Dad orders his omelet, and Doreen scoops up our menus and goes.

"Okay, then," Dad says. This is always the best moment of these meals, when we transition from the jokes to the real stuff. "How's everything with you, Mags? How you recovering from that heartbreak? I hate thinking of you having to feel that."

Dad knows about my relationship with Carter in broad strokes: that I was dating someone I really liked and that we broke up. But he doesn't know, for example, the part about my boyfriend being the forever-teenager, who recently regressed a year and forgot that I exist. I told Dad I had to end it because it wasn't working. Technically true!

"I'm actually doing a lot better," I say, and I really mean it. "It's still hard, but—"

"Well, hello there," my older sister says, appearing from nowhere and sliding into the booth next to Dad, giving him a kiss on the cheek. "What's still hard?"

"Viv, you're here!" Dad says, putting an arm around her shoulder and squeezing as she shimmies out of her parka.

I try to make words, but it comes out more like a mangled mix of "Hey" and "What?"

"Nice to see you too, Mags," Vivian says, laughing and taking off her deep purple wool hat. She smooths down her vibrant, always-luscious dark brown hair.

"No, yeah, I'm so happy you're here," I say. "I just— You said you couldn't make it."

"Yeah, well, plans changed. Is that okay?"

"Of course. Of course!"

"Better than okay," Dad says. "I love when the whole trio is together!"

"Hey." Vivvy reaches across the table and puts her hand on mine. "Everything all right? What's still hard?"

No no no. Bad. Must change subject.

"Did you and that guy Chord break up?" Vivian asks.

"No, Chord and I are good. Great, even. Dad and I were talking about . . . other stuff. Nothing, really. It's not— It's stupid."

"Okay." Vivian's on to me. Maybe it's time to go to the bathroom.

"Oh! Viv." Dad reaches under the table again. I'm so relieved. "I thought I left it in the car, but it was in the same bag as Maggie's. This is for you."

He pulls out an actual canvas this time—about half the size of our table's surface—upon which is painted an absolutely gorgeous scene of a woman emptying clothes from a dryer.

"What the . . . ?" Viv stares down at it. "Ohmigod, Dad, is this based on *Lost Sock*?"

"It is," Dad says. "I felt really inspired."

Lost Sock is a short film Vivian wrote and directed in the spring last year, a dark, funny story that takes place during one load of laundry. Like everything Vivian does, it's fantastic.

"Thank you," Vivian says, her eyes teary.

I look down at my cardboard Billy Beaver and suddenly feel silly. Like, Vivian gets this masterpiece you could easily envision in an art gallery, and I get . . . a cartoon rodent.

"I actually just submitted it for six more film festivals," Vivian says. "So, fingers crossed."

"Man!" Dad says. "You're so on top of it. I was horrible at that with my own work. Still am. It's like you got all of my creative artist stuff plus all of Mom's type-A-get-shit-done stuff. A killer genetic brew. I'm jealous."

"I dunno about that." Vivian flicks a hand in the air. "I think more likely I have a powerful combo of both of your unique anxieties."

Vivian's so consistently good at downplaying these moments. But the damage is already done. She's the gorgeously rendered painting; I'm the goofy, bucktoothed cartoon.

"Well, whatever it is," Dad says, "it's working!" He turns to me. "Not sure what genetic mix *you* got."

Oof. I know this is Dad's sense of humor, but I'm not in the mood for it right now. My stomach clenches, and I wildly blink to stop tears.

"I'm kidding, I'm kidding!" Dad says. "You're incredible too, Mags. You know that."

"She is, Dad." Vivian is also very good at coming to my defense. "Did you see those videos from her show? Seriously unreal. I'm sorry I couldn't be there."

"Oh god, yes," Dad agrees. "Of course I saw the videos! Maggie's a straight-up rock star, I already told her that. Didn't I already tell you that?"

"You did," I say. I'm still fuming even though I do appreciate the compliment.

"The catering gig was a mess," Dad says. "I would have much rather been at your show."

"You know what you want, hon?" Doreen says, appearing at the table now that Vivian's arrived.

"Uh, can I see a menu?" my sister asks.

Dad and I give her deadpan stares.

"What? I wanna deviate!"

Doreen trudges to the front and returns with a menu. After fifteen seconds of frantic looking, Vivian says, "Okay, I'll do the avocado toast, light on the salt."

"Glad I brought this," Doreen says, winking as she takes the menu back and walks away.

"I really did think I'd try something else," Vivian explains. "But then you were all looking at me, and I panicked."

"We're not judging you," Dad says. "We got our usual shit too."

"Maggie's definitely judging me."

"Me?" I say. "Judge my older sister? Never." Even as I'm saying it, I have no idea if I'm joking or not. The thing is, I *don't* consciously judge Vivian that much; I'm too busy comparing myself to her and feeling inferior. If anything, I'm always feeling like Mom and Dad and Vivian are judging *me.*

"Speaking of judging," Dad says, "can I ask you girls a question?"

Vivian and I exchange a look. We know what's coming.

"Is it okay if we say no?" Vivian asks.

"Unfortunately not." Dad grins as he takes a sip of his coffee. "I'm wondering what you make of this wedding situation. With Mom."

"'This wedding situation'?" I say. "That's what you're calling it?"

"What else would I call it?"

"Maybe just 'Mom getting married'?"

"Fine," Dad says. "What do you—"

"I think it's really great," Vivian says, punctuating her thought with a sip of water. "Mom seems happy. So."

Vivian's always been firmly Team Mom when it comes to our parents' relationship, whereas I'm more wishy-washy, siding with both of them at different times. Maybe it's because I was eleven when they divorced, and Vivian was fifteen, so she understood better the nuances of what was happening. Or maybe it's because I know my parents will love Vivian no matter what she says or what stance she takes, and I don't feel like I have the same luxury. Like, of course they won't stop loving me, but they get annoyed by things I say in ways they don't with Vivian.

Or maybe that's in my head. I don't even know.

"Yeah," I say, with less enthusiasm than Vivian. "Mom does seem happy."

"Wow, okay," Dad says, flipping up his eyebrows as he takes another sip of coffee. "I knew she and Ron were . . . enjoying each other."

"Ew, Dad," Vivian says.

"It just didn't even occur to me that they might get married."

"A lot of things don't occur to you, Dad," Vivian says as she pats his arm.

"Ouch." He rubs the spot Vivian touched as if she's left burn marks.

"It's okay to feel weird about it," I say. "I definitely do."

"Apparently not weird enough to stop you from agreeing to be the entertainment, though," Vivian says, which I find supremely annoying.

"The entertainment?" Dad asks. "What do you mean? At the wedding?"

"It's not a big deal," I say as my insides shrivel up into a ball. "My band is just gonna play some songs."

"Oh geez, wow, that's . . ." Dad is thrown. Maybe even a little hurt. I wish Vivian had kept her mouth shut. "That's great, Mags. Wow."

I shrug, looking toward the entrance to the kitchen. *SAVE US, DOREEN.*

"Hey, as long as you promise to one day play my wedding too," Dad says, trying to smile but unable to keep the sadness out of his voice.

"Of course, Dad."

"Not that that's happening any time soon," he adds, staring at his folded napkin as if the meaning of life is embedded somewhere inside.

"Are you still seeing . . . ?" Vivian leaves the question hanging because I'm sure she can't remember who Dad was last seeing. It is hard to keep track.

"Nadia. No. That ended. It's a long story."

"Oh," Vivian says, finally feeling bad for the guy. "Sorry, Dad."

"It's all right, Viv."

Dad unfolds his napkin, placing it in his lap like it's a burial shroud, while Vivian joins me in staring longingly at the swinging door to the kitchen. WHERE IS OUR FOOD? Seeing no hope there, Vivian turns to me.

"But in brighter news, you said things with you and Chord are going well?"

"Oh. Yeah. They are. He's really sweet. And attractive."

"We love to see it," Vivian says with a smile. "And whatever you were talking about when I first got here . . . I mean, it's none of my business, but I'm just saying, I'm here if you need me. I've known some heartbreak, know what I mean?"

It's like Vivian is peering into my soul. Like she can see everything.

My pits are sweating. I should take off my sweater.

Later. I'll do that later.

If I do it now, it'll seem too much like I'm panicking and trying to hide something.

Because I am.

Panicking and trying to hide something.

From Vivian. From Dad.

Even from myself, if I'm gonna be completely honest.

The thing is, Carter Cohen did indeed heartlessly dump somebody the night before this whole horrible looping business began.

But the person he dumped was not Layla Banerjee.

No.

It was Vivian Spear.

My older sister.

"Okay," I say. "Yeah. Great. Super. Thanks."

Vivian is about to say something else when—thank the sweet

lord—a feta spinach scramble touches down in front of me, followed immediately by Dad's and Vivian's plates dropping into place.

"Food's here!" I shout.

"Well, aren't we enthusiastic today," Doreen says.

CARTER

Sure let's talk

The message is just three words long, but I can't stop rereading it.

My desperate nudge worked.

Layla Banerjee finally wrote back.

"Dude," Bodhi says, jabbing an elbow into my side. "The point of coming to the girls' basketball game to take pictures for the yearbook is to take pictures of the girls' basketball team for the yearbook."

"Oh, yeah, totally," I say, looking up from my phone and remembering that I'm in a packed gymnasium, cheers and hoots ricocheting off the walls, the aroma of dirty socks and Sun Chips wafting around us. We're sitting in the first row of bleachers, Lizzy on the other side of Bodhi, and Tatiana Robinson next to her. My fancy-ass camera is on a strap around my neck.

"Janessa Suher just had the most amazing finger roll of all time," Bodhi says, "and you completely missed it."

"Oh man, I suck. I'm sure she'll do something else cool."

"Also," Bodhi adds, "instead of being all up in your phone, maybe you want to sit over there with Tatiana. At some point."

"Yes. Definitely."

"What were you even doing? Randomly scrolling?"

"No. I just got a notification because . . . Big news. Layla wrote back."

"Whoa, for real? Old Layla who you dumped?"

The crowd erupts again. Janessa Suher just stole the ball. I lift my camera to my eye and snap a shot of her heaving it down the court to her sprinting teammate. I pull the camera down to check out the view screen. It's a blurred mess. You can't even tell it's a basketball game.

"Yeesh," Bodhi says, peering over my shoulder. "You need to focus the lens."

"I know, I know. I'm not used to action shots! It's different than taking pictures of you and Robbie walking past a tree."

"You'll get better. You did last year, anyway."

"Right. Maybe." It's weird feeling jealous of myself.

"So, that Layla lady, huh? What did she say?"

"That she's down to talk."

"Dude!"

"I know."

"That's not big news, it's humongous! She finally hit you back!"

"I nudged her again last week. So."

"Persistence! I like it. So what're you gonna tell her?"

"I'm gonna say yes, let's find a time to talk ASAP."

"Ooh, yeah. That's a good response."

There's a groan in the crowd as a towering girl on the other team blocks a shot from Ridgedale's star forward, Elise Alexander.

"It's good you didn't take a picture of that," Bodhi says. "That would be embarrassing for everyone. Especially Elise. Imagine showing your yearbook to your grandkids and being like, 'Oh, and here's when I got dominated in the paint and felt horrible about myself.'"

"There should be a whole yearbook of bad memories," I say,

laughing. "Just everyone's worst moments of high school captured in one book."

"Here's when I failed my geometry test."

"Here's when my crush told me they just want to be friends."

"Here's when I got cast as a cactus in the spring musical."

"Here's when I woke up and found out I was stuck in a horrible nightmare, reliving my sixteenth year over and over again."

Bodhi stops laughing. So do I. "Aw man," he says. "Don't worry, dude, this Layla thing is really promising."

The buzzer sounds, and the second quarter ends.

"What were you guys laughing so hard about?" Lizzy asks, smiling, and I realize she and Bodhi are holding hands. They might not be *concerned with labels*, but everything they do in public seems like it should come with a giant one that reads, *We are a couple!*

"Mostly how bad I am with this camera," I say, holding it up.

"Oh!" Tatiana hops up and comes around to the open space on the bleachers next to me. "Gimme."

She holds out her hands. I take the camera off my neck and pass it to her.

"My mom is all up in the world of photography," she says, staring down at all the buttons and dials. "So I know a lot of shit."

"Oh. Amazing."

She scrolls through the images I've taken so far. "Huh. These are . . ."

"Bad. I know. You can say it."

Tatiana lets out a loud laugh and leans her shoulder into mine. "I was gonna say *photographically challenged*, but okay, yeah, if you're gonna let *bad* fly, let's go with that."

Tatiana and I have had this flirty relationship ever since Shana's party where—so I'm told—we made out. She's really cute and smart and fun, so I could see us making out again, though, to be honest, I'm not feeling it as much as I want to be.

But Maggie is probably kissing Chord on the cheek and/or mouth at this very moment.

"I've been getting better at pictures where people aren't moving fast," I say, "but once people are running or jumping, I have absolutely no idea what I'm doing."

"Guess it's lucky I'm here, then."

Tatiana proceeds to take me through every feature on the camera, different speeds, how to focus the lens to create a variety of effects and styles. The whole time our bodies are close to each other, and Tatiana keeps putting her hand on my arm, and she smells like an ice cream sundae intermingled with lilacs, and if we weren't in the stands at a basketball game, we'd probably be kissin—

Maggie.

Not in my head. Actual Maggie.

I'd glanced to my right to see if Bodhi and Lizzy were still here (they're not; they must have gone to get snacks or something), and instead I see Maggie sitting alone farther down the bleacher just behind us. Staring at me. I don't think she was expecting me to turn my head at that moment because her eyes are open deer-in-headlights wide. She gives me a wave without smiling.

I cautiously wave back, in case she's actually waving at someone behind me.

She lowers her hand. She was waving at me.

Our first interaction since the concert. Which was more than a month ago.

I'm turning my head to look back at Tatiana, who's now also

looking toward Maggie, but Maggie raises her hand and gestures for me to come over to her.

I point to her like, *You want me to come over there? To you?*

She shrugs, like, *I guess I do, yeah?*

"Tatiana, just hold on a sec," I say.

She was in the middle of showing me two variations in depth of field on shots she just snapped of the empty court. "I'm gonna go say hi to, uh—"

"Yeah, I know," she says. "It's cool." But it doesn't sound like she's *so* cool with it.

"Um, okay." I feel kinda bad, but I can't ignore Maggie's beckoning. "I'll be right back, this'll just be a second."

I slide down the bleacher toward Maggie.

"Hey," I say.

"Hi," she says.

"I didn't think we were, like . . ."

"No, I know, we haven't been, but I just thought . . ."

I don't finish her sentence because I don't know what she thought.

"That we could, like, say hi for a second," she says, looking down at her Chuck Taylors. "Since it's been a little while."

"Oh. Yeah. Sure. Definitely. Hi."

"Hi." Maggie scrunches her mouth to one side and flicks her eyebrows up, like, *Well, this is kinda weird!* It's really adorable, but I try not to think about that.

"Are you here . . . alone?"

"No, with Shana. But she went to pee. She and Janessa are friends. The point guard?"

"Oh yeah. I know. I was there when she caught the speaker at Shana's party."

"I don't know what that means."

"I don't fully either, actually. I just have a vague memory. A speaker fell, I guess."

Maggie awkwardly runs a hand through her hair. "Speaking of that party . . . You and Tatiana have reunited, huh?"

"Oh. Well." My face goes full beet farm. "She's just showing me how to use my camera."

"Gotcha."

"Yeah." I don't really know what the point of this conversation is. But since we're here . . . "I saw you and Chord. On his profile."

"Oh. What? Oh." Now Maggie's cheeks turn tomato. "That was . . . I told him not to post that, but he liked it. So."

"You didn't like it?"

"No, I was fine with it. I mean, things with Chord are going great. But I'm just more private about . . . I don't know, it doesn't matter. I'm sorry if seeing that was . . ."

"Seeing it was totally fine."

"Okay. Right. Yeah."

"Ahem." Shana steps onto the bleachers behind me, then sidles past Maggie and sits down on her other side. "Well, hello, Carter Cohen."

"Hey, Shana," I say. "I was just leaving."

"Don't go on my account," she says. "I just didn't think you two were even talking."

"We haven't been. But Maggie waved me over."

"It was an accident," Maggie says, as if talking with me is a huge mistake. It pisses me off.

"Yup. Total accident," I agree. "Incidentally, though, you might be interested to know that I finally heard back from Layla. You remember, right? Layla Banerjee?" I say the last part real sarcastically.

Can't help it, I'm so annoyed. Seeing Maggie's face go pale is both gratifying and horrible.

"Who's Layla Banerjee?" Shana asks, her face contorted like she's just gotten a whiff of someone's fart.

Maggie doesn't tell her, so I don't either.

"Anyway," I say, toning down my hostility, "Layla said she's down to talk, so I'm gonna apologize to her. Like, who really knows, but maybe that will end all . . . this." I gesture to myself. "So thank you for your help."

Maggie nods. "Yeah. You're welcome. But . . ."

"But what?"

Maggie looks to Shana, then back to me. "Nothing. That's great. I'm glad for you."

I nod a few times. "Okay, then. Peace out!"

I move thirty steps across the bleachers toward Tatiana, Bodhi, and Lizzy as the basketball gets inbounded and the second half begins.

"Carter!" Maggie says. Nearly shouts, actually.

I turn back.

"I'm not . . . I'm not sure apologizing to Layla would actually work. To, you know, unstick you."

I walk closer to her, doing my best to crouch so I don't block the view of the people behind me. "Well," I say. "Whether it does or doesn't, it can't hurt to try and make things right. Right?"

Maggie opens and closes her mouth a couple of times before words come out. "I guess. Making things right is probably good. So. Yeah."

It looks like she might say more, so I hover there, waiting.

"Sit down!" some girl behind me shouts.

Maggie gives me a silent shrug. Weird. I give her a shrug back and skitter to my seat in between Bodhi and Tatiana, just in time to see Janessa Suher fire a pass to Elise Alexander that's so powerful, it bounces off Elise's fingers and tumbles out of bounds.

I do not get a picture.

MAGGIE

I don't know what I'm doing.

Something happened when I saw Carter sitting there all cuddly with Tatiana.

What happened was this:

I didn't like it.

I didn't like it at all.

Which, I know, is incredibly unfair. I'm the one who's made it very clear Carter should not be associating with me, and now I see the vaguest wisp of a new relationship forming, and I'm ready to destroy it, a sandbox bully kicking down barely begun castles.

It's demented.

Because I wasn't lying when I said things are going great with Chord. He's sweet, he's smart, and, sure, he gets a little trigger happy with the social media, but I really like spending time with him.

There's only one major problem, as far as I'm concerned:

He's not Carter.

It's also possible that seeing Carter with Tatiana took me back in time.

Back to a summer day many moons ago.

When I first saw Carter with Vivian.

MAGGIE

I was eleven years old when I first learned of the existence of one Carter Cohen.

It was the beginning of August, and I'd just gotten home from four weeks at sleepaway camp. They were good weeks for me, very good weeks, and I felt like a new person: more confident, more empowered, more worldly-wise. I'd had my first relationship, a week and a half of steamy hand-holding with Ryan Fischer, topped off the last night by a slobbery kiss in the shadows outside my bunk—yes, my *first kiss*—followed by a promise to stay in touch on the interwebs. In retrospect, Ryan was not at all my dream guy, and he was overly obsessed with talking about the stars and pointing out the same constellations every freaking night, but at the time, he was *it*, man.

And I couldn't wait to talk to Vivian about him.

Mom and Dad picked me up from the camp bus in the afternoon, and even though they put on a good face, it was clear they were both in shitty moods. This was about a month before they officially called it quits. So neither of them could really take in New Maggie. And I certainly wasn't going to rub my joyful dalliance with Ryan in their sour faces.

Once we pulled into the garage, I bolted out of the car and into the house, leaving Mom and Dad squabbling in my wake. I left my duffel bag at the foot of the steps and hightailed it upstairs, where my heart sank as I discovered Vivian's room was empty.

"Where's Vivvy?" I shouted down to my parents.

"Oh shoot, I forgot," Mom said. "She's working today."

My effortlessly cool sister had spent the first two weeks of the summer at an intensive music camp and the time since then working a part-time job at Ridgedale's best ice cream place, Scoops 'n' Sprinkles.

It was the spot where tons of kids from our high school hung out in the summer, loitering in the parking lot till the sun went down.

"Want to go over and say hi?" Mom shouted up to me. "We can get some cones."

Hell yeah I wanted to go say hi.

We pulled up in Mom's green Honda CR-V, loud teenagers amassed on the front benches like a colony of ants, only a couple of them actually eating ice cream. I stepped out of the car with my New Maggie confidence, ready to turn heads and take on the world.

The door jingled as we stepped inside and were aggressively enveloped by AC. I spotted my sister behind the counter and went through a slot machine whirl of emotions, starting with excitement and landing, finally, on a bright yellow disappointment lemon. The thing I hadn't accounted for was that my sister might *also* have turned into a new person while I was away.

Vivian was chatting happily with a customer, tapping their order into the iPad register, her dark brown hair pulled tight into a ponytail, sporting a blue employee T-shirt—with its classic image of a dripping three-scoop cone covered in sprinkles—that fit her perfectly. She looked . . . *radiant*. It was the most appropriate word

I could think of. She somehow looked older than her fifteen years, just the way she was carrying herself.

Her glowing newness made mine seem . . . small. I should've seen it coming.

But it wasn't just that.

There was someone else behind the counter with her.

A boy.

He was radiant, too, bouncing around with a genuine smile plastered to his face, dramatically flipping the stainless steel scoop in the air before muscling misshapen spheres onto a cone, his blue shirt speckled with mint chocolate chip (or pistachio?). He was an adorable human. Like a character straight out of a Netflix show about teenagers that Vivian would let me watch with her, except he was slightly less perfect-looking, with a crooked nose and green eyes a bit too large for his face. Which only added to his aura of hotness.

"What do you think you're gonna get?" Mom asked as we joined a line of six people.

I couldn't even answer. I was too fixated on the dynamic between Vivian and The Boy. They were *flirting* with each other. Exchanging glances, muttering things that made the other crack up, engaging in tiny arm touches, scattered like glitter amid the sand of their interactions with customers.

I watched as The Boy took a small clump of rocky road that had affixed itself to his shirt during the scooping process and mushed it into Vivian's nose. I thought she'd be horrified, and she did scream, but it was with glee. Sure, she said, "You are a fricking jerk!" but the tone was much more like, "Please do that again, I never want to be apart from you!"

"Yup," Mom said, seeing what I was seeing. "Vivvy's got a boyfriend now."

The words reverberated in my head like a taunt, even as I knew it was ridiculous to feel anything but happy for her. But here I was, ready to show Vivian who I had become over the past month, and, even in this, she'd somehow found a way to outshine me.

That's what Vivian did. And still does. She shines.

Vivian's obvious sparks with this scoop-flipping boy made my time with Ryan Fischer seem like a puddle. One of those small, flat ones you barely notice until you've stepped in it.

"Ahhhhhhh, Mags!" Vivian said when we made it to the front of the line. She reached across the counter to hug me and kiss the side of my head. "I missed you!"

"Missed you too," I said.

"She really did miss you," The Boy said as he grabbed an empty cone. "Won't shut up about you, actually." He leaned over the counter and offered me a fist to pound. "I'm Carter."

"Maggie," I said, pushing my knuckles into his, smiling in spite of myself.

"Oh, uh, good to see you, Mrs. Spear," Carter said, directing his charm spotlight onto my mom, who also couldn't help but grin.

"Hi there, Carter."

We ordered. "I want to hear all about camp!" Vivian said, straining to scoop my chocolate chip cookie dough. "Was it good?"

"It was." The invincibility I'd felt a mere five minutes earlier was nowhere to be found. "Really good."

"Yay! That's the best news. You need to tell me all about it when I get home."

"Definitely."

"My shift ends at five, but then I seriously need to know everything."

Vivian didn't get home until ten that night. She thought she'd end up hanging out with Carter for a little first and completely lost track of time. I, meanwhile, spent the evening pitying myself, bingeing *Fuller House* while trying to tune out the sound of Mom and Dad arguing about money, specifically Dad's inability to make enough of it.

Thus began the Days of Vivian and Carter. My sister was around far less than usual the rest of the summer. The silver lining was that her cameo appearances were always accompanied by a disturbingly good mood. Her absence was a buzzkill, though, not helped at all by Mom and Dad sitting us down on the couch the Saturday morning of Labor Day weekend, less than a week before the start of school, to let us know they were going to separate. Mom would stay with Vivian and me in the house; Dad would get a nearby apartment and visit a lot.

Vivian was upset. I was *wrecked*.

Somehow, in spite of the perpetual cloud of snark and resentment that had settled in our home, I hadn't seen it coming. Divorce was something on TV, something for other people, not for *us*.

It was a tough fall. As if seventh grade wasn't already a struggle without throwing a divorce into the mix.

One of the worst parts was that, once school started, Vivian—who'd never encountered an extracurricular activity that didn't appeal to her—was around even *less*, which I hadn't thought possible. So there was a lot of me and Mom hanging out. We'd transformed, practically overnight, from a vibrant family of four into a wise-cracking mom-and-daughter duo. Like a poor man's *Gilmore Girls.*

Mom seemed sad but mainly relieved. "It was really for the best," she'd say. "Your father and I have different ideas of what it means to be an adult, if that makes sense. We weren't a good team anymore."

For some reason I always pictured my parents in field hockey jerseys when she said that, shouting at each other while flailing their sticks around.

Some of my favorite moments during that lonely time were when Vivian was home long enough to hang out with me, even if we were just lying on a couch watching movies we'd seen a zillion times already, like *Love, Simon* or either of the *Frozen*s. I could temporarily forget that we'd undergone this wrenching shift, what felt like a prank: me coming home from camp, thinking I'd changed and then realizing it was actually the rest of my family that had.

Ha ha. Good one.

My *other* favorite moments that fall were when Carter came over for dinner.

It only happened twice, but those meals—with him, Mom, Vivian, and me—were, I don't know . . . fun. Bright. A lovely distraction.

"Do you think I can balance this on my finger?" Carter asked at one of them, holding out the plastic ketchup bottle he'd just used to squirt a splotch next to his fries.

"Which finger?" I asked. "Like, your index finger?"

"Probably start with that, yeah. Then work up to doing it with my pinky."

"No," I said, smiling. "I don't think you can."

"Cart, don't actually do it," Vivian said, laughing.

"Don't worry, don't worry," Carter said, putting out a calming hand, directed mostly toward Mom, who was giving him a skeptical look. "I'm very experienced."

He stuck his pointer finger up in the air and, like a professional magician, slowly lowered the bottle of Heinz onto it.

"Voilà!" Carter shouted, releasing his hand. The bottle balanced there for almost a full second before toppling over and landing with a thud in the Caesar salad.

"Carter!" Vivian shouted with glee.

"Oh god, sorry," Carter said, genuinely mortified. "That's never happened before. I seriously practice all the time."

"All the time?" Vivian asked, cracking up.

She and I couldn't stop laughing the rest of the meal. Even Mom, who was obviously annoyed, eventually laughed too.

I definitely wouldn't call what I felt for Carter at that time a crush. I mean, he was four years older than me and dating my *sister*, so the word *crush* didn't even really occur to me. I just liked when he was around.

"You look pretty," I told Vivian as I sat in her room one late afternoon in December watching her put on sparkly lip gloss. "Are you going to a party?"

"No, just to Carter's," she said.

"Oh."

"It's his birthday tomorrow, so we're starting the celebration tonight."

"Fun."

"Do you like him, Mags?"

She asked it in this pointed way that made me self-conscious.

"Carter?" I said. "Yeah, what do you mean? Of course I like Carter."

"Okay, good." Vivian took out the dangly earrings she had in, exchanged them for hoops. "You always seem kind of bummed when I mention him."

I felt a hot blast of embarrassment. I hadn't realized Vivian was picking up on that.

"I'm not— I mean— Well, yeah," I said. "I just . . . miss you. These months with just me and Mom have kind of sucked."

"Oh, Mags." Vivian wrapped me up in a hug. "I know. I'm sorry. I've gotten kind of swept up in it. And then with Dad living somewhere else . . . It's tough. I know it is. I didn't mean to abandon you."

"It's okay."

Vivian pulled back from the hug and looked at me. I couldn't take my eyes off her glittery mouth. She looked so grown-up. I couldn't imagine how I'd ever get to be like that. "I love you so much, sis."

"I love you too."

Vivian nodded and tapped my nose, like she was putting a period at the end of that topic of discussion. "Do you want to hear something weird?"

"Sure."

"I think I might say those words to Carter tonight."

"What words?"

"Well, that sentence that has an *L*-word in the middle of it."

It took me a long moment to decode what the hell she was saying. Once I did, I just kind of blankly nodded. I knew from movies and TV that it was supposed to be a big deal for people to say that in a romantic way. But it didn't seem that surprising to me—I'd kinda thought they were *already* saying it.

"You think I shouldn't say it?" Vivian asked, a rare and surprisingly satisfying moment of insecurity.

"No, I think you should totally say it." I tried to take on a tone of expertise, as if all those episodes of *Fuller House* had prepared me for exactly this moment. "If you feel it, you should say it."

"I feel it," Vivian said. "I've felt it for a while."

Hours later, I was in my usual spot on the couch (for the sake of my own dignity, let's pretend I was watching something this time that wasn't *Fuller House*, something British), when I heard Vivian come in and head straight upstairs to her room, slamming the door behind her. It was only a little after eight, earlier than she'd usually come home from a Carter hang. Mom looked up from her laptop at the kitchen table, and we shrugged at each other.

When my episode ended, my sister had yet to emerge.

"Vivvy?" I said, knocking on her door. "You okay?"

"Not now, Mags," she said, her voice strained and wobbly in this scary way I'd never heard before.

"Ohmigod, are you hurt?"

"No," Vivian said. "I mean, not physically."

"Can I just come in? Please let me come in."

There was a seven-second pause, and then: "Fine."

Walking into my sister's room that night was every bit as shocking as when I'd first seen her and Carter together at Scoops 'n' Sprinkles. Vivian was a mess, curled up sideways on her bed, her face red and raw, her chest heaving, her breath uncatchable.

"Vivvy." I sat next to her. I rubbed her back.

“I shouldn’t have said it,” Vivian said. “It was a mistake.”

“What happened?”

“I told—” She was seized by a fresh cascade of sobs. “I told Carter I loved him, and he . . . He said . . .”

“What? What did he say?”

“He was such an asshole.”

“What did he say?”

“He said, ‘That’s really awkward because I actually want to brayyyyyyuhuhuh.’”

“Um . . .”

“BREAK UP!” Vivian violently wiped the tears off her face. “He said he wants to break up, Mags! He dumped me.”

“What?” It seemed impossible. As inconvenient as their relationship was for my life, I knew how happy it made Vivian, and I’d gotten so used to it. And I liked Carter being around! How could it just end all of a sudden?

“His reason was so stupid too,” Vivian said. “He said now that he was almost seventeen, he’d been thinking about life and stuff, how he wanted to be with a lot of different people while he was still young. Screw that. So immature.”

“Yeah,” I said, even though I wondered if maybe Carter had just stopped liking her. That’s what had happened with me and Ryan Fischer from camp. One day in October his DMs started to seem annoying instead of cute. And he way overused the tongue-smile emoji. “What a stupid farthead.”

“He *is* a stupid farthead,” Vivian said, plopping onto her back. “I hate him. I hate him so much.”

“Maybe he made a mistake,” I suggested. “Maybe he’ll change his mind.”

"I doubt it. That's not Carter's style. And even if he did, I don't date stupid fartheads."

"True."

We sat there talking for at least another hour, and then Vivian asked if I could sleep in her bed with her. It was the best night I'd had in a long time.

The next morning, Vivian felt nauseated by the idea of going to school and seeing Carter, and she was right to, because when he passed her in the hallway after biology, he didn't even acknowledge her existence.

So Vivian was single again. Single and heartbroken. Mom was appropriately sympathetic but also strangely delighted to hop on the Carter Hate Train, loving the idea that she and her daughter could bond over their respective breakups. I found myself experiencing yet another jarring family shift, another sudden rearrange that left me on the outside. I tried to get in on it by invoking my situation with Ryan Fischer—"Men are ridiculous. Look at these emojis!"—but we all knew it wasn't the same.

Even when Vivian returned to school in January after winter break and learned that Carter had been stricken by some mysterious condition that left him unable to remember the past year, she and Mom still referred to him as The Jerk.

"I don't want to say it," Mom said at one point, shrugging, "but maybe it serves him right."

"I think that's too mean, Mom," Vivian said. "I feel really bad for him."

"Yeah, you're right. I take it back."

But I knew Mom really meant it. Her anger at Dad seemed to

have gotten intertwined with her anger at Carter.

Cut to three years later, and I was now in Carter's grade, both of us sophomores. Like Vivian, I felt bad for the guy, but I also knew I wanted nothing to do with him. We had no classes together, so that was easy enough to accomplish. I went the rest of sophomore year and most of junior year with minimal Carter Cohen contact (MCCC).

But then, that June, I started working at Scoops 'n' Sprinkles. Just like Vivian had.

And everything changed.

Look, considering the history, did some part of me understand that getting a job there might mean an encounter with Carter? Possibly! But I'd gone there so many times the previous summer, and he was definitively not an employee. And it always seemed like such a fun place to work!

During my second shift, a sunny Tuesday after school, Carter walked in five minutes after me. I froze like a gallon of moose tracks.

"Hey," he said.

"Hi." It was my first time talking to him since he'd asked if I thought he could balance a ketchup bottle on his finger, and he looked *exactly the same.* Which meant, yes, he retained a goofy, distinctly adorable quality; even after my immersion in a yearslong anti-Carter propaganda campaign, I could still see that.

But I didn't want to say anything more to him than *hi.*

I really didn't.

It felt too gross, like I was betraying Vivian.

It was just the two of us working, though—other than our supervisor Lloyd, who spent most of his time in the back on his phone—so how could I not speak to him? If only as a coworker?

"Have we ever met?" Carter asked, once he'd officially punched in on the iPad.

I didn't have a response to that.

"I only ask because I've worked here in past years, though not last year, I don't think, but I have this weird condition where—"

"Yeah. I know," I said. "About your condition."

"Right, yeah." He grinned, but there was more sadness than joy in it. "I guess most people do."

"But, uh . . ." *Of course I've met you!* I wanted to say. *My sister* loved *you. We've spent literal hours talking about you and analyzing you and cursing your name and calling you a stupid farthead!* "I don't think we've met."

"Okay. Cool."

I didn't feel great about the lie, but I also didn't think I owed this heartbreaker anything. In a way, I was protecting Vivian. That's what I told myself.

But, as Carter and I talked the rest of that shift, I was betraying Vivian too.

He just didn't seem like such a villain to me, though. I liked talking to him. I liked his jokes. I liked the way he playfully nudged me with his elbow.

And, let's face it: I liked that I had somehow become Vivian behind the ice cream counter in that scene engraved in my brain from when I was eleven. Now the floodlight of Carter's affection was directed at *me.*

It felt amazing.

So what was the harm in making a joke back?

Or in talking about how annoying my mom had been that morning?

Or in hanging out with Carter after a shift sometimes?

The first time Carter tried to kiss me was in his car on the first day of July. I dodged his lips and made up a reason why I had to go.

I'd let things get out of hand, and I felt horrible.

But the more I thought about it, the more it seemed silly to run from whatever this was. Vivian was with Carter *five years ago*. She was so far past that now, in college living her best life, hooking up with all sorts of people. And Mom was a year into her relationship with Ron, still, somewhat sickeningly, reminding me of Vivian when she was first dating Carter: always in an incredible mood, her mind constantly on Ron even when he wasn't around.

So, really, screw them. Carter was pursuing *me.* And chances were, he wouldn't remember any of what had happened with us five months from then anyway.

So, a week later, I kissed him.

We kissed a lot after that.

And, for the first time in my life, I got to see what it was like to be the one in the relationship.

The one who couldn't get someone out of their head.

The one in the incredibly good mood.

And I was. I really was.

Carter was funny. And hot. And charming.

And he liked *me.*

Not Vivian.

Me.

I told Mom about it in September. She was pissed. *Do you not remember what he did to your sister?* But I told her how happy I was, how I'd never felt this way before about anyone. Mom sighed and hugged me. We agreed that Vivian shouldn't know unless it got more serious.

Soon after, it occurred to me:

What if Carter was stuck in this loop *because* he dumped my sister?

And what if I could do what Vivian couldn't—get Carter to say *I love you* back?

I knew I was probably kidding myself to think it was that simple, but I couldn't shake the idea from my head. Especially because I felt like maybe I *did* love Carter, a thought that filled me with elation and shame and terror.

And so:

On that last night together, I told him I loved him. And he said it back. He actually said it.

But it didn't matter. It didn't work.

So I was done.

At least Vivian never had to find out.

And yet.

And yet and yet and yet.

There was Carter with Tatiana, and all I could think was:

He should be with ME, dammit.

But of course he shouldn't. That's over. And I'm with Chord.

There is, however, this Layla Banerjee problem.

I knew from Vivian that, before her, Carter had briefly dated—or hooked up, or *something*—with Layla, which was why I used her name as a decoy in the car that night. Very smooth.

And then That Carter told This Carter about Layla's existence, so now he's going to apologize to the wrong person, and it's my stupid fault.

Which means *I'm* the one who should be worrying about making things right. I need to tell Carter the truth before he humiliates himself on that call.

And then I say goodbye to him forever.

I sit up in bed—Shana dropped me at home after the game—and, since I don't want to text him and reveal my phone number, find Carter's profile on Instagram.

There's just one photo on his grid, a selfie he took of him and Bodhi, with the caption: *Walking around a random neighborhood like creepers bc we're too early to a party. We are cool I swear.* Must be from the night of Shana's party.

It would've been easier if he hadn't been there.

I open up a blank message field and type the words quickly, like I'm ripping off a Band-Aid.

Hey when are you talking with Layla?

I hover my finger over the purple Send button and close my eyes tight.

I hear Carter in my head: *"It can't hurt to try and make things right. Right?"*

I tap the button.

CARTER

"Oh," I say, stunned to see that it's Maggie Spear standing outside my front door and not some random delivery person.

"Hi," she says.

"What, uh . . . ?"

"I could have just called, I know. But I wanted to tell you something in person. If that's all right. You haven't talked to Layla yet, have you?"

"Well, no, but I will in . . ." I look down at my phone—5:19. "Eleven minutes."

"Whoa," Maggie says. "Okay, I'll be quick."

As confused as I am by this turn of events, I'm also delighted. It's hard not to feel delighted when I'm near Maggie. "Do you want to come inside?" I ask.

"Oh. Sure." She slowly steps over the threshold.

Maggie Spear is in my house.

Even though she's of course been here before, probably many times, which is confirmed when Mom comes out of the kitchen.

"Oh my! Maggie!"

"Hi, Mrs. Cohen," she says, taking off her sneakers without being asked. "Er, Wendy."

"Yes. Please call me Wendy, you know that. How are you, sweetheart?" She wraps Maggie in a hug. "I'm surprised to see you."

"I am too," I explain. "She just came to tell me something. So it's not like we're . . . Yeah."

"Fine with me," Mom says, hands in the air. "As long as it's what you both want, it's not my place to butt my big head in."

"Your head's not big, Mom."

"Thank you, Carter. Do you want to stay for dinner, Maggie?"

"Oh, no. Thanks, Wendy." Underneath her coat, Maggie's wearing a dark green jumpsuit. It's cool as hell. "That's sweet, but . . . I won't be here long."

"We're having quesadillas," Mom says, walking back into the kitchen.

Maggie and I stare at each other for a few awkward seconds, during which I remember that my FaceTime with Layla is imminent. I'd been incredibly nervous, but then Maggie came and distracted me from all that. Now I feel jittery all over again.

"I should probably go up to my room to start setting up for the call," I say. "But you can . . . you know . . ." I point upstairs.

"Come with you?" Maggie says.

"Only if you want to."

"For the call?"

"Well, yeah, or just talk to me for the next five minutes while I'm setting up and making sure my room looks presentable. But actually, if you're down to stay, I wouldn't mind the moral support." It would also make me feel like less of a creep. Like, *Look, Layla! This girl doesn't think I'm an asshole, so you shouldn't either!*

"Stay for the call?" Maggie asks again, as if I've asked her if she'd care to dissect a cat.

"Or not, if that weirds you out. I'm just really nervous."

"No, of course, yeah."

"Either way, I really do need to go upstairs."

"Okay," Maggie says. "Yeah, I'll follow you up there."

"Okay. Great."

I lead the way, Maggie right behind. I bet she's having memories of coming up here with me before. I furrow my brow, like maybe I can activate some of my own deeply buried memories, creak open some trapdoor wedged between my brain folds, some secret entrance into past incarnations of myself.

Nope.

We step into my bedroom. I'd already started cleaning it so Layla wouldn't get background glimpses of me being a mess of a person.

"Sweet banana peel," Maggie says, pointing below my desk.

Dammit, missed that.

"That's supposed to be there," I say. "For good luck."

"And good fragrance."

"Exactly." I pick it up and shoot it like a basketball across the room toward my wire wastebasket. I miss.

"Nice one," Maggie says, taking a cross-legged seat on my bed, real casual, like it's something she's done dozens of times before. She shrugs off her winter coat as she's looking around my room, and I can tell she's having Feelings. Perhaps regret for coming here.

I'm having Feelings too. Maggie looks real good in that jumpsuit. Like the world's hottest auto mechanic.

"So, yeah," I say, drumming on my thighs like a dweeb. "I guess there's not much else to really do before the call. What did you want to talk about?"

"Right." Maggie looks down, and I notice there's a red-hooded E.T. on each of her socks. So cool. She also has some kind of sparkly lip gloss on. I remember it from Shana's party.

Makes it hard to stop staring at her lips.

"Is it about Layla?" I ask.

"Not really," Maggie's mouth says. "Kind of."

"Oh god. Is there something else assholey I did that I should be apologizing for? I'd prefer not to do more than one call with her, you know? Get it all apologized for at once."

"Ha, right. No. There's nothing else you did to Layla. That I know of."

"Okay, good."

"Yeah."

I glance at my phone—5:28. "So . . . ?"

"So . . . Okay." Maggie pets my blue comforter like it's an animal. She's almost zookeeper-like in that jumpsuit, come to think of it. World's hottest zookeeper. "So you heard about the Layla breakup from yourself, right?"

"Right."

"And yourself heard about it from m—"

My phone vibrates in my hand, like a bomb is about to explode.

Layla. One minute early.

"It's her!" I shout, embarrassingly loud. "You're gonna stay for this, right?"

"Uh . . ." Maggie says.

"You have to! Please stay."

"Okay, okay, I'll stay!"

"Great! Thank you. So I'm going to pick up now, okay?"

"You got this."

"Do I?"

"I think so?"

"Wait, there's a chance I don't got this?"

"No, no, you do, you do!"

The phone keeps buzzing. I'm so confused.

"I have to do this, right?" I ask. "Layla might be the key!"

"Okay! Yeah! Sure!"

I accept the call, and Layla Banerjee fills the screen.

She's wearing a light blue workout top, her thick black hair in a ponytail. She is just as hot on FaceTime as she is on her grid. But, similar to Chord, she's, like, adult hot. Which instantly makes me even more anxious than I already was.

"Hi!" she says.

"Hi, Layla," I say.

"Oh my gosh, you look . . . exactly how I remember you looking."

"Well, yeah. That's kind of my thing."

She smiles, with warmth and pity. "Right. Of course. Sorry."

"It's okay. My friend Maggie is here too," I blurt out, turning the phone toward her. "Just so you know. Maybe you know her? Maggie Sp—"

"Hi, Layla!" Maggie says, her voice more high-pitched than I've ever heard it. "You probably wouldn't know me because we went to school so many years apart. But hi!"

"Nice to meet you, Maggie," Layla says. "I actually have someone here with me too." She pulls a furry head into frame, all floppy ears and sad eyes. "This is Chester. He's my roommate till we find him a home, aren't you, boy?" Her voice goes even higher than Maggie's just did. "You're such a very good boy too. The very best boy."

Chester barks right into the phone.

"You and your family wouldn't happen to be on the lookout

for a dog, would you, Carter?"

"Uh . . ." I'm not connecting with this dog the way I did with Peaches. And I don't even understand how adopting Chester would be logistically possible. Would Layla drive him across the country?

"His name is kind of like yours, actually! Chest*er* . . . Cart*er* . . . Could be a sign."

"Oh, funny." I exchange a quick look with Maggie, who vehemently shakes her head while trying not to laugh. "Yeah. No, I don't think my family wants that. Right now. Unfortunately. But definitely a cute dog. Very cute. Very good. Good boy."

"He is a good boy." Layla rubs her nose against Chester's one last time before sitting up and shifting the view back to just her. "So, look, Carter, I'm sorry I didn't respond sooner. You sent that first message, and I saw it, but I thought maybe it was someone impersonating you or something, and I just let it be. But then you wrote back again and I realized it probably *was* you, and I'd been leaving you hanging for so long. I felt bad. I'm sorry."

"Oh." I'm shocked that somehow she's the one apologizing to me. "That's completely fine. Like, beyond fine. I mean, the whole reason I wanted to talk actually was to apologize to *you*."

"To me?" Layla says. "Oh god. That's very sweet, Carter."

"Of course. I heard that stuff with us, years ago . . . ended with me being kind of a dick. And I'm sorry about that."

"Well, apology accepted. And not even necessary. You've gone through enough over the past years without having to worry about that too. We had our thing, it ended, I was kind of annoyed, and I got over it. It's seriously all good."

"Oh. Okay." *Kind of annoyed*. That's like how I feel after I lose a race I know I should've won in *Mario Kart*. I can't believe apologizing was this easy. I look over to Maggie, and she seems pretty surprised too. "That's great. Thanks, Layla."

"Of course! And, if you don't mind me asking—are you doing okay otherwise? Do the doctors . . . you know . . ."

"Think I'll ever age again?"

"Right, yeah," Layla says, smiling sheepishly. "I guess that's what I was going for."

"They have no idea. But, I mean, I feel hopeful." I shoot Maggie a smile like *Maybe this very conversation is going to help me age!* but she still has that shell-shocked expression on her face and doesn't smile back.

"I'm glad," Layla says.

"Yep." I nod. We sit in a few excruciating seconds of FaceTime silence. "So I guess—"

"You know, Carter. This is an embarrassing story, but . . ."

"I love embarrassing stories," I say, wondering what the hell she's about to say.

"Okay." Layla smiles big. Her teeth are so white. "When we were in second grade, Ms. Berkovich's class, we were in the same reading group. Do you remember that?"

"Kinda, yeah."

"So, there was this one day—remember I said this was embarrassing—when I was, well . . . picking my nose when I thought no one was watching. But Ollie Fusco-White saw, and he was loudly like, 'Ew! Gross! Nose-picker, nose-picker! Layla's a nose-picker!' And the rest of our group was also horrified, so they joined in, and I was, like, collapsing into myself as I prepared for it to spread to the whole class. I saw this new future identity unfolding before me. But then you were like, 'So what? I pick my nose all the time.' And then you started picking your nose right there in front of everyone."

"Ohmigod, yes!" I say, laughing. It's such a relief to actually remember a moment someone is talking about. "And then they started saying *I* was gross, so I put a booger on my finger and started waving it in their faces."

"Yes!" Layla says.

"Ew," Maggie says.

"And then Ms. Berkovich got mad and made you sit at a desk by yourself while reading group finished. And no one in our group brought up my nose-picking again. Ever. I was so grateful to you for that."

"Oh," I say. "Wow." I never realized I was being heroic in that moment. I just liked chasing people with my boogers.

"So, honestly," Layla says, "that's what I remember about you even more than what happened between us sophomore year. Hopefully that's not insulting or anything, but—"

"It's not insulting at all," I say. It's like a backpack filled with boulders has just slid off me. "It's really great. Like, really. Thanks, Layla."

"Also worth mentioning," she says, "I don't pick my nose anymore. Just to make that clear."

"All good with me either way."

"But I really don't."

"Okay."

"Great. And, by the way, Ollie Fusco-White is apparently in some FBI training program now. So, go figure."

"Well, that's unsettling."

"It is." Another torturous pause. "So I guess I'm gonna go now. Unless you have other questions?"

"Yeah, no, sounds good. Thanks again for doing this."

"My pleasure. And thanks for the apology. I release you!" She makes an almost magical gesture with her hands when she says that, and I get a full-body chill, almost as if those specific words have just unstuck me. Can that be? Am I going to turn seventeen now? From this six-minute conversation? Much of which was spent watching Layla kiss a dog?

"Thanks."

"Great to see you, Carter. And nice to meet you, Maggie!"

I clumsily flip the camera toward Maggie again.

She waves. "You too!"

"Ohmigod," Layla says. "I just put it together who you look like. You're Vivian Spear's younger sister, aren't you?"

Maggie doesn't respond. Then she starts coughing.

"Do you want water?" I ask, turning the phone back toward myself.

"No, I'm okay," she says. "I've just been . . . fighting this cold thing. Sorry. I am Vivian Spear's younger sister, but I actually should go. Probably need more cold medicine."

"No problem," Layla says. "Tell Vivian I said hi, though. Haven't seen her in a while. I assume, Carter, that you've—"

"Oh!" Maggie says, coughing again so hard that she bumps into me, and I drop the phone. "I'm sorry, so sorry."

"It's fine," I say, picking up the phone. "Thanks again, Layla, I'm gonna go help Maggie."

"Of course. Good luck and be well!"

"You too!" I end the call.

Maggie is still coughing away into her elbow. I fill up my water glass in the bathroom and bring it to her. She chugs the whole thing in one go.

"You all right?" I ask.

"Yeah, this cough comes and goes," Maggie says. "I feel so stupid."

"Don't," I say. "Everybody coughs sometimes. And that went really well! She totally accepted my apology!"

"Uh-huh." Even though Maggie is sort of smiling, she also looks like she wants to throw up.

"Oh man, you seem pretty sick. Want me to go get cough medicine?"

"No. No. Could you . . . Could you sit down with me for a second?"

"Sure. Absolutely." I slowly lower myself onto the bed next to Maggie. I'm instantly aware that there are only a few inches separating us. And, again, my eyes are drawn to her lips—her glossy, glittery lips—even now, when she's liable to cough phlegm into my face at any moment.

Maggie doesn't speak, so I do. "I appreciate you sticking around. That was helpful to have you here."

"You did a good job."

"Thanks. It feels nice."

Maggie nods.

"Do you want to say what you came over here to say?"

"It's just . . ." Maggie takes a deep breath and rubs one of her closed eyes. "I feel like a bad person. For . . . reasons. And I hate this feeling."

"You think *you're* a bad person? Maggie, I'm the one who

sucks so bad I got myself stuck in a time loop. Have *you* ever gotten yourself stuck in a time loop?"

She shakes her head, eyes glassy, the tiniest of smiles appearing on her face.

"Like, if what I did to Layla caused this," I say, "think how bad I must have hurt her. *That* is some serious bad personing right there. Though, she honestly didn't seem like she thought it was a big deal at all. So that was weird. Time heals all wounds, I guess. But, look, even an asshole like me can find redemption! She released me!"

"You're not an asshole, Carter," Maggie says.

I shrug. "I think everybody has asshole potential if you catch 'em at the right moment."

"Maybe. But I'm sorry I've had to be such an asshole to *you*."

"You haven't!"

"Avoiding you. Lying to you. So shitty."

"I get it, though! You're doing what you have to in order to protect yourself."

"But maybe that's silly." Maggie reaches her hand out and puts it on mine.

I look at her.

I hold my entire body still, even as my insides are engulfed by a tidal wave.

"Well," I say.

"What I came over to say," Maggie says, moving her fingers lightly along the back of my hand, "was . . . that it wasn't . . ."

"Wasn't what?"

I stare into her eyes, trying to understand what she's getting at.

Finally she speaks.

"Sometimes I still want to kiss you."

“Oh.”

Maggie inches slightly toward me. I remain a statue.

Of course I want to kiss her. Like, obviously.

But.

“What about Chord?” I ask. “I mean, I wouldn’t want him to, like, get frayed.”

“That doesn’t— It’s not— Don’t worry.”

It’s a highly unconvincing answer, but then I’m completely convinced anyway, because Maggie’s glossy lips are on mine, and mine are on hers, and it’s finally happening.

We’re finally happening.

I am the tidal wave, we are the tidal wave, and we lose ourselves as we crash down upon the shore.

APRIL.

MAGGIE

So I went to Carter's house to make things right, and instead I just . . .

Kissed him.

I know, okay?

I know.

I thought the truth would come out naturally during the call with Layla.

It did not.

I wanted to tell Carter about Vivian after that, I really did.

But I also wanted to kiss him.

Like, a lot.

So I did.

And he kissed me.

And it felt right.

I'm tired of trying to convince myself that not being with the guy I've liked more than anyone in my whole life is a good thing.

So we made out that night. I thought maybe I'd regret it afterward.

I did not.

So we made out the next night.

And again a couple days after that.

And a bunch of other times in the past few weeks.

Including right now.

Yes. We are making out right now.

“I can’t stop thinking about you,” Carter says, his lips brushing mine, his hand tangled up in my hair.

“Hard same,” I say, more or less lying on top of him, as much as that’s possible in the back seat of his not-so-large vehicle, Toro. We’re parked under some trees at Brisby Brook Park, which has become a regular spot for us. I like it because it’s romantic. And also hidden.

“Let’s stay here till tomorrow,” Carter says, his hand sliding down my back toward my butt.

“I wish.” I move my mouth to Carter’s neck, then kiss a ladder back up to his lips. “I have to leave in a bit. Going out to dinner with Mom and Ron.”

“Just skip it. They’ll be fine.”

“Trust me, I would love to. But it’s, like, a celebration.”

“Oh.” Carter moves his head to the side. “Of what?”

Dammit. Why did I say that word? I want us to keep kissing.

Maybe I can make up some other good news Mom, Ron, and I would be celebrating. Like, that we got a puppy or something. A miniature schnauzer! Named Dipsy!

I have to tell him.

“I, um . . . officially decided to go to Delaware.”

“Oh man!” Carter says. “That’s really exciting, Mags.”

“Thanks.” But already I see his mind spinning, his light dimming. I try to kiss the brightness back into him. “Are you okay?” I ask.

“Yeah, of course,” Carter says, staring past me at the car ceiling. “I just . . .”

“I know.” I shift my body off his, and we both sit up. “I’m sorry.”

The few times college has come up since we got back together, it's had this effect on Carter. I get it, but I'd prefer not to talk about it. I want to focus on how his tongue tastes. On how good it feels when he touches me. When it's just the two of us, escaping the rest of the world. No talk of the future. Or the past. Just the present.

"You don't have to apologize," Carter says. "It's great. You're going to college. You *should* go to college. Like Lincoln. Like Manny. And I'll stay here, and when my birthday comes, I'll probably loop back and forget you anyway, so it's whatever, you know? And, unlike this time, I won't even see you in the hall at school, so—"

"Hey," I say, putting a hand on each side of Carter's face and looking into his eyes. His beautiful green eyes. "Maybe don't think about that yet, okay? Let's just . . . Let's be here together now. You know?"

After a moment, Carter nods, giving me such a sweetly vulnerable look that I must kiss him again immediately. Our lips touch, and something inside me uncoils. He's very good at kissing.

"Do you think," he says between kisses, "apologizing to Layla might actually be the thing?"

I pull back and stare at him.

"That gets me out of this?" he clarifies, as if I don't understand what he's talking about.

"Well," I say, because of course I know there's no way that apology will do what he's hoping it will. "I mean, I think . . . DUCK!"

"What?" Carter says.

I tackle him down to the seat so that we won't be seen by the people I know who are walking perilously close past our window.

"Whoa!" Carter says. "What's happening?"

"I'm sorry," I say, an inch from his face. "This girl Renata from school was passing by with some other folks. Renata's friends with Marigold, and Marigold's friends with Chord, so, you know . . ."

"I see," Carter says, a smile in his voice. "Not intense at all."

"I feel bad, okay?" I say, laughing.

"But you did break up with him, right?"

"Of course!" I ended things with Chord the day after Carter and I first made out. (I haven't been cheating on him this whole time. I'm not a total monster.) "But I didn't say it was because of you, so I . . . I just don't want him to know about us yet."

"Fine, all right," Carter says, resting his hands lightly on my back. "But that doesn't explain why your mom can't know about us either. Unless you're worried she's gonna tell Chord during one of their regular FaceTimes."

"Ha!" I say. "Touché. I guess it's like . . . I don't know. Everything's so bonkers with Mom's wedding coming up. She's out of her mind enough already. I want us to be able to figure out what this is before bringing other people—and their opinions—into it."

"Will your mom have an . . . opinion about me?"

"I'm not really sure," I say, scrambling for words. "But she knows how painful it was for me last time when you . . ."

"Yeah, I get that." Carter's hands slide under my shirt, up along the skin of my back. "Though, I hate to break this to you—I'm pretty sure my parents are on to us."

Seeing as I've been to his house three more times since that first night, always hanging out in his bedroom with the door closed, that makes sense.

"I know." I slip my hands under Carter's T-shirt, up along his chest. I move my mouth closer until it's a millimeter from his.

"And soon everyone else will know too. Okay, Carter Cohen?"

"Okay, Maggie Spear." He presses my body toward his before kissing me again. "I gotta admit," he whispers into my ear. "The hiding thing *is* kinda hot."

CARTER

"Link! Hey!" I shout into my phone. "You're actually there."

Lincoln's been so busy with school that we've barely been in touch, just short text exchanges here and there. He doesn't even know Maggie and I are back together. But in mid-April, I finally get ahold of him.

"I am," Lincoln says, sitting alone on his dorm room bed. "Getting some reading done."

"Wow, college seriously seems like a never-ending string of work." I plop down onto my own bed. "I don't know if I wanna go, even if I do find a way to age up."

"Ah, it's not as bad as it seems." Lincoln smiles, but it seems kind of fake. "So what's up?"

"Not much. I've been watching different time-loop movies. Like, for research or inspiration or whatever. *Palm Springs. Groundhog Day.* Just finished *Big.* Which isn't a time loop, but, you know."

"And . . . ?"

"Eh. The loops in *Palm Springs* and *Groundhog Day* are just a day, not a year. And it's the *same* day, over and over, and both those guys remember everything that happens."

"Right," Lincoln says.

"And *Big* was a wish he made that turned him into an adult. But I doubt I wished for *this*. Why would I do that?"

"Yeah, I mean . . ." Lincoln runs a hand through his curls and over his scalp. "They're just movies. So."

"Geez, all right. Thanks for your support, bro."

"I do support you!" Lincoln says, having picked up on my heavy sarcasm. "But, to be totally honest, this isn't the first time you've watched those movies . . ."

"Okay, see?" I say, trying not to look as disappointed as I feel. "That's helpful, Link! I need to know this stuff so I'm not just repeating the same tactics. It's eight months till my next loop—time is of the essence!" I get up from the bed and walk out of my room, across the hallway. "Which is why when you're home this summer, you're gonna bring me up to speed on everything, and we're gonna figure this shit out! Am I right?"

"Uh." Lincoln tries to smile, but it looks more like a constipated grimace.

"Look where I am," I say, flipping the phone around. "Your room! It misses you so much, won't stop yapping about you. I keep telling it to calm down. You'll be home in like a few weeks, right?"

"Not . . . exactly," Lincoln says. "I . . . I got this internship."

"Oh." I flip the phone back toward myself. "What does that mean?"

"It means . . . A slot just opened up, and I got it. It's cool, actually. I'm gonna be helping this psychology professor I love. On campus."

I stare past the screen, at Lincoln's pristine bed, this eerily clean room, devoid of life. "Congrats," I say, fighting hard not to unleash another snarky comment. "That's great. So . . . what? You're not gonna be here? All summer?"

"Well," Lincoln says, visibly squirming, "unfortunately not

much. I'll be home for a bit here and there, but yeah. Mostly I'll be in campus housing. Can't exactly commute from New Jersey to Pennsylvania every day, you know?"

I nod, unable to form words, a ragged knot in my stomach. I assumed Lincoln would be home soon, that we'd have a few months when things would finally feel closer to normal.

"Totally," I say, impressed by how steady my voice seems. "Makes sense. I mean, I definitely think your room is devastated right now." I aim my phone at the wall above his bed. "So sorry you had to hear that, Lincoln's Room. I'm sure Lincoln will make it up to you somehow." I turn the screen back to myself. "But I, on the other hand, am proud of you, little bro. You're doing such cool stuff. I'll probably be spending lots of time with Maggie this summer anyway. We got back together. I've been meaning to tell you."

"Oh," Lincoln says, eyebrows raised high. "Really? Wow. Okay."

"Yeah. Really. And it's been amazing."

Lincoln nods a bunch. "Okay then. I mean, if . . . Yeah. Congrats."

"Why are you being weird about this?" I ask, the words leaping out of my mouth without permission. "It's good news. I'm happy about it."

"Of course, CT," Lincoln says. "It is good news. It's just—Maggie literally messaged me the day you looped back to tell me I shouldn't mention her name to you. Because she didn't want to be with you again. So I'm . . . I don't know."

"She changed her mind!" I say, pacing past Lincoln's desk. "Is that not allowed? I know I'm stuck this age forever, but let's rejoice about the things that *can* change, right? Instead of being a buzzkill? Like with this Layla apology, too. I'm all excited for what that could mean, and you barely seem to care."

"No," Lincoln says, massaging the side of his face, "that's because— Honestly, I just find it frustrating that you think I don't care when I've spent the past five years being here for you in every way possible. I'm almost literally a human search engine for every question you have about Maggie or the past or whatever. Meanwhile, you barely ask me anything about my life."

It's as if he's stuck a hand through the screen and flicked my nose.

"A human search engine? Geez, sorry that I sometimes turn to my brother to try to figure things out! Didn't realize that was so offensive."

"It's not offensive!" Lincoln throws his head back, looks up at the ceiling, then back to me. "That's not what I'm trying to say. I'm just telling you how I feel. But you've never been able to take that in. So why start now?"

I'm frozen to the floor, vibrating with anger. "Is it that you don't like seeing me happy? Is that it?"

"I gotta go, CT."

"No, seriously," I say, "are you so used to me being down in the dumps that it's, like, hard to see me actually experiencing joy now that I'm with Maggie?"

"Yeah, fine, you got me," Lincoln says, his voice drained of all emotion. "Let's talk another time. Okay?"

"Works for me."

Lincoln shakes his head and sighs, and the call ends.

I stare for a moment at the screen where he used to be, trying to breathe through the itchy, raw feeling in my stomach.

"You should be glad he's not coming home," I say to the walls. "Because he's being a huge dick."

I pounce onto my brother's bed and mess up the covers as much as I can.

MAY.

MAGGIE

"Coco!" I say, laughing as Carter kisses me. "I seriously need to go."

"It's all good," he says, gesturing to his baseball cap and sunglasses. "I'm in disguise, remember?"

We're in his car, parked on my street, and I'm late to band practice. At my own house.

"Yes, and it's so effective even I can't tell who you are," I say. "But since my mom thinks I was just hanging out with Shana, who is now literally in my home without me—undoubtedly super pissed that I'm late—I must leave this car."

"At least you have the apology Munchkins." He points to the box in my lap that I just raced into Dunkin' to acquire.

"And thank god for that. Now I go."

"Okay. I'll miss you."

Carter kisses me again, one hand on my cheek. His lips are so soft.

I finally extract myself from Toro and run as nonchalantly as possible into my house, then down the basement steps.

"I know you've been late a lot recently," Shana says in between string plucks while tuning her guitar. "But *you live here*."

"I'm really sorry," I say, walking into our practice area, which, until recently, was the part of the basement that's meant for storage. We lazily repurposed the space by pushing stacks of bins and boxes to the sides, so it's kind of like playing music in the middle of a hoarder's fort. "But look: Munchkins!"

"Hooray!" Ember shouts as they shift their bass drum into place.

"I've literally been gluten-free since September," Shana says.

"Ah shoot, you have!" I say, passing the box to Ember. "My bad, Shane. I don't think Dunkin' does gluten-free Munchkins."

"I don't care about the Munchkins!" Shana lifts her hands from the guitar like she wants to strangle me. "I'm just annoyed. That you're late *again*."

"I know," I say, taking off my coat and sitting down at my keyboard. "I suck, okay? I said I was sorry."

"But I'm more annoyed that you've been back together with Carter for weeks and haven't bothered telling us."

"Oh." It's like she just pointed out I'm wearing nothing but underwear. "Well. How did you know?"

"Uh," Shana says, "because we have eyes? And brains? And because it made very little sense to me why you would break up with Chord until I put the Carter thing together."

"That's not the only reason I broke up with Chord!"

"So, you're, like, doing this again?" Shana gives her guitar a big, boisterous strum that bounces off the basement walls. "And you're okay with that?"

"I am. I think." I know I should have told Shana and Ember sooner. But I was worried—correctly, it turns out—that Shana would disapprove and try to convince me to stop. "I mean, being with Carter feels . . . right. So, yeah. But I wasn't . . . When it started again, it was because I had just ended up at his house, and—"

"You went to his *house*?" Shana says. "What did you think was going to happen at his *house*?"

Ember laughs as they step on the bass drum's pedal and make adjustments.

"I know, I know." I play a quick G major scale on my keyboard, as if that might somehow reboot our entire conversation. "But I actually went over there to tell him the truth about . . . You know." I point upstairs.

"The truth about your mom? What is the truth about your mom?"

"No! My sister," I whisper.

"You told him about that?"

"Well, no, I didn't, because we ended up making out instead."

"I see the logic," Shana says. "If I had to choose between making out with the tragic boy I'm in love with or telling him a long-kept secret he might not like at all, it would be a very easy decision."

"I know I need to tell him. I will."

"Wait, what is this about your sister?" Ember asks, lightly tapping a cymbal with their drumstick.

"Carter used to, like, date her," I say. "A long time ago."

"Right before he developed his disorder," Shana helpfully adds.

"No way!" Ember says. "That's insane!"

I don't go out of my way to tell people about Carter and Vivian. Took me a long time before I even told Shana.

"And Carter doesn't know that?"

"Not yet."

"Whoa." Ember shakes their head, as if they can't believe their bandmate is such a psychopath. "That's . . . Did you tell him in the fall? The last time you were dating? And he's just forgotten?"

"No," I say. "But what does it even matter?" This band practice is feeling more like an intervention. I don't like it.

Ember answers with a shrug and a bite of a glazed Munchkin.

"Marigold says Chord is still gutted, by the way," Shana says.

"'Gutted'?" I say. "Seriously? We dated for like a month. People are overusing that word."

"I'm just telling you what she said."

I let my lips puff out as I exhale, trying not to let myself feel as horrible as I know I should. I pop a powdered Munchkin into my mouth.

"She also said he still can't believe you broke up over text."

"All right," I say, trying not to wince, crumbs bouncing out of my mouth. "Chord looks like an adult and acts like an adult, so why can't he deal with this like an adult? Life sucks sometimes. Get over it, dude. Stop passing messages through your friend to make me feel guilty."

I do feel guilty. Obviously. But I couldn't handle making my breakup with Chord into a big, dramatic thing—I've had plenty of those as it is—so I just told him in a text that he's great but I didn't think it was working out and I was really sorry.

Oh, he texted back. *Could you explain why exactly?*

It felt like a homework assignment. Or a standardized test.

I did not respond.

But hey, I could've not texted at all. I could've just ghosted the guy!

I'm not a bad person.

Am I?

I might be a bad person.

"He's not passing messages, Maggie," Shana says with this fire in her eyes that scares me. "He's expressing his feelings to a friend, who is then mentioning them to *her* friend. You don't have to be so mean about it. You dumped the guy in a text, what did you expect?"

I know there are probably legitimate points buried in what she's saying, but I'd prefer not to dig them up. "I'm not sure, Shana. I guess I didn't expect one of my best friends to so vehemently defend this random dude instead of me. But maybe that's too much to ask."

Now Shana looks like I've smacked her with a dueling glove, and I'm straight-up terrified. Ember, seated behind their drum kit, looks pretty freaked too.

"I have been here for you in every possible way," Shana says, her left hand gripping the neck of the guitar so tight, it looks like it might snap. "Keeping your secrets. Cheering you on. Having your back. Trying to stop you from having any interaction with Carter, including when he showed up at my stupid party. So don't talk to me about not defending you."

"Fine," I say, trying to seem like a tough, brave person. "I won't. Can we start rehearsing some of these songs?"

"I dunno." Shana shakes her head. "I might be too annoyed by you right now."

"I'm sorry! I'm an annoying person, what can I say?"

"Yeah, okay." Shana pulls the guitar strap over her head, kicks open the case on the floor, and places her acoustic inside it.

"Uh. You're leaving?" I feel tears quivering, threatening to jump ship.

"I am." Shana clicks shut the case's latches one by one, a devastating barrage of snaps.

I look to Ember for help. They look petrified.

Is it weird that I had minimal awareness of what a shitty friend I've been? Maybe being with Carter has led me to develop my own strange disorder. Of the brain.

"I'm sorry I offended you, Shana," I say, standing up from the keyboard. "I really am. Don't leave. The wedding is like a month from now! You haven't even heard this new song yet."

"Thank you for that very genuine-sounding apology"—she sounds sarcastic, so I must not have sounded as genuine as I was trying to—"but I can't rehearse right now. The vibes are wrong. And bad."

"Are you quitting the band?"

"No, I'm not *quitting the band,* I just don't want to be here right now! Stop talking!" Shana walks out of the storage area of the basement with her guitar. We hear her marching up the carpeted steps.

I turn to Ember again, still frozen behind the drums, drumsticks crossed on their lap. "You couldn't have tried to stop her?"

"I don't know, man," they say. "You're both in full beast mode right now."

"Yeah." I sit back down at the keys. "That's fair."

"I do think it's cool that you and Carter are back together," Ember says.

"Thanks. I think so too. But I've—"

"Hey there," Mom says, popping her head in and totally startling me. "Are you already done rehearsing?"

"No," I say. "Shana just had to go do something."

"Oh. All right. How's it been going?"

"Great. Really good."

"You're going to be all set for the wedding, right?" Mom seems nervous, like she's regretting asking us to do this. Like she wishes she'd asked Vivian to sing some jazz standards instead.

"Mom! Of course. Yes. We're going to honor your and Ron's love in an epic fashion. We will be the musical equivalent of fireworks spelling your names."

Mom smiles. "Well, you don't have to be *that*. I just want to make sure you're not in over your heads."

This is how my mom sees me, as perpetually in over my head.

Maybe she's right to see me that way.

"We got this, Mrs. Spear," Ember says, this time heroically stepping in to get my back, even though they don't realize Mom goes by her maiden name now. "You were at our gig—it's gonna be like that, but way more amazing. Because we keep getting better."

"Oh, good," Mom says, sighing and wiping imaginary sweat off her forehead with the back of her hand. "That's nice to hear."

Of course she believes it now that she's heard it from someone who's not me.

"Well, I'll leave you to it, then," Mom says. "Let you keep getting better."

"Thanks," Ember says.

Mom is staring at me as she walks out, as if waiting for my response, but all I can do is nod because I'm too angry to talk.

CARTER

"Are you sure you're okay to miss prom?" I ask for the twenty-second time.

"Carter," Maggie says, reaching across the table for my hand. "The only place I want to be right now is here. With you. At our non-prom."

"Okay." I give her a goofy smile.

Going to prom wasn't really an option, as Maggie still isn't ready for the world (meaning Chord and her family) to know about us. I keep telling her she could go on her own. You only get one senior prom. And, if you're me, you might never even get that.

But she insisted on skipping, so we drove several towns over to this seafood restaurant where we won't know anyone. We're sitting outside on a beautiful spring night, twinkle lights strung above, as a cheesy cover band called Beachy Bill and the Bobcat Boys provides background music. I'm wearing one of the two ties I own—this one has Spider-Man on it—and Maggie is in a yellow sundress, her hair up so I can see every freckle on her shoulders.

It's hard to imagine that any prom could be better than this.

"Hey," I say once we've ordered, "can I ask you something kind of funny?"

"What kind of funny are we talking about?" Maggie asks, her eyes narrowing. "Hilarious? Uncomfortable? Embarrassing? Strange?"

"Maybe all of those?"

"Okay, yeah. Go for it."

"So, I guess I'm wondering . . ." I unfold my cloth napkin. "What was it like the first time we dated?"

"Aha," Maggie says, and I can tell she's the slightest bit uncomfortable. We've been secretly hooking up for almost two months now, and it's been pretty much the best thing that ever happened to me. (At least, as far as I can remember.) But this is the part of being with her I've enjoyed the least, having a history that only she knows, needing SparkNotes for my own relationship. "What was it *like*?"

"Yeah," I say. "Like, the first time we dated. And when we first met. Your first impression of me. What we did on dates. Stuff like that."

"Oh." Maggie takes a sip of her water and crunches an ice cube. "Well, I mean, we met at Scoops 'n' Sprinkles. Which I think you already know."

"And was I an attractive scooper?"

"The most attractive," Maggie says. "My god, such dazzling scoop work."

"Were you, like, immediately into me?"

"I . . . I was. Yes." Maggie shifts in her chair. "But can we come back to this topic? Another time? I just feel sort of put on the spot. Or something."

"Oh," I say. "For sure. I wasn't trying to . . . Sorry."

"It's totally fine." Maggie squeezes my knee under the table, which only slightly eases the curdling sense that I've messed up somehow. "Will you dance with me?" she asks, standing up and extending her hand.

"Here?"

"Yes, here! Beachy Bill needs us." She points at the fiftysomething white men with instruments, who have just started playing a buoyant and aggressive rendition of "Brown-Eyed Girl."

"Yeah, okay." I reluctantly rise. Maggie lifts my arm and spins herself underneath it, which makes me laugh.

I spin Maggie close and wrap my arms around her waist.

She puts her arms around my neck.

"I like you so much," she says, as we sway back and forth to some of the most unsubtle *sha-la-la*s I've ever heard in my life.

"I like *you* so much," I say.

"Okay, good," she says, her breath tickling my ear. "Glad we're agreed."

We dance beneath the twinkle lights until our food arrives.

It's one of my favorite nights of all time.

And we emerge from it closer than ever. Over the next couple weeks—other than when Maggie goes away for the weekend with her family for her sister's commencement—we hang out almost every day.

Never at school, sometimes in my car, but mostly at my house.

And it's not just making out!

We also watch classic nineties movies and play *Super Smash Bros.* on Nintendo Switch (Maggie, despite never having played before, is exceptionally good at it) and sing along to throwback playlists of hits from ten years ago (so that I have a shot at knowing the lyrics).

But okay, yeah, it's a lot of making out. In my bed. With the door shut tight.

"Hey," I say now, my free hand moving up and under Maggie's T-shirt as my lips descend from her mouth to her chin to her neck. "I have a question."

It's something I've been wanting to ask for a while, but since she shut down all lines of inquiry at our non-prom, I've had a hard time finding the right moment. It feels more urgent every day, though.

"Uh-huh," Maggie whispers.

"Did we ever, you know . . . do it?"

"You mean have sex?" she asks. "Almost. But no. Not yet."

"Maybe we should," I say, my lips still grazing her neck. "One day. At some point in the next six and a half months. Not that I'm keeping track of time or anything."

I'm expecting Maggie to laugh at this, but she just says, "Yeah. I would like that."

OH HELL YEAH.

"Okay. Cool," I say. I shift upward, so I can look into her eyes, but she pulls away and propels herself from the bed.

"Hold on, sorry. I keep hearing my phone buzz." Maggie digs around in her bag on the floor, then crouches staring at her phone with an increasingly disturbed look on her face.

"Everything okay?" I ask.

"Um, it seems my dad is . . . coming to my mom's wedding?"

"Is that bad?"

"Well, it's not good!"

"Okay." I sit up, recognizing that our make-out session is going to be on hold for a moment.

"I mean," Maggie says, finally standing up out of her crouch, "I wrote a song for my mom and Ron, all about their love and stuff, and now I have to perform that in front of my dad?"

"Will he be . . . jealous? Does he want to get back together with your mom?"

"No. It's not that." Maggie slowly paces around the room. "They were . . . They weren't the right fit. But I know he's bummed about the wedding. Like, six years after the divorce, Mom is moving on and he's . . . not. I didn't think he'd want to be there to watch, though."

"Your mom invited him?"

"No, he asked her if he could come, which is so my dad. He said he wanted to see my band play. And see my sister officiate. 'Cause she's, like, the one leading the ceremony."

"Oh. That's cool. What is her name again?"

Maggie pauses at the window, staring outside. "My sister?"

"Yeah."

"Vivian."

"Vivian . . . Was she in my grade?"

"Um. Year below you."

"Vivian Spear . . . Oh yeah! I think I remember who that is. She's pretty."

"Mm."

Maggie's voice has gone cold, and I realize maybe it's not the classiest thing to tell the girl you've just been making out with that you think her sister is attractive.

"Not as pretty as you, though!" I backpedal. "At all! Obviously. You're the hottest girl I've ever known. I was just trying to be nice."

"Thanks, Coco." She doesn't sound mad. Just kind of sad. Or something. She turns around from the window and sits back down next to me. "Anyway, Ron told Mom she should tell my dad he's welcome, that it could be healing for the whole family if he's there, so she did." She chucks her phone onto her bag. "Kinda makes me want to barf."

"Feel free. Just aim for the carpet and not my lap."

Maggie falls backward onto the bed, arms sprawled out above her. "Why is everything so stupid?"

"I ask myself that all the time. Don't move." I grab my camera from the dresser and frame Maggie, adjusting the focus.

"Hey, I didn't grant permission for this."

"I'm sorry, your breathtaking beauty made me forget myself. Can I take your picture? In honor of you graduating in less than a month?"

"I guess so." She stretches her mouth into a giant smile. "Anything in my teeth?"

"Nope, you're golden." I snap a pic, then another and another. Maggie's completely goofy at first but gradually relaxes into something more natural. I snap a few more, then look at them in the viewfinder. The end-of-day light is shining onto her in this almost ethereal way. It's like she's glowing.

"Can I see?" Maggie is up on one elbow.

"Not yet." I surprise myself with how decisively I pull the camera away.

"Come on!" Maggie paws at my shoulder. "Why not?"

"Because I'm worried I actually suck at this."

"So what if you do?"

"Then I'll feel stupid and embarrassed and not want to take photos ever again?"

"You're insane," Maggie says. "Take one we're both in."

I mess around with the depth of focus, then grab Maggie around the waist with one arm and hold my camera out with the other. I snap a few pics.

"Yay! Can I at least see those?" Maggie asks.

"Nope."

Maggie sighs and drops back onto her side. "You wouldn't let me see your pictures in the fall either, even though you'd obviously gotten very good at it."

"How about this," I offer. "When you tell your family and the rest of the world about us, then I'll show you these photos."

Maggie sighs. "I am going to tell them, okay? I promise. Just not yet."

"Okay. But I could be your date at the wedding. I could follow you around with a barf bag."

Maggie sits up and throws her arms around my shoulders from behind, nestling her head next to mine. "I appreciate that. And I'm so happy about this. About us. It's just . . . My mom and dad and sister don't want me to be with you a second time for the same reason I didn't want to. They know I'll likely get hurt again."

"I know, I know," I say, turning myself around so I can face Maggie again. "But maybe you won't! Like, maybe my apology to Layla really did shift something. And either way, we're feeling good *now*, right? Doesn't your family care about that? Instead of just you being happy in the future?"

Maggie looks into my eyes with this unreadable expression. Maybe hopeful. Maybe scared. "Is it okay if I just say no on this? For . . . reasons?"

"It is," I say.

She kisses me, and I kiss her, and the make-out hold is officially lifted.

"One sec," Maggie says, lifting her hand off my thigh and bending down to reach for her bag. "I just—" She pokes around in her bag for a moment before stepping over to my desk. She opens the drawer and studies its contents. "Aha!" She triumphantly lifts up a pack of wintermint gum. "Still here!"

"Ha, what?"

"I left this in there in the fall! For moments like this!" She unwraps a piece and pops it into her mouth. "I love that it's still here. You want?"

"Uh . . . I don't think so."

"Okay. I feel better now, thanks." She sits back down and leans in, and we're kissing again.

But I'm still thinking about the gum.

Like, that's my desk. And I didn't even know that was in there. But Maggie did.

She stops. "You all right, Coco?"

"Yeah. Totally." I clutch the edge of my mattress, trying to shake off this feeling. "You know, I have no idea why you call me that."

"Coco?"

I nod. "It's like an inside joke between you and the old me."

Maggie is silent for a moment. "Yeah. I'm sorry," she says finally. "When we first started hanging out, I was using both your names a lot. Like calling you Carter Cohen, just in everyday conversation. And then that shortened to CarCo, but you complained that it sounded like a discount car brand."

"It does. CarCo is the worst nickname I've ever heard. Also sounds like a rotting—"

"Carcass. Yes. That was your other line of complaint. So I switched to Coco as a joke. Which you also kind of hated, but maybe secretly sort of loved?"

"Huh. I do like that Pixar movie. And I'm kinda like that kid. We both wear hoodies a lot."

“Actually,” Maggie says, folding my fingers into hers, “I would joke with you about that song Miguel sings to get his great-grandma Coco to remember her dad. ‘Remember Me.’”

“Oh. Yeah. More relevant than the hoodies.”

We both go quiet, reminded of the horror of our situation. Because, once I looped, I definitively did *not* remember Maggie. And I’ll likely forget her again. I sort of *am* Coco. But no song, not even that one Maggie wrote about me, is going to snap me out of it.

I must lighten the mood.

“In that case,” I say, “maybe I should call you Maguel.”

“Please, no,” Maggie says, gently shoving my chest. “You tried to do that last time too.”

“Of course I did. Because it’s a brilliant nickname. Why do you get to call me Coco but I can’t call you Maguel?”

Maggie throws her head back and sighs. “Fiiiiine. I guess you can if you really, really need to.”

“I do, Maguel. I really, really do.”

Maggie narrows her eyes, touches her forehead to mine, and growls.

I growl back.

Her gum slides into my mouth as we start kissing again.

JUNE.

MAGGIE

When I come downstairs on the morning of Mom's wedding, she's in the kitchen, hovering over the counter with Ron and Vivian, who's pointing to her iPad and talking them through the ceremony.

"Morning, Mags," Mom says without looking up. "Vivvy is making sure we're not a clueless bride and groom."

"A rehearsal breakfast, if you will," Vivian says in her big, cozy lavender hooded sweatshirt.

"Cute." Out the window over the sink, I see that the caterers are already in the backyard, setting up tables and dozens of chairs beneath an ominous blanket of gray cloud. "Exciting day."

"I know," Ron says, putting an arm around Mom and giving a gentle squeeze. "I barely slept. Just can't wait to be married to your mom."

"Awww," Mom says.

"I thought the bride and groom aren't supposed to see each other until the actual wedding," I say, with more downer energy than I'd intended.

"Oh, that's just a silly tradition," Mom says.

"Yeah," Ron agrees, dipping a pita chip into a container of lemon dill hummus. "We don't need to hide from each other. We have nothing to hide!"

"I always thought it was about, like, building up suspense," I say. "Or drama."

"We've all had enough drama," Mom says. "No more drama!"

"Okay, let's get back to it," Vivian says. "Eyes on me. We're up to the rings."

"As you were," I say, feeling my phone buzz in the front pouch of *my* big, cozy hooded sweatshirt as I investigate the contents of the fridge. I grab a slice of sourdough bread and throw it in the toaster before pulling out my phone.

Can't wait to see you dazzle em today, kiddo

It's Dad. Ugh, so much for blocking out the fact that he'll be at the wedding.

Thanks, I type. *You sure you want to be there for this?*

I can't send that. I replace it with a *See ya soon!*, then plop the phone into my pocket and retreat upstairs to my room as Vivian points outside and tells Mom and Ron where they'll walk after their kiss.

"Check check, one two," I say into the microphone while Misty, Shana's dad's friend who owns Bean-Age Dream, bends over the portable speaker system she's lending my parents for the wedding. She fiddles with a couple of the knobs as I continue saying words. "Check check, sound check. Wedding. Love. Anxiety. Barf. Check check."

Misty throws a rigid thumb into the air. "Yup." She returns to a standing position, adjusting the light gray suit jacket she's wearing. "Levels sound great. Keys and vocals, both solid."

"Okay, cool," I say, nodding to Shana and Ember. Things are better between Shana and me, though still not perfect. I apologized for being a shitty friend and for putting so much of my focus on Carter, and I meant it. Though I also had no choice since our band needed to be on good terms so we could do this wedding.

I feel even more nervous for this performance than I did for our first gig.

It's just past one, and guests will start arriving at two. The ceremony is first, followed by a brief cocktail hour, then us. I'm not sure where my panic attack slots in. Hopefully after the performance.

"You plugging in your ax?" Misty asks, pointing to Shana.

"Oh," Shana says. "Sure?"

Misty gets to work, pulling a black device out of a tote bag and putting it into Shana's acoustic. The confidence radiating off Misty is intimidating but also calming. It's almost enough to offset the extreme uneasiness I feel every time I notice the charcoal sky. The caterers have set up a big canopy thing for if/when it starts raining. I'm holding out hope it won't, though.

"Oh yeah, now you're in the pocket," Misty says, responding to Shana strumming the opening chords from the new song I wrote. I get a little lightheaded. I'm not sure I can go through with playing it. Our other originals and the assorted covers we've learned—weird eighties shit Mom and Ron requested, like "Always Something There to Remind Me" and "I Melt with You"—all feel doable, but the new one is a tribute to them, and, at this particular moment, I might prefer to literally jam a knife into Dad's back instead of playing this in front of him. I need to stop writing intensely personal songs about people I love.

"All righty, then, Angry Infant," Misty says, "you should be good to go. Have a great show."

None of us has the heart to correct her. I'm in such a vulnerable place, it leaves me wondering if Angry Infant is actually a better name; maybe we should officially switch to calling ourselves that.

As Misty strides away, I pull my phone out of the skinny green purse I've brought out especially for today. Carter has texted.

You are a star, Maguel. And I love the new song

Thanks Coco, I write. *I'll letcha know how it goes. Hopefully won't besmirch my family name*

COME ON, he texts back immediately.

"You good?" Shana asks, sidling up next to me. "You've been looking a little pukey."

"I'm okay. I'll be okay."

Ember whacks one of their cymbals, continuing to warm up.

"I feel like I should be more, like, unconditionally happy about today," I say. "Vivian seems thrilled."

We glance over at my sister, in an animated conversation with one of the caterers.

"She's just a good actor," Shana says. "I'm sure she's feeling a lot of the same things you are. Have you talked to her about it? About them getting married?"

"A little. Not really. I don't know. She usually just points out how happy Mom is and says it is what it is."

"Oh, she's walking this way. Hey, girly!"

"Hi hi hi," Vivian says, her dark hair perfectly stacked into this magnificent spiral bun thing. She looks gorgeous and put together in a way that makes me want to pull out my phone again, use the camera to look at my makeup. "How did sound check go?"

"Amazing," I say. "Misty was very pleased."

"Great. So why do you look . . ."

"Pukey?" Ember offers.

"I was gonna say worried," Vivian says, "but yeah, *pukey* works."

"I just . . ." I'm hesitant to finish the sentence. Shana gives a little flip of her chin to nudge me forward. "I feel strange about doing the song. In front of Dad. The whole thing is, like, about how happy Mom is since she met Ron."

"Mags." Vivian takes my hand. "It's beautiful. It's a beautiful song. Mom and Ron will love it, and today is for them, so that's all that matters. Dad chose to be here, so if he can't handle it, that's on h—"

"Vivvy!" Mom emerges from the sliding door in the back, looking panicked and pretty in her simple, long-sleeved white dress.

"Yeah?" Vivvy says, dropping my hand.

"Do you know where the rings are? Ron says you know where the rings are."

"Yes, Mom, rings are safe, don't worry."

"Okay, thank god. Could you just come in and go over everything one last time with me and Ron?"

"Mom, it'll all be clear during the ceremony, I promi—"

"Please, Vivvy! We're flipping out a little!"

"Ron's flipping out?"

"Well . . . Mainly me. But please?"

Vivian sighs and gives a comic roll of her eyes. "Okay. Let's go."

Mom applauds. I try to silence the voice in my head wondering if she's ever needed *me* that badly.

"You got this, Mags," Vivian says, squeezing my shoulder before turning to Shana and Ember. "You all do. I can't wait to finally see Angry Baby." Glad she got the name right. We definitely shouldn't switch it.

I nod, and Vivian makes a beeline to the house, a swagger in her step not unlike Misty's.

How does one achieve such a swagger? I may never know.

"Let's go inside and hide in the basement till this starts," I say.

It's a gorgeous ceremony.

Of course I expected nothing less from something engineered by Vivian, but, sitting there in the front row next to Shana and Ember, I'm still thrown by how moved I am. It helps that I haven't seen Dad arrive yet, so I don't have to feel uncomfortable as Vivian talks about when Mom and Ron first met at Barnes & fricking Noble, of all places. Mom was holding a book about Cleopatra, and Ron said it was really great, even though he'd actually read only a third of it, and they'd proceeded to stand in the aisle chatting for over an hour (leaving me wondering where the hell Mom was and what the plan was for dinner, but I've forgiven her). Vivian talks about Mom and Ron's lake walks. She talks about how Mom seemed like a giddy teenager during that first year of dating, topped only by Ron, who literally clicked his heels together one night when they were waiting for a table at Vincenzo's.

It's all so charming and hilarious that I start to feel like the song I wrote is actually not *enough* of a tribute, that I'm yet again going to offer up the dinky supermarket frozen pizza as Vivian presents a coal-fired pie made on premises with 100 percent fresh ingredients.

Somehow Vivian's wizardry has even kept the granite boulders in the sky from releasing their haul of raindrops, which leaves the canopy feeling like an artful framing of the space rather than a crowd-size umbrella.

But the real triumph of the ceremony is when Mom and Ron read the vows they wrote for each other. This is another win that belongs to my sister, as Mom was fiercely resistant to the idea, saying again and again that she's not a writer, pushing Vivian to look online and find some vows there. Vivian wouldn't let it go, though, and Ron started to get really into the idea, enough so that he was eventually able to convince Mom.

His vows are very moving, but it's Mom's that send me spiraling into a snotty mess. I've never known her to write anything more involved than a to-do list or a two-sentence birthday card, so it's sort of a revelation. She, too, talks about Barnes & Noble, how taken aback she was when this handsome man started chatting her up, partially because she found it shocking that a man would actually read a book. (I wince at this not-so-subtle dig at Dad, who famously hasn't read one since college.) She says she felt better about her instincts when she later learned Ron hadn't actually finished the Cleopatra book, but then was stunned all over again seeing Ron in the act of reading enough times that it was clear it wasn't a charade.

The part of her vows that really gets me, though, is when she starts to get choked up and says that Ron saved her. "You really did," she tells him, and he's starting to cry too. "I was feeling so blocked. So stuck. And you helped me move again."

And of course I start thinking about Carter. I mean, I've *been* thinking about him all throughout today, but now the thought is this:

I wish he were here. Sitting next to me. Holding my hand. Laughing quietly with me at the parts of the ceremony that are funny, and even more quietly at the parts that are unintentionally funny.

And another thought is:

Maybe Carter saved *me.* I think about those months before we met: Vivian immersed in her junior year of college; Mom immersed in the world of, well, Ron; and Dad immersed in . . . the usual alternate plane of existence he chooses to reside on. I was feeling so alone.

And then . . . there he was. Scooping right next to me.

"You may now kiss each other!" Vivian shouts, pulling me out of my own brain to watch as Mom and Ron share a gentle kiss. Vivian's right—they are so happy together. They walk down the grassy aisle together as Misty cues up this Ben Folds song called "The Luckiest" that Ron is obsessed with, and all seventy or so people in the audience stand up.

"That was so great," Ember says, wiping at their cheek.

"They're so damn cute together," Shana says.

"I know," I say. "They really are."

"I cannot wait to explode this crowd's collective brain," Shana says.

We're about twenty minutes into the cocktail hour, ten minutes before Angry Baby will start playing, and spirits are high. Shana, Ember, and I are huddled behind the drum (secretly) sharing a beverage called a greyhound that Vivian kindly snuck to us. It has grapefruit juice and vodka, and though my drinking experience is limited, I think it's the best-tasting alcoholic thing I've ever had.

"Hey, go easy on that," Ember says, eyeing us with genuine concern. "You need to still be able to play chords."

"Ember, my love," Shana says, one hand on their shoulder. "It's one drink split among the three of us. I think we're gonna be okay."

"This is my last sip," I say, taking a large chug that goes down rougher and grosser than I was expecting. "Yowza-dowza!"

Shana, Ember, and I all crack up. I'm not feeling nervous about performing anymore. And it's not (just) because of the vodka! I'm riding high on the wave of Mom and Ron's love, on the relief that Vivian is emanating now that the hard part of her day is done and it went so well, on this deep feeling I have that being back with Carter is the Right Thing, no matter what doom awaits us in six months.

Plus, it still hasn't rained, and the sky has taken on a lighter shade of gray.

"Oh!" Shana says. "Maggie, question: the chords going from the chorus into the bridge . . . Is it B-flat right into C? Or does it bounce to F first, then C?"

"Lemme think." I hum through the song in my head. "It bounces to . . ."

In the middle of the sentence, I see him, wandering through the yard.

Dad has arrived.

"Bounces to what?" Shana gives me a playful shove. "F?"

"Yes," I say. "F. As in *F* my life because of what I *C*."

Dad is wearing a black sports jacket over a light blue button-down, along with jeans and his black Chuck Taylors. He grabs a dumpling off a server's tray and pops it in his mouth, right before he spots me.

My nerves come rushing back.

"Magpie!" Dad says, arms wide, giving me a hug that I mostly reciprocate. "I'm in time for your set, right? How'd the ceremony go?"

"Hey, it was great," I say. "Really beautiful. Did you miss it on purpose?"

"Eh," Dad says. "More or less, yeah. I wanted to see Vivvy in her element, but . . . There's only so much weird I can handle, you know?"

"That makes two of us."

"You didn't want to see it either?" he asks, unable to hide his excitement.

"No, I'm talking about right now, Dad," I say. "You. Being here."

"Oh. Yeah." Dad scratches his cheek and looks around. "Well, your mom and Ron were really cool about it. I already missed your last gig. Couldn't miss this one too. They get that. You look fantastic, by the way. Great dress. I—" Dad turns to acknowledge my friends, as if he's just noticed them. "Hey, Shana! Ember! Long time, no see!"

"Hey, Mr. Spear," Shana says at the same time that Ember says hi.

"Heard you all tore it up big-time at your coffee shop gig. Consider me hashtag proud, as you kids would say."

"No one says that anymore, Dad."

"Ha! Okay." Dad lowers his voice to a conspiratorial whisper. "Magpie, is it too much for me to be here? Should I go?"

I'm about to say, *Yes! It's way too much! Please leave immediately!*, but we're interrupted by Ron strolling up hand in hand with Mom.

"How's our all-time favorite band feeling?" Ron asks.

My internal organs panic and try to run but instead bump into each other, tangling themselves into impossible knots.

"Oh, hey there, Danny!" Ron smiles and extends a hand toward Dad. "Glad you made it, buddy."

"Thanks, Ron," Dad says, looking both sheepish and grateful. "Big congrats to you! And to you, Laurel. Exciting day. Really appreciate you welcoming me."

I look to Mom, ready for some shit to go down. But to my astonishment, she's not in cold, bristly mode. In fact, she seems completely unfazed. Maybe even *glad* to see my dad, which is something I don't think I've seen since before the divorce.

"Hey, Danny," she says as she leans in to give Dad a hug. "You're not going to believe how mind-blowing Maggie and her band are."

"Oh. Yeah," Dad says, and I can tell he's also a little thrown by Mom's genuine ease in his company. "I can't wait. Heard Vivvy led a beautiful ceremony too."

"Incredible," Mom says.

"Beyond," Ron agrees.

"You talking about me?" Vivian says, putting an arm around Dad's shoulders.

"Hey, kiddo, way to kill it," Dad says, giving her a hug.

Everyone's nodding and smiling at each other—it's a little uncomfortable but mostly a warm continuation of the glowing vibes that have surrounded the entire wedding so far. Mom wasn't kidding in her vows; Ron really has helped her move forward.

Which means I'm the only one who actually has a problem with Dad being here.

Guess I should get over that.

"Five minutes till go time, Infants!" Misty says, appearing from nowhere, voice booming like she's our coach.

"Oh god," I say.

"All right, gang," Ron says with a couple of hand claps. "Let's give this band a little time to get in the right head space for the performance of a lifetime. All of us stans absolutely cannot wait."

Mom and Dad separately wish us broken legs before she drifts away with Ron and he with Vivian—who gives me one more confidence-transmitting nod, a beacon of calm and maturity as always—and the three of us are left on our own.

"Time to kill," Shana says, hand on my back. "You okay?"

"I am," I say. "Everything's great. Is there any of that drink left?"

"Yeah." Shana puts the glass in my hand.

I take a deep, disgusting, delicious swig.

"We really don't have to do that new song," Ember says, tapping their drumsticks together. "If it feels weird, I mean."

"Yeah, screw it," Shana says. "We'll explode brains even without that song."

"That's sweet," I say, "but we should probably—"

"Excuse me, miss," a voice says behind me as a hand touches my lower back. "Sorry to interrupt, but I'd absolutely love to get your autograph."

It's Carter, crouched behind me in a full tuxedo.

"Oh Jesus no," I say.

CARTER

Maggie is not pleased to see me.

This is evident not only in her body language but in her language-language as well.

"Oh Jesus no," she says.

"I came to cheer you up," I say to the person upon whom my presence seems to be having the exact opposite effect.

"Carter," Maggie says, literally smacking her hand to her forehead. "You're in a tux. My god. You look so good. Even though it's a little big."

"Facts," I say, grinning. I bought the best option the Salvation Army had: a slightly oversize tuxedo with a dark purple bow tie and cummerbund, which is currently pressing into my belly button in the most irritating way.

"But why are you— I told you not to come!"

"I know. I know you did, but . . ." What is the end of this sentence? Coming here made so much sense in the moment—my gut was telling me that Maggie was nervous, that she needed me, and that maybe I needed to put myself out there, make the big, selfless gesture—but now I'm seeing the alarm on Maggie's face and all I can think is WHY THE HELL DID I COME HERE? "I thought I could . . . Like, just now, I saw how thrown you were by your dad. I didn't want you to be alone in that."

"She's not," Shana says, not so mean but not so nice either. She and Ember are standing on the other side of Maggie, positioned in a way that, intentionally or not, blocks me from the view of the other wedding guests.

"Yeah," Maggie says, eyes shifty, clearly terrified that I'll be spotted. "I appreciate you being here, it's so sweet, but— It's really not good if— I just—"

"I also brought my camera," I say, pointing at the device strapped around my neck. I figured if anything went awry, I could just say I was here to help out by taking some photos. It's hard to argue with that, right? It's a nice gesture!

"You have to leave, Carter," Shana growls, with a conviction that is highly persuasive. "Okay? That's what she's saying."

"Yeah, okay." I try to sound chill even as a small crack ripples down one of my heart chambers. "I get it. Sorry."

"It's not you, Carter," Maggie says, her voice wobbling. "It's really not. It's just my—"

"Family," I finish for her. Part of my logic had been that maybe Maggie's family would be *most likely* to accept us as a couple again here, at a wedding, when everyone's in a spectacular mood. Like when I was in fifth grade at Uncle Jed and Uncle Flip's wedding, and Mom and Dad were so happy, they let Lincoln and me sit at the table and play on their phones for, like, two hours. Unheard of! I broke my high score in *Tiny Wings* by so much.

"Guess I didn't think this through," I say. "My bad." I take a few steps backward toward a large tree. A fat raindrop plunks onto my neck.

"Oh, great," Maggie says, flinching as she gets hit by one too.

"Operation: Canopy Relocation is a go!" It's the older woman from Bean-Age Dream, wearing a suit, all business. She points to

Shana. "Grab your ax." She turns to Ember. "I'll help you move your drum kit. Maggie, you take your keyboard with the help of . . . You!" She points to me as I try to casually position a hand on the tree trunk. "Be a pal and carry this keyboard with Maggie over to the canopy."

"Oh," I say. "I probably shouldn't—"

"Come on, man, this ain't brain science! She picks up on one side; you get the other! Before the rain turns it into a useless piece of junk."

"He, um, was actually just leaving, Misty," Maggie says, nodding me away, "so I'll find someone else to—"

"Fine, fine!" Misty says, hefting Ember's bass drum into the air and walking it across the yard with quick, tiny steps as Shana and Ember follow with, respectively, a guitar and a high hat. "Just move it!"

The raindrops are picking up. I look to Maggie, like *You sure you don't want me to move it with you?*

"Go, Coco! Please! Just leave!"

And I'm about to go, I really am, but then:

"Here, pick up your side," an older girl says, gesturing to the keyboard, "and I'll get this . . ."

Her sentence peters out. I realize this is Maggie's older sister, who I vaguely recognize from when I was fifteen. She is staring at me.

I could run away. I probably *should* run away.

But Vivian Spear seems to have already identified me.

I decide to address the problem head-on.

"Hi there," I say with a wave.

"What're you— What is he doing here, Maggie?"

“Oh, him?” Maggie asks, and I can tell she’s flipping out, like maybe on the verge of a panic attack. “I don’t . . . Um, I think he said he was just . . .”

“Here to take pictures,” I say, holding up my camera. Hell yeah, backup plan!

“We have a professional photographer for that,” Vivian says, eyes shifting back and forth between me and her sister.

“You’re gonna wanna get this keyboard under the canopy pronto,” Ron says, joining our horribly awkward gathering with a huge white umbrella held overhead.

“They actually say rain during a wedding is good luck,” Maggie’s mom says, huddling next to Ron. “But we should—” There’s a thick, terrible pause as I’m spotted. She looks to her younger daughter. “Maggie?”

I have to speak up. For myself. For Maggie. For both of us.

“This is my fault,” I say, stepping away from the tree toward the group. “Maggie specifically told me not to come, and I should have listened, so I’m really sorry.”

“Oh my,” Maggie’s mom says, under her breath but loud enough to hear.

The rain starts coming down a little faster, like someone has nudged the sky’s shower handle.

“Carter,” Maggie says, somehow more panicky than ever, not calmed at all by my openhearted attempt to take control of the situation. “Please. Don’t say anything else. Just go. You heard— We have a photographer, okay?”

“That keyboard should not be out here,” Maggie’s dad says, wandering up to our circle.

“I’ve been saying that this whole time!” Misty shouts, having returned from dropping off the bass drum. "Come on, come on!" She and Maggie's dad crab-walk the keyboard over to the canopy.

"Here's the thing," I say. I need to cut to the chase if I want to win over Maggie's family. "I completely get why you wouldn't want Maggie dating me again."

"Again?" Vivian says.

"Maggie tried not to date me this time! She really did. But somehow we were drawn together again."

"Ohmigod," Vivian says.

"I know, I know." I put up a hand toward Vivian, which is meant to be calming, but she mostly looks like she wants to punch me. Must try harder. Must persuade better. "Here's what I'm starting to realize, though: Maybe connection is connection, whether you ultimately remember it or not, you know?

"So maybe it's not a waste for me and Maggie to have this time together. Maybe it can still be a beautiful thing, to be with someone you like being with, to laugh with them, to confide in them, to see them for who they are and know they're seeing you for who you are too. Even if it ends, or reboots or whatever, maybe it's all still worth it. You know?"

There's a nightmare of a pause as everyone stares at me.

Finally, Ron breaks the silence.

"I have no idea what specifically you're talking about," he says, "but I love the sentiment."

No else seems even slightly won over by my speech. Vivian and Maggie's mom both seem kind of shocked, and they're not even looking at me anymore. They're looking at Maggie.

"Last point to make," I say, trying to adjust my cummerbund lower because it's a suffocating accessory with a ridiculous name, "and then I'll stop talking, I swear. It's possible I *won't* erase on my next birthday. This loop may have started because of the way I broke up with Layla Banerjee the night before, but I apologized to her—"

"STOP TALKING!" Maggie shouts.

I look over, and she's soaked. I can't tell if she's shaking with anger or from the cold. Possibly both.

"I told you not to come here, and I told you to stop, but you wouldn't and you didn't, and I don't know why you won't stop talking!"

"You're dating Carter," Vivian says, now also holding a white umbrella.

"I was trying not to date him, I swear!" Maggie says, suddenly sobbing. "Vivvy, I'm sorry!"

"Did you know?" Vivian asks their mom.

"Well," Mom says, looking to Ron for a way out of this, "not that it was happening again!"

"Wow," Vivian says.

I'm beginning to think there's more to what's going on right now than I'm aware of.

"What you were talking about at the diner," Vivian says, looking so disappointed in Maggie it makes *me* want to hide behind the tree again. "That was about him."

"I wanted to tell you!" Maggie says, pushing away the open white umbrella that a server is trying to hand her. "But I just . . . What else can I say but sorry?"

"I'm not sure," Vivian says, raising her voice over the rain. "Maybe *I don't know why I decided to date the one guy in the world who's ever broken your heart*. Maybe that would be helpful for me to hear?"

"Don't mean to be a party pooper," Misty says, "but I think we'd all be best served shifting this conversation to somewhere beneath the canopy."

"I'm sorry," I say, choosing to ignore Misty, as it seems everyone else standing here is also choosing to do, "but can we go back to that last part? Because it *sounded* like Vivian said I was the one guy in the world who's ever broken her heart. But that definitely feels like something that Maggie would've told me." I turn to Maggie. "Right?"

She's still crying. She doesn't seem angry anymore. Just sad.

"Maggie, right?" I repeat. "Can you catch me up on what the hell is going on?"

Maggie chokes back another sob and shakes her head, looking like she's just climbed out of a carnival dunk tank. In the distance, there's a clap of thunder. "Layla wasn't the one you dumped that night," she says. "It was . . ." She can't get out the name so she just gives a weak nod in Vivian's direction.

The yard spins. I almost topple over.

"Why did . . ." I say once I've regained my balance. "This isn't a joke?"

"No," Vivian says, her voice cold.

I can't look at her.

"So you lied to me," I say to Maggie.

"I don't know," Maggie says. "It just . . ."

"You straight-up *lied* to me. As if this shit isn't hard enough already."

"I know! I know it's terrible. But people always like Vivian more than me. And I worried that you'd . . . I did it wrong. I'm sorry, Carter. I'm so sorry."

"You sat there," I say, "and watched me give a big apology to Layla Banerjee, knowing she wasn't even the right person!"

"I was gonna tell you that afternoon—"

"But you didn't."

Maggie shrugs and shakes her head, crying too hard to speak.

"This is . . ." I don't know what else to say.

I need to leave.

"Apologies to all if I ruined this special day," I say, too overwhelmed to look anywhere but at the grass as I back away. I came here to put myself out there, and instead, I seem like a complete idiot.

"Carter, wait," Maggie says.

I break into a jog, then a run, then a sprint, feeling the weight of my waterlogged tuxedo.

Guess I'm soaked too.

I hop into Toro and drive away, yanking off the stupid cummerbund and tossing it onto the floor.

JULY.

CARTER

"Dude," Bodhi says, in the voice memo he sent several hours ago, "I know you'll probably say no to this, but you should come out with me and Lizzy tonight. We're gonna hit up that new ghost movie."

I'm planted on the family room couch in front of the TV, which has become my regular Friday night routine. And my Saturday night routine. And Sunday night. Really, all the nights. And some of the days too. It's been about a month since that shitty wedding, and, at least since school ended, most of that time has been divided between two locations: couch and bed. I don't have the energy or enthusiasm to be anywhere else.

My parents would prefer this wasn't the case.

Not my problem.

Only five months till I loop away from all this.

It's funny that I thought apologizing to Layla Banerjee might solve my situation. Obviously it was never going to do anything. Even if she *was* the person I'd broken up with, it all sounds so ridiculous now. Which is why I won't be apologizing to Vivian Spear either.

Can't make it, I text Bodhi as I keep half my attention on this weird-ass Netflix show about the circus. A fire-twirling woman just cheated on her muscular acrobat husband with the charming, androgynous ringmaster. Pretty fucked-up.

My bro's about to come home, I type. *Have fun buddy.*

Lincoln *is* about to come home from his internship for a couple days to celebrate Dad's birthday with us, but not till tomorrow. So it's a weak excuse. I don't feel like being a third wheel tonight, though. Nor do I need to watch a movie about ghosts. That's already my life now anyway.

I've ghosted myself from everything. Because it feels better.

You put yourself out there, you try too hard, and you just get fucked over.

I also stopped going to therapy. Soren's mustache was annoying the crap out of me.

And Maggie finally stopped texting too. For the best, really.

After her many messages over the weeks—and once even showing up at my house; I had Mom tell her I didn't feel like talking—I get how bad she feels.

But I hated how that all went down.

On the TV, the fire twirler and ringmaster are hooking up again, this time in a grunty, fully clothed sex scene in a grimy dressing room. Seems like a ridiculous place to do that, they're obviously going to get caught.

"What're you watching, bud?" Dad says, appearing behind the couch. I race to hit the Pause button. He and Mom don't mind if I watch stuff like this, but I definitely don't need to watch it *with* them. "Oh! *Three Rings!* This season was so good. Are you into it?"

"Um, yeah, it's fine, I guess."

"I was always obsessed with the circus when I was a kid," Dad says. "So it was cool to see what's actually going on behind the scenes."

"Uh. You realize it's not a documentary, right?"

"Come on, Carter," Dad says, ruffling my hair. "I'm old, but I'm not *that* old. I felt so bad for Stefan during this plotline."

"Stefan?"

"The acrobat guy. Whose wife is humping someone else on-screen right now."

"Dude!"

"What? I always find adultery plotlines uncomfortable!"

"No, just— Don't say *humping*, Dad. Never say *humping*. We've talked about this."

"I know, I know." Dad pats my shoulder. "I was hoping it might make you laugh. It's good to see you smile for a second."

I shake my head and sigh. That wasn't quite a prank, but it was close enough, so I gotta give him credit for that. I grab a handful of Cheez-Its and a couple of Swedish Fish from the snack platter Mom kindly assembled for me.

"I see you've entirely given up on the Ayurvedic diet," Dad observes as I turn my finger into a fishing rod and try to hook the gummy fish chunk that's just gotten stuck between my back teeth.

"Yeah," I say. "Sorry, Dad."

"I get it," Dad says, coming around the couch and plopping down next to my legs. "But if you're serious about wanting to solve this, then—"

"Pete, let it go," Mom says, shouting from her home office.

"I know, I know," Dad shouts back. "Can I get out this thought, though?"

I hear Mom's chair roll backward, and then she pops out of her office. "I think he's *heard* that thought already. Many times. So have I. He doesn't want to do the diet. So you need to stop bothering him about it."

"Wend," Dad says, standing up from the couch as Mom walks into the room. "It's not like I'm bothering him about taking an art class or playing lacrosse or something. This could make a genuine difference with his . . . condition."

"I know," Mom says. "But right now—not sure if you've noticed—he's been in a bit of a funk. To say the least. And I don't think passing on two Swedish Fish will be the difference maker on finally cracking this thing."

BOOM. I love when Mom has my back.

"Sure," Dad says, "but—"

"If Cart's forced to be stuck like this," Mom interrupts, "we can at least allow him to enjoy himself occasionally."

Amen to that. I hate being here when Mom and Dad argue about me, but I appreciate that I don't have to be the one arguing.

Dad throws an arm in the air, huffs, and goes silent for a moment. "I know you're enjoying *yourself*," he finally mutters. It takes me a moment to realize he's talking to Mom. "Maybe we can find a way to get Lincoln stuck too; we'll all live here together forever. That's the dream, right?"

I get a queasy feeling in my stomach when I see the way this has landed with Mom.

She's angry. Incredibly angry.

Her eyes get shiny, and she slowly turns and leaves the room.

"Wendy," Dad says, following her. "I'm sorry, okay? That was too much. I know that was too much."

I go to unpause the circus non-documentary, but I feel so tired.

I pull the blanket tighter around me and roll onto my side.

I close my eyes.

★ ★ ★

When I wake up the next morning, I'm still on the couch, and Dad has been replaced by Lincoln. He's wearing a maroon hoodie and sipping from a mug while looking at his phone.

"Morning, bright eyes," he says.

"Link," I say. "You're home. How'd you get here so early?"

"Well, first of all, it's 11:12, so I don't think it's as early as you think. Also I caught an early train."

"Oh. Cool." I clumsily sit up and get my bearings. My tongue feels caked with Cheez-Its. I've been dreading seeing Lincoln. He's another bullet point on the list of People I've Decided to Ghost.

"Why are you sleeping on the couch?" he asks.

"I don't know. I do it sometimes. It's just easier, I guess."

"I see." There's so much judgment packed into those two words. My little brother takes a long sip from his beverage, and I'm tempted to smack the mug right out of his hands. "You haven't been responding to any of my texts," he says.

I shrug my shoulders. "Sorry."

"It's okay." Lincoln takes another sip. "*I'm* sorry about you and Maggie."

"Are you?"

Lincoln raises his eyebrows and looks around the room, as if he's saying *Yeesh* to an imaginary studio audience. "Yes, CT. Of *course* I am."

"I know you were annoyed by us being together. And I *also* know that you were fully aware I'd already dated and dumped Maggie's older sister, but I guess that never seemed worth mentioning to me, huh?"

Lincoln groans and puts a hand over his face, looking pained. "I know. It's . . . I'm just glad Maggie finally told you."

"She didn't! I found out by mistake."

"Oh god."

"You're awake!" Dad says, peeking into the room from the kitchen. "The Cohen brothers, reunited!"

"That's right," Lincoln says. "Get ready for *Fargo 2*."

"Can I make you something to eat?" Dad asks me.

His fight with Mom from last night rises to the surface of my brain. I push it down.

"Eggs? Pancakes?"

"I'm good," I say. "I'll get myself something in a minute. Also, happy birthday."

"Thanks, bud."

I'm weirdly jealous of how simple his birthday gets to be. He wakes up, he's a year older. Easy. Dad goes back into the kitchen and says something to Mom. Thankfully, the vibes between them seem pretty chill.

"I'm sorry I didn't tell you about Vivian," Lincoln says, tugging at both ends of his hood's drawstring. "I wanted to, but . . ."

"But what?"

"Well, last summer with Maggie, when that first happened, I felt like, *Oh man, Carter needs to know he dated her older sister.* But then . . . I don't know. You just seemed so happy."

"Oh."

"Like, happy in a way I hadn't seen you in a long time. So I didn't want to ruin that, you know?"

I nod, but I only feel more infuriated. I don't need to hear about how happy I was with Maggie. "So what about this time? Why lie to me this time?"

"I wasn't trying to lie!" Lincoln stands up from the couch and paces away, then back toward me. "I didn't think it was my place to tell you if Maggie wasn't going to, you know? Maybe that was wrong. I don't know! This whole time, CT, again and again, year after year, I'm trying to help you. But it feels like whatever I do just seems to piss you off!"

"How about trying to be *honest*!" I shout, rising to my feet. "It's not that hard. Just say, *Hey, bro, you actually dumped Maggie's sister, Vivian, and then all this shit started, so maybe there's a connection there! Maybe apologizing could help all this!* That would be a GREAT thing to say!"

"That wouldn't do anything!" Lincoln shouts.

"You don't know that," I say. "It might!"

"I *do* know, CT! That's not the reason you're stuck."

He says it so confidently, it's almost confusing.

"How do you— What?"

"You're not stuck because you dumped Vivian Spear." Lincoln floats down to the couch, as if he's just opened a parachute. "You're stuck because of me."

LINCOLN

THE NIGHT BEFORE THE FIRST LOOP

I was playing *Mario Party* in my room with Prateek when you dumped Vivian.

We actually didn't know right away that you were dumping her. We thought you two were making out. Prateek wanted to eavesdrop. I told him that was gross and bumped up the volume on our game.

But then we heard a yelp. Prateek gave me one of his ridiculous grins, which quickly disappeared once we realized it was a sob. Vivian was crying.

We heard you saying something about it not feeling right. Like, since you were turning seventeen, you didn't want to feel like you were already married. You wanted to be with a lot of different people. Vivian said something we couldn't hear, then called you immature. You responded, but you were both talking too quietly after that to understand what you were saying. A couple minutes later, your bedroom door flew open, and Vivian speed-walked out in tears.

You walked out too, but you stopped at the top of the stairs, watching Vivian leave the house. You seemed shaken up. Not crying but definitely rattled. Prateek and I looked at each other. He gestured at me like, *Go see if he's okay.*

So I did.

I called out to you in the hallway, asked if you were okay.

You looked at me, and something switched in your eyes, and

I immediately wished I hadn't said anything. "I'm fine," you said. "Why wouldn't I be?"

And you walked into my room.

You asked us if we heard what happened. Prateek and I said not really, we were too busy playing, just that it sounded like you and Vivian got in some kind of argument.

"An argument?" you said. "Look at you, so smart!" You paced around the room—it was really more like a prowl—and I remember wishing so deeply that this moment could be over, that I could fast-forward to the part where Prateek and I were back to rolling digital dice and throwing cartoon pies.

"I'm sorry," I said, "we don't have to talk about—"

"Prateek," you said, "this is something funny about Lincoln you might not be aware of. He actually wet the bed until age eleven. Eleven! Did you know that?"

I couldn't believe you'd said those words.

Prateek was silent. He just sat there looking at the Switch controller in his hand.

I pretty much died inside.

You kept speaking. "For someone so smart, you'd think this kid would know what's a bed and what's a toilet, you know?"

"That's mean," I said, barely audible.

"It's a *joke*!" you said.

"Jokes are funny," I said, louder now. "And that's just mean!"

"It all depends on your sense of humor, I guess," you said.

And then the dread inside me transformed.

"You *are* immature!" I shouted. "I get why Vivian said that!"

"More immature than a bed-wetting eleven-year-old?" you asked.

"You're just proving my point by saying that!" I took a few steps toward you. "*You* are like an eleven-year-old, stuck in a sixteen-year-old's body. You're turning seventeen tomorrow, and it doesn't seem like that at all, it really doesn't."

I saw on your face, only for a moment, that I'd hurt you.

And I liked that.

"Well, maybe I'll never be mature!" you yelled. "Maybe I'll be this way forever. Maybe I *want* to be this way. So get used to it!"

You stormed out of the room.

I didn't see you again until the next morning.

CARTER

I stare at Lincoln, the weight of his words sinking in.

He's avoiding my eyes, staring at the coffee table.

"So you're saying you did this to me."

"I really don't know." Lincoln looks up. His voice is shaking. "But I'm sorry, CT. You'll never understand how much I wish I'd never said anything to you that night."

"You think I've been living this nightmare because you got mad about a stupid joke I made? Did I also punch you or something?"

"No," Lincoln says. "I know it seems like a small thing, but . . ." He wipes at his eyes, inhales some snot. "You humiliated me in front of my best friend. And then you . . . You said you wanted to be like this forever."

I stand up from the couch as anger rises in me like a slowly filling bathtub. "Why didn't you tell me this earlier? What is with everybody? You and Maggie and everyone, just fucking burying the lede."

"I *have* told you this before, Carter!" Lincoln says, also rising from the couch. "The first time you looped, I couldn't keep it to myself anymore, so I told you what had happened. And it . . . It didn't do anything! It just made you hate me. So I decided I was going to support you and be there for you and do everything I could to—"

"No," I say. "I don't buy that. Do Mom and Dad know about this too? About our fight?"

"I mean . . . Kind of. Not all the details, really."

"Doesn't even matter." I shake my head and stumble off the couch, trying to get away. "I'm surrounded by liars. Thanks for ruining my life."

Even as I say it, I realize my own hypocrisy.

I'm the one who said I wanted to be this way forever.

Which means *I* did this to me.

"CT," Lincoln says as I barrel up the stairs.

"Enjoy the rest of your fucking internship," I shout.

MAGGIE

"They don't hide," I sing. "They don't hiiiiiiide. They don't hiiiiiiide from each other."

I really belt out that last line, my fingers still pressing on the keys as the final chord of the song rings out, along with the shimmer of a cymbal crash and the bright bounce of a guitar strum.

The crowd goes nuts. Shana, Ember, and I exchange grins.

Angry Baby is back.

It's our first performance since our set at the wedding, which, as you might imagine, didn't go so great. I can't even tell you what we played. Carter had just dashed off, so I was trapped in my head the whole time, thinking about what a horrible person I am, all the relationships I'd ruined, as Shana and Ember carried me through the set.

Vivian did not watch.

Afterward, I tried to give Mom and Ron their money back. They insisted we'd earned it.

That was a month and a half ago, but it easily feels like it could have been a year. And now, here we are, playing a set in Shana's backyard for the graduation/going-to-college party her parents are throwing her. Mom and Ron are here, standing toward the back, beaming. It's nice to see.

This is probably the first moment since their ceremony that I haven't felt like a pile of rotting garbage. My days have not been wonderful.

Vivian and I haven't talked much since the wedding. I texted her a long apology that night. She responded: *Thanks*. That felt a little worse than if she hadn't written back at all. Then she unexpectedly decided to go stay with Dad for a little while. That's when I knew things were *very* bad. A few days into her time there, I sent a rambling, eight-minute voice memo. She texted back: *It's ok, Mags. I just need a minute.* When she finally came back to our place a week or so later, she and I hugged and started talking again, mostly about the unsettling lack of hand soap in Dad's home and not at all about Carter.

No, we don't talk about Carter.

Soon after that, Vivian left yet again, this time to go backpacking in Europe with a few friends. We got a postcard from Venice last week. *By 2040, maybe all cities will be like this!* she wrote. *Miss you, fam*. I felt bummed that I didn't get my own message, but maybe that would've been the case even if I hadn't dated her ex-boyfriend and never told her about it.

Carter, meanwhile, doesn't talk to *me*. That night after the wedding, I ran to his house to apologize in person, my attempt at a big, bold gesture of love (and also because my car was blocked in). His mom answered the door and said, with an expression not dissimilar to the emoji yeesh face, that Carter didn't want to see me. It was a really fun walk home.

I texted him every day after that. Never any response. Then I switched to every other day, and then finally, a couple weeks ago, I gave up. I don't really blame him. I probably wouldn't respond to a rotting pile of garbage either.

But I miss him a lot.

"I love our band so much!" Shana shouts now as Ember and I stand up from our instruments and meet Shana in front to do an awkward bow, which I guess is Angry Baby's thing now. People hoot and cheer some more, and Ron does his two-fingered whistle, loud enough to cut through everything.

"I love *you guys*," I say to Shana and Ember.

They are great friends. Even in the moments when I've become the literal manifestation of our band name.

"Hey," Ember says, nudging my elbow with their drumstick as the applause ends and people return to loud conversations. "That new song killed. It was really beautiful."

"Thanks," I say, not even trying to conceal how meaningful it is to hear that. "You both sounded so good."

"In full agreement about the new one," Shana says, putting an arm around my shoulder, "but must be honest, love: I missed playing 'Stuck.'"

"Same," Ember says.

"I know, I know," I say. "I do too. But . . . I'm glad we didn't play it. Performing a song about him when he's not even talking to me feels kinda gross."

"Rock stars probably do that all the time," Ember says. "If that makes you feel any better."

"It doesn't, but thank you."

"Come on, though," Shana says. "Lots of boys get stuck lots of places, you know? We could just say the song is about, I don't know—"

"A boy stuck in earthquake rubble in Morocco," I say.

"Yes! Totally! That's brilliant!"

"Shane. Ember. We'll do 'Stuck' again one day. Just . . . not now."

Shana squeezes my shoulder hard. "Integrity looks good on you, girl."

"Thank you so much," I say, giggling for the first time in a while.

"Well, that was damn impressive." It's our old pal Marigold, her faux-hawk now light green instead of light blue.

"Yeah. Really incredible." Chord appears from behind her, looking as handsome and impeccably dressed as ever, and I have a moment of panic before I remind myself that things with us are okay now. In my recent attempts at being a less horrible person, I sent Chord a lengthy text explanation about why I broke up with him, including everything that had happened with Carter. He was surprisingly sympathetic.

"Thanks, buddies," I say, giving Marigold and Chord hugs. I spot Mom and Ron over Chord's shoulder. "I'm gonna go say hi to my mom."

"Go for it," Chord says. "I think I see a passionfruit LaCroix with my name on it anyway."

The new song Angry Baby played, "They Don't Hide," was, of course, written for Mom and Ron—a redo of the one we never even ended up playing at their wedding—inspired by the way they literally didn't hide from each other that morning before the ceremony. And figuratively don't hide from each other either.

"Oh, honey," Mom says as I approach, rising from her seat at an umbrella table and giving me a hug. "That was so wonderful."

"Did you . . . like the song I wrote for you?"

"Are you kidding? We *loved* it. Ron was bawling."

"I was," Ron says, nodding proudly behind her. "The whole set was . . . It was even tighter than the one at our wedding."

"Well, that's not hard to do," I mutter.

"It really was fantastic," a familiar voice says, and then, screw my new song, I have the desperate urge to hide. Somewhere.

Anywhere. Beneath the table! In Ember's bass drum! In that big-ass beverage cooler over there!

"Ah, why are you here?" Mom says, giving Vivian a huge hug. "I thought you were back tomorrow!"

"I switched my flight to come home a day early," Vivian says. She's wearing a sleeveless black top and hoop earrings and somehow looks stunning in spite of traveling here from another continent. "I mean, after missing Maggie's first two performances, I couldn't miss *this one* too. That felt unacceptable."

"You were watching?" I asked, sounding dazed even to myself. "I didn't see you."

"More like lurking. I didn't want to distract you."

"Oh," I say. "Thanks."

"Glad you finally got to witness the magic for yourself," Ron says.

"Me too," Vivian says.

"Can we talk?" I ask, the words popping out of my mouth like it's a jack-in-the-box.

"Me and you?" Vivian has this panicked look in her eyes that people other than me probably wouldn't notice. "Of course, sure. You mean right now?"

"I do," I say.

"Okay. Yeah. Let's talk."

We look around Shana's backyard, scoping out a spot for this conversation we're both terrified to have. Finally, I take a few steps, and Vivian follows.

I would still prefer to hide in that gigantic cooler with the seltzer cans, but I keep moving forward instead.

MAGGIE

Vivian and I find a spot a healthy distance from the rest of the party, sitting on the worn-down patch of grass where Shana's family swing set used to be. Her parents finally got rid of it last week to make more space in the yard for this party. Shana said her dad cried as he disassembled it.

"You want some?" Vivian asks, holding out some fancy bottle of sunscreen. "It's bright out here."

"I'm good, thanks." I definitely have not sunscreened yet today, but I can't start this conversation by admitting weakness.

"Okay, good." She cracks open a grapefruit LaCroix—I guess she pulled it out of one of the big pockets on her pants?—and takes a sip. "Feel free to have some if you want."

"Thanks. I hydrated a lot before the show."

Vivian nods.

"So you're back from Europe," I say. I can't lead with the Carter stuff. Need to warm up into it.

"I am."

"How was it?"

"It was great. It was really great."

"Nice!"

"Yeah."

I pull out a blade of grass. I try to tie it into a knot.

"As great as living with Dad for a week?" I ask.

Vivian smiles. "Maybe even a little greater, if you can imagine that."

"Wow." If I don't bring this up now, I might avoid it forever. "Vivvy, I'm sorry I dated Carter."

Vivian sighs, takes a long sip of seltzer. "It's not . . . I think keeping it a secret from me for so long was even more offensive than you being with him."

"I know." I grab the LaCroix out of her hand and take a chug; she made it look so good. "But I didn't want to hurt you. I was trying to protect you. And instead it was the biggest betrayal."

"Not the *biggest*," Vivian says, swiping the can back. "I mean, it wasn't good. But it wasn't— Do you think I'm so pathetic that I couldn't handle you being with someone I dated when I was a sophomore in high school?"

"It wasn't just *someone you dated*! That breakup was a big deal. We talked about it a lot! Because it sucked!" My face feels hot, from my passion but also because, well, we are getting a ton of sun. "And, Vivvy, to me you are the *opposite* of pathetic. That's part of the problem! You're a goddess, and I'm, like, this street urchin."

"What? That is not— That's not at all how I see it."

"Can I have that sunscreen actually?"

"Of course." Vivian hands it over, and I squirt some into my hand.

"You were right about the brightness," I say, rubbing it into my cheeks and my neck. "You're right about everything."

"Maggie. Come on."

"No, really! You are. And you know what to do in every situation, and people love you, and that's just what it is. Another reason I never wanted Carter to know he dated you. I was worried he'd be like, *Oh seriously? What am I doing here with this street urchin? Lemme make* that *happen again.*"

"That's silly."

"But it's how I feel," I say, and dammit, here come the tears. "I stopped trying to match up to you a long time ago. You set the bar so high, and Mom has always made that very clear, and I can't . . . I can't compete. I can never compete."

"Oh, Mags." Vivian reaches out a hand; I take it as I cry. "I wish I had a tissue to give you—"

"No!" I say, wiping snot away with my available hand. "I'm so fucking glad you don't have a tissue! Please. It's such a relief to hear there's something you haven't thought of."

Vivian laughs. "Fair enough."

"But even though I can't compete," I say, "it doesn't mean I, like, want you to feel bad. So when Carter first started flirting with me, and I was maybe starting to like him, I knew how shitty he'd been to you. So of course I wasn't going to be with him. But then it . . . I don't know, it kind of felt nice to think that Carter might be into me. That I could be on your level."

"You're *always* on my level," Vivian says, gripping my hand tighter.

"I'm not. You don't have to say that. You went to an Ivy League school, you're good at lots of things, people are drawn to y—"

"Maybe, but I'm also kind of a mess!"

"Nice try," I say. There's a roar of laughter from near the appetizer table.

Vivian doesn't seem to notice it. "No, really," she says, looking down at our joined hands. "I've always admired that you don't feel constantly compelled to hold yourself to this ridiculously high standard."

"Uh," I say. "Thank you?"

"I'm being serious, Maggie!" Vivian is so animated that she accidentally knocks over the LaCroix. "Oops."

It leaks into the grass before she lets go of my hand to pick it back up.

"Sometimes I see how you're not uptight about things like I am, or obsessed with doing things perfectly, or pleasing everybody, and I'm so jealous. And honestly, when I understood at the wedding that Carter was there for you and not me, I think I . . ."

Vivian taps a finger to her lips. It's her thing when she's thinking deeply.

"You think you . . . ?"

"I think that part of me, for just a minute, went back to my sixteen-year-old self and felt completely stunned and embarrassed and pissed that you were with the first guy I ever loved."

"See, that's what I was terrified of!"

"But then I came back to myself," Vivian says. "Me now, who understands I was with Carter a long time ago." She picks a blade of glass and tries knotting it like I did. "And when I saw Carter at the wedding, I felt like . . . Like *you* have all the things I don't that *do* make you a good fit for him. Like how funny you are. And spontaneous. And messy."

"So many backhanded compliments coming at me right now," I say. "Not sure what to do with this wealth of riches."

"You know what I mean, Mags!" Vivian throws her grass knot at me, and it bounces off my cheek. "It's not like I have any desire to be with Carter now. It was just feeling envious that, you know, these qualities that you have might . . . make you . . . more lovable than me. In general."

It's the most vulnerable thing Vivian has said to me in years.

Maybe ever. She's tapping her fingers on her thighs, possibly about to cry, and it breaks my heart.

"Vivvy." I put an arm around her and cuddle up close. "Are you kidding me? You are the most lovable."

"No one's ever crashed a wedding to declare how much I mean to them," Vivian says, her voice quiet.

"Well, that's very specific."

"I'm done with college, and I still have no clue how to do love right."

"That's 'cause people are fools," I say into her ear. "And they're probably intimidated by you. And in awe of you. Like me."

"No," Vivian says, "you make fun of me for dumping people when things start to get serious, and that is literally what I do. I know it is."

I'm not sure what to say to this. The only advice I can think of is, *Well, maybe try not doing that!* Which seems unhelpful.

I realize Haim is playing through the speakers, so I point to the air. We love Haim.

"Yeah," Vivian says. "*Days Are Gone*. It's been on this whole time."

We listen to "Go Slow" for a minute.

"You know," I say, "I'm not as spontaneous as you think. I was essentially trying to control my whole relationship with Carter. It's why he hates me now."

"He definitely doesn't," Vivian says, lowering her head into my lap.

"No, he does. He thinks I'm untrustworthy. And he's not totally wrong!"

"So talk to him."

"I've tried. A lot. Texts. Voice memos. Surprise appearances at his home. His position is a very clear: *Get out of my life, Maggie*."

"Hmm," Vivian says.

I run a hand through her hair as "Let Me Go" plays.

"Maybe," she says, "you need to send him a piece of Billy Beaver art in the mail. Along with an inspiring message. *I'm so dam sorry*. That should win him over."

"Great idea," I say, laughing. "Not creepy in the slightest."

The vibrations of Vivian's laughter move through my body. Best feeling in the world.

"I think he's gonna come around, Mags," she says.

"I unfortunately don't." I twirl my sister's hair into a bun, like I've done hundreds of times before. "But I sure am glad *you* did."

CARTER

I shove four Swedish Fish in my mouth as I lie in bed looking at Maggie's Insta grid.

She finally accepted my follow request when we got back together in March, but for a long time after the wedding, I resisted checking it.

I really didn't want to see her.

But last week, I got curious. Like, what has she been up to? How is she?

So I looked.

Since April, she's posted exactly one thing:

A short video from an Angry Baby concert. It went onto the grid on July 19, just a few days before I checked. It looked like they were in Shana's backyard, playing a song I didn't recognize.

"They don't hide," Maggie sang, her voice like an arrow to the torso. "They don't hide from each other."

After the first time I watched, I had to put down my phone and catch my breath.

Was she sending me some kind of message?

I've seen it a few times (or twelve) since then, and I watch again now.

I love the way her eyebrow rises when she sings.

I keep thinking she'll post something else, a story at least, but she hasn't.

I scroll down to January, linger on a selfie Maggie took with Shana and Ember during a rehearsal.

I hop out of bed and slide open my closet door.

I grab my camera from the shelf beneath my hanging clothes where I stashed it the night I got home from the wedding. Haven't really been in the picture-taking mood.

But I want to see Maggie.

I sit on the edge of my bed, staring at the small screen as I scroll through.

The first shots I see are from the wedding, minutes before I snuck up on Maggie and tapped her on the back. When I first peeked into the backyard, I saw her standing with Shana and Ember, passing around a glass and laughing, lit up with joy.

She looks so beautiful. It makes my stomach hurt.

I keep scrolling through, and I find the shots I took in my bedroom earlier that week: first the selfies of the two of us, then the shots of Maggie lying on the bed, staring right at me.

She looks simultaneously goofy and ethereal and breathtaking.

And suddenly I realize I'm not angry at her anymore.

I know she cares about me. It's so obvious in the photos.

She wasn't trying to mess with me. She was in an impossible situation, and she fucked up.

I fuck up all the time.

I put down my camera and pick up my phone.

Hey, I type. *I really miss you.*

I'm about to send it when it occurs to me:

I can't do this to Maggie again.

She's about to leave in a few weeks for her first year at Delaware, and I'm going to try to start things up again? Why? So we can have a really painful goodbye, followed by a few tortured months of a long-distance relationship, followed by an even more painful goodbye after which I straight up forget her? *Again?*

That's insane.

I gasp as the phone starts vibrating in my hand and, for a moment, I think it's Maggie. Like we mind-melded or something.

It's not, though.

"Hey, Mom," I say, after I pick up.

"Hi, sweetie. Just my midday check-in. You doing okay? Have you eaten lunch yet?"

"I have," I say, staring down at the almost-empty bowl of Swedish Fish next to me on the bed. "And I'm fine."

"Okay, good. Maybe you want to get out of the house today. It's beautiful out. Sunny but not too hot. And Dad's at his conference, and I won't be home from work till six. So maybe go hang out somewhere with Bodhi."

"Maybe." For the first time in a while, I'm not just saying that because I know it's what she wants to hear. Doing nothing might be getting old. "Mom?"

"Yeah?"

"You know last month, when you and Dad were arguing? And he said that you're, like, enjoying that I'm still living at home, still a teenager. Is that . . . true?"

There's a silence for at least five seconds. It feels really long.

"Carter, I don't . . ." Mom sighs. "I don't want this for you. Or for us. At all. But . . . I guess I also don't want to spend all my time wanting things to be different than they are. If that makes sense. This has been my reality—*our* reality—for a while now. And, though there's a lot about it that feels awful and unfair, there's also . . . some perks. You know?"

"Yeah," I say. "I get that."

"One of the reasons I called, actually," Mom says, "is because I bumped into Shawn this morning when I was getting coffee."

"Shawn?"

"The guy who runs Scoops 'n' Sprinkles."

Bodhi's been working there this summer, and he's been telling me at least once a day for the past week that some people are about to leave for college and they would totally hire me again.

"He wasn't sure if Bodhi had passed along his message."

"Oh, yes. Many times."

"You should think about taking the job. Could be fun."

"Maybe, yeah."

"And Maggie's definitely not there this summer. I'm sure Bodhi told you that, but I asked anyway."

"Oh. I . . . Yeah. Thanks, Mom."

"Of course. Okay, I've gotta go. Love you. Step outside the house!"

"I will. Love you."

As soon as the call ends, I go to FaceTime and scroll down to Bodhi's name. I tap it before I have time to overthink.

"Hey, hey, my dude!" Bodhi says, picking up instantly. He's got on his usual backward cap along with a gaming headset. "Did you mean to call me or is this a butt dial?"

"Dude. I meant to." It's embarrassing that I've become such a recluse my closest friend can't imagine me intentionally calling him.

"Whoa! That's great!"

"Yeah. Look, I . . . I'm sorry I, like, fell off the face of the earth the past two months."

"Hey, that's okay," Bodhi says. "I know this Maggie stuff has been hard. I'm sorry I kept bugging you to do stuff even though you obviously didn't want to do stuff."

"No, I'm glad you did."

"Yo, shut up!" Bodhi says. I realize he's talking into his headset microphone. "I need another minute!" He shakes his head. "Sorry, Carter. Amir and Robbie are whining at me. I should go in a sec. You can join us if you want!"

"Thanks," I say. "But I was actually thinking . . ."

"Yeah?"

"I might take that job at Scoops."

Bodhi screams with joy so loudly, the sound glitches out for a second.

AUGUST.

MAGGIE

"My dad got choked up while we were at the fricking Container Store," Shana says, turning us onto Route 81.

"Yikes," Ember says. They're sitting shotgun with their hand out the window, feeling the breeze on this humid afternoon. "That's sweet, though."

"It wasn't, it was disturbing," Shana says. "He's, like, standing there holding a shower caddy and silently convulsing. I'm like, 'Dad, what is happening?' He's like, 'I'm fine, I'm fine.' I'm like, 'Are you? You're silently convulsing.' And he's like, 'I just can't believe my little girl is going to college,' and I'm like, 'Can we talk about this literally any other time but now?'"

I laugh from the back seat. The three of us have been doing drives like this all summer—roaming around with no specific destination, cracking each other up, singing along to MUNA at the top of our lungs—and I love it. Nothing's been better at getting my mind off you-know-who.

But soon this, too, will be done. Ember leaves for Berklee College of Music at the end of this week, then Shana's off to the University of Michigan two days after that, and then the next day, I go to Delaware.

"I'm kind of scared," Ember says. "To go."

"Kind of?" Shana says. "I'm *terrified*."

"Same," I say. I always feel like a child when I'm sitting back here, like Shana and Ember are my parents and I'm trying to get their approval. But I *am* terrified to go to college. Also excited. And sad. Like Shana's dad. "We're still gonna talk and stuff, though, right?"

"Hell yeah, we will," Shana says. "Lots of talk and lots of stuff."

"Teela thinks I'm gonna kiss someone else as soon as I get there," Ember says.

"Will you?" I ask.

"I don't *think* so," Ember says. "I mean, that's not my plan. I want to stay together with her."

"Tell Teela she must be thinking of *me*," Shana says. "I'm gonna kiss *everybody*."

"That sounds unhygienic," I say.

Shana shrugs. "Possibly."

I look out the window and see that we're turning into the parking lot of the Old Valley Shopping Center.

"Why are we here?" I ask, trying not to panic. "You need more earbuds from Tech Haven?"

"Nope," Shana says. "I thought maybe we could get some . . . ice cream." She looks back at me with a devilish grin.

"Oh god, what? No." Scoops 'n' Sprinkles is in this shopping center. And apparently Carter works there again.

"I'm sorry, Maggie, my dear," Shana says as stores blur by and we get closer to the place I must avoid. "But you have been a wreck about this all summer. Don't you think you could use some proper closure? See him one last time before you go?"

"Shane, he hates me," I say. "So, no, I don't think that's necessary."

"He doesn't *hate* you," Shana says. "There's no way."

"Agreed," Ember says.

"We don't even know if he's there right now," I say.

"Actually, we do." Shana stops the car, with Scoops 'n' Sprinkles just up ahead. "Lizzy told me he and Bodhi have a shift together."

"Oh." My heart is flipping out. "Then maybe . . . Okay, fine. Inch us forward a bit."

"On it." Shana drives again, slowly rolling to a stop once we have a view into the store.

And there he is, behind the counter.

And here I am, eleven years old, seeing him for the first time.

Carter Cohen.

His dark hair has gotten longer. Messier. It only makes him more attractive.

The store is empty right now, just him and Bodhi.

I want to dash out of the car. I want to kiss him.

And I'm about to.

But then I take in how happy he is.

He and Bodhi are laughing about something.

Was he ever that delighted when he was with me?

Bodhi tries to send a crumpled-up ice cream cup into the trash with a jump shot. He misses, and Carter laughs harder than ever.

If I go in there, I ruin this moment.

Why would I once again force him to confront the fact that he doesn't like a Spear sister as much as she likes him?

That's what got him into this mess in the first place.

A pack of rowdy middle school doofuses stomps past the car and into Scoops 'n' Sprinkles.

Just as well.

"Shane," I say, staring at an empty bottle of Peach Tea Snapple on the floor. "It's not happening."

"Why? Because of those kids? Who cares—"

"Let's go," I say. "Please. Drive."

She does, as I silently convulse.

CARTER

"Cookies and cream," Bodhi says, counting on his fingers. "Chocolate chip. Strawberry dream."

Apparently, all summer he's been trying to memorize every ice cream flavor in the exact order they appear in the Scoops 'n' Sprinkles display. Unclear why. But he's taking advantage of this rare quiet moment on a hot August afternoon to try to prove that he can recite them all without looking.

"Blue monster," Bodhi says, bouncing in place as he nears the finish line. "Fudge swirl, black raspberry, pistachio, MOOSE TRACKS!" He throws his arms in the air. "That was it, right?"

"That . . ." I hold for a dramatic pause. "Was it."

"YEEEEEEESSSS! In your face, ice creams!" Bodhi shouts into the freezer. "You thought I couldn't do it, but I COULD!"

"Congrats," I say. "I didn't realize the ice cream had been doubting you so much." I grab my camera from my backpack in the break room to capture the hilarious moment. After I took it out of the closet a couple of weeks ago, I started playing around with it again.

I snap a pic of Bodhi as he lets out an extended victory cry, during which a woman in a tank top cautiously opens the entrance door for her and her five-year-old.

"Welcome," I tell them. "Don't worry about this guy, he's just excited."

"Yeah!" Bodhi says. "Because I did something unprecedented!

Do you know what the word *unprecedented* means, little buddy?"

The five-year-old buries his head in his mother's legs.

"He doesn't," the woman says, clearly annoyed.

"Sorry," I say. "Just ignore my coworker. What can I get you?"

She orders a cookies and cream kiddie cone, which Bodhi eagerly starts making. After I ring her up, I snap a couple of quick shots of Bodhi as he scoops.

"Yo, lemme see!" he says, reaching for my camera once our customers have left.

"Ehhh," I say, looking down at the viewscreen. "They're not great. I'm still shaking off the rust."

"Man! You think all your stuff isn't great," Bodhi says. "Even when it is. You're good at this, dude! And it's important for me to see what my flexed triceps look like with some sick filters on 'em."

I put my camera back into my backpack. "I'll think about it."

"Please do," Bodhi says, wiping down the counter. "I'd love to put one of those pics in a going-away card for Lizzy."

"I thought you and Lizzy are breaking up before she leaves for college."

"We are." Bodhi flips the towel over his shoulder. It slides off and lands on the floor. "But I still want her to be, like, thinking of me. Speaking of which: Have *you* been thinking of Maggie at all?"

This is the one downside of working shifts with Bodhi. The other Scoop 'n' Sprinklers don't ask me weighted questions about my personal life.

The answer to this one, of course, being *yes*.

I've been thinking about Maggie all the freaking time.

"I mean," I say to Bodhi now. "I've thought about her a little. I guess."

"A little?" Bodhi says, poking my belly in a way that makes me giggle. "A *little*?"

"Yo, quit it!" I'm cracking up, even though I'm so annoyed.

"I can't believe you haven't reached out to her yet," Bodhi says, scooping himself a kiddie cup of black raspberry. "This is insane."

"Not really. She's probably leaving for Delaware in, like, a week or something. Reconnecting now would just be cruel."

"Okay," Bodhi says, spooning a hunk of ice cream into his mouth. "Whatever you say."

"I'm trying to evolve here," I say.

"Ha!" Bodhi snorts out a little black raspberry onto my sleeve. "You think that's what you're doing?"

"Yeah." I grab a napkin and wipe my shirt. "Totally. It is."

"All right, Hookup Guy, let *me* hook you up with some advice. Totally free." Bodhi crumples his empty kiddie cup and three-point-shoots it toward the trash can in the customer seating area. He misses by a lot. "You didn't see that."

"I did," I say, laughing. "And I don't need your advice."

"So you think this is, like, a selfless act of love, right?" Bodhi vaults the counter. "But to me, it seems more like you're avoiding the whole situation so you don't have to deal with it. So you don't have to acknowledge your *emotions* and Maggie's emotions and all of that." He picks up the misshapen kiddie cup. "Just like you don't want to show me the photos you took. Because then I might judge them, and you'd rather stay in your happy little bubble." He emphatically dunks the kiddie cup, along with his spoon, into the trash. "Without the mess."

The front door swings open. Eight sweaty middle school boys in basketball shorts shout, screech, and shove each other as they approach the counter and start barking out orders.

"That is *not* what I'm doing," I tell Bodhi a minute later as we scoop side by side.

"Again," Bodhi says, eyeing his flexed triceps while he wrestles with an impenetrable mass of dulce de leche, "whatever you say."

CARTER

I feel very creepy right now.

I heard from Bodhi, who heard from Lizzy, who heard from Shana, that Maggie leaves today. So I'm sitting in Toro, parked on her street, five houses down from hers, watching as she packs up the car with her mom, Vivian, and Ron.

And, in case my spying isn't sketchy enough as is, I also have photos in my lap of Maggie.

They're the shots I found on my camera.

I had them developed. As a goodbye gift.

I'll have to get out of the car soon to deliver said gift, but it's hard to know what the right moment is.

So, instead, I've opted to watch as box after box is loaded into the back of Ron's green Subaru. Maggie and Vivian emerge now from the garage gripping either side of Maggie's keyboard, laughing as they clumsily make their way to the trunk. Whatever tension there was between them after my wedding ambush appears to have been worked through. They seem incredibly close. It's like the opposite of me and Lincoln.

I flip through the photos in my lap, the pics from the wedding and my bedroom, including the selfies I took of the two of us. I want Maggie to have these, but I'm questioning the logic of my half-baked plan.

Like, what if I crash this sweet moment and completely kill the good vibes? What if I just create a fresh wave of sisterly drama?

Maggie's mom pulls Maggie aside for a hug. She whispers something into her ear, Maggie nodding and tearing up. It's an intense moment I probably shouldn't be witnessing. But I can't look away. Finally, Maggie's mom finishes talking and leans back to look into her younger daughter's eyes.

"Thank you, Mom," Maggie appears to say. "I love you too."

I shift in my seat.

Am I seriously about to interrupt this major family milestone?

Wasn't that exactly what screwed up everything so badly a few months ago?

What is wrong with me?

I start the engine.

I love Maggie too much to keep exploding her life.

Oh. Wow.

Love.

Did I actually mean that?

Yeah.

I love Maggie Spear. Which is why I can't go through with this.

I chuck the photos onto the passenger seat and calmly K-turn the hell out of there.

CARTER

Was that the garage door opening?

No. Not yet.

I sit at my desk, nervously bouncing my knee as I wait to hear the telltale mechanical hum.

Dad went to go pick up Lincoln from the train station. He'll be here for a few days before heading back for the fall semester.

Yesterday, as I drove home from Maggie's, feeling a twist of shame and sadness in my gut, I couldn't stop thinking about how sweet she and Vivian were together.

Lincoln and I have barely talked all summer.

Sure, it started because I was angry at him after he finally told me what happened the night before I first looped. But then it turned into something else:

I just don't really know what to say to him.

I want to say *something*, though. We can't go on like this.

So last night, lying in bed, I decided it will happen today.

I'll talk to Lincoln.

If I put it off this afternoon, I know I won't do it. I'll make excuses. I'll avoid. I'll find ways to convince myself that *Welp! Timing just didn't work out. Maybe next time!*

But I can't carry this feeling around for three more months.

There's the garage.

They're here.

I look at myself in the full-length mirror on the back of my door, as if my appearance is going to affect how this goes. I look pale and worried. So glad I checked.

Downstairs, Mom is in the kitchen assembling a sandwich. "I'm throwing this together for your brother. You want one?"

"Um, no, I'm good," I say. Whatever I put into my stomach right now will likely pop right back up.

The door to the garage opens, Lincoln entering first with a travel bag over his shoulder, Dad trudging behind him. Neither of them are speaking.

"Hi, sweetie," Mom says, giving Lincoln a hug.

"Hey, bro!" I say, maybe a bit too exuberant.

"Hey," Lincoln says, eyes on the tiles. "I'm just gonna go to my room for a bit."

"Oh, all right," Mom says. "I have a turkey sandwich here if you want it."

"Maybe later." Lincoln moves straight through the kitchen and up the stairs to his bedroom, closing the door behind him.

He's still pissed at me, I guess. Damn.

"Is he okay?" Mom asks.

Dad sighs, but I don't listen to the rest of what he says. I'm not letting this go. I am going to talk to my brother.

I run up the stairs and am about to knock on the door when I hear sounds from inside.

Deep breaths. Sniffles. Sobs.

"Link . . . ?" I say quietly.

No response. I say his name again.

"Not now, CT," Lincoln says, his voice thick.

"I just wanted to tell you I'm sorry about being such a—"

"This isn't about you!" Lincoln shouts. "Hard as that may be to believe. Just go away. Please."

"Oh."

I would *love* to go away, but something keeps me standing there.

"Are you okay, though?" I ask.

"No! Obviously not!"

"Right. Yeah. Sorry."

I stand there another minute, listening to Lincoln cry.

I speak again. "Would it help if I—"

"Terrell broke up with me last night, okay?" Lincoln says. "And it fucking sucks."

Oh god.

I don't know what I was expecting, but it wasn't that.

"That's . . . I'm sorry, Link. That's . . . That's bad."

"No offense, CT, but you are not helping. Like, at all."

"That's fair," I say.

But still, I don't want to leave. I sit down, my back against the door.

"This is, like, totally Terrell's loss," I say. "You know that, right?"

Lincoln doesn't respond.

"For real," I continue, "you're the most amazing person I know, Link. That's what I was gonna . . . I mean, I'm just really lucky you're my brother."

More silence. Then the door opens, and I fall backward into his room.

"Oh shit," Lincoln says, laughing. "I didn't realize you were leaning on the door."

"I was," I say, lying on my back.

"Well, just come in," Lincoln says, gesturing for me to scootch my legs out of the way so he can close the door. "You're so damn persistent today."

"Trying something new." I rise from the floor, feeling triumphant, like a vampire who's just been invited in. This quickly dissipates when I see Lincoln plop down on his bed and cover his face. "Hey," I say, sitting next to him. "I'm really sorry. What, uh . . . What happened?"

"It's not even interesting," Lincoln says. "Terrell's going abroad to Barcelona this semester. And I thought we were staying together, and he was, like, *Nope*!"

"What an idiot. Good luck finding someone as rad as you in Barcelona, buddy!"

"No, he probably will," Lincoln says. "Spain is literally known for having the most beautiful people in the world."

"Oh," I say. "Seriously?"

"I don't know." Lincoln falls back onto the bed, curls up with his pillow. "That's what people say."

"Well, fuck that!" I lie down next to him. "You have beauty *and* radness."

"Meh."

I stare at the ceiling, hands on my stomach, listening to Lincoln breathe. This room is so much better with him in it.

"Stuff like this hurts so much," I say. "And nothing I tell you will really change that."

"I also feel stupid, you know?" Lincoln says. "That I didn't see it coming. I had my plan all ready for how we'd be in touch. The best times of day for us to talk with the time zone difference. It's just embarrassing."

"Welcome to my world, bro. Forget about what's coming, I

don't even know what's *going*."

Lincoln laughs, and I feel so proud. Like, for the first time I can remember, I'm actually there for him the way an older brother is supposed to be.

"That was kinda funny before," Lincoln says, propping himself up on an elbow. "When you said I was the most amazing person you know."

"Well," I say. "I meant it."

"Oh." Lincoln blinks twice. "That's nice."

"No, it's just *true*. I've been thinking so much lately about . . . You know, I've had all these relationships over the years, right? Like, Vivian. Layla. Maggie. God knows who else. But, through all of them, there's only one person who's always been there."

Lincoln sniffles. "Are you trying to get me to cry again?"

"Always. But for real, I just feel lucky you've stuck with me all these years. Because man, what a pain in the ass for you."

"It's not so bad."

I give Lincoln a deadpan stare. "Come on. You said I treat you like a search engine."

"Well, yeah, I was pissed, but it really isn't so bad! I'm lucky too."

"Now *you're* just being nice," I say, "but I'll take it."

I take a deep breath. One last Band-Aid to rip off.

"What happened to me," I say. "What's still happening to me . . . It's not your fault, Lincoln. Not even a little."

"Don't—"

"You were trying to be there for me that night. The way you always are. And I . . ."

I feel the tears coming, but I push them back.

"I'm sorry about what I did to you, Link. What I said that night. You were right to get pissed. I did this to myself. It's my fault."

"WHAT? No, it isn't!"

Lincoln and I both flinch at the voice that just shouted at us through the door.

"Mom?" I say.

"How long have you been listening?" Lincoln asks.

"Sorry," Mom says. "Just a few minutes. Dad is here too. We were worried about you guys, so we . . ."

"Yeah," Dad says. "So we came and put our ears to the door."

"That's . . . really odd," Lincoln says, "and pretty inappropriate. But I'm intrigued, so you may enter."

The door swings open, revealing a sheepish Mom and an equally sheepish Dad behind her. They slowly walk forward, then lower themselves onto the foot of the bed we're still lying in.

Mom takes a deep breath, runs a hand through her hair. "The night before Carter's seventeenth birthday, before any of this started, Dad and I were doing dishes. Remember?"

"Not really, no," he says.

"Well, we were, and we were wondering how you kids got so old so quickly. And I made a joke, like . . . saying we should find a way to stop this. And Dad played along, like, *Sure, let's look into it*, and I said . . ." Mom closes her eyes and shakes her head. "I said maybe we could google *Is there a way to make your kid stay sixteen forever* and then do whatever it says."

We're all silent.

"Did you actually google it?" I ask.

"No!" Mom says, grabbing my foot. "But I did say those words! And then the next morning . . ."

"Wendy." Dad puts a hand on Mom's shoulder. "I told you that was a ridiculous theory back then, and I still think it is now."

Mom nods, and I see that she's crying.

"I'm the one who can't seem to find the right doctors to help you, Carter," Dad says.

"Well, look, maybe it's not Carter's fault, or my fault, or Mom's fault," Lincoln says. "Maybe it's *everyone's* fault. Some kind of freak mystical wishing catastrophe." Lincoln points to me. "Like the movie *Big*! Except with more wishes. And, I mean, mathematically, if it's everyone's fault, that would also mean it's *no one's* fault."

There's a pause as we try to process that.

"Is this the first time in all my loops that you guys are talking about this?" I ask. "Like, has this conversation happened before?"

"No," Mom says.

"Definitely not," Lincoln agrees.

"Wow," I say. "That is really fucked-up."

Dad starts laughing. "You're not wrong."

Then Mom cracks up, and so do Lincoln and I.

I can't tell if the situation is actually that funny or if we're all just relieved to finally be honest with each other.

Whatever it is, it feels very good.

SEPTEMBER.

CARTER

"Hey, Ms. Jones," I say as I walk past my pantsuited principal toward the front doors of Ridgedale High.

"Welcome back, Carter," she says, with a nod and a small smile.

Inside, the halls are thick with first-years, yammering in high frequencies and moving at a glacial pace.

"Carter Cohen!" a voice shouts through the masses. I turn to find Ms. Himberton, eternally caffeinated as always, walking next to me. "Yearbook will start up in a few weeks. You're in, right?"

"Definitely," I say. "I've been taking a lot of pictures lately. So. I'm excited."

"Yes, Carter!" Ms. Himberton says, her short purple hair bouncing. "I'm excited too!"

I'm about to say *I can see that*, but she's already sprinted onward.

I spot Bodhi, Amir, and Robbie gathered near the lockers ahead. Before I can reach them, though, someone grabs my shoulder.

"Dude! Hey!"

It's long-haired Everett, one of my best customers from last school year.

"Oh hey. I actually, uh . . . I'm not doing the hookup thing anymore," I tell him. "Just taking more time to focus on other stuff. Like photography."

"No, man, that's what I wanted to tell you," Everett says. "I couldn't stop thinking this summer about what you said that one time. How vaping is destructive to my health. So I looked it up. You were right! It's, like, really bad!"

"Oh. Wow."

"Yeah, man. So I don't do it anymore!" He holds up a hand for a high five, which I give him. "Hey, do you ever do photography on skaters?"

"Uh, I haven't. But I could."

"That would be sick, man! I'll hit you up soon." Everett pats me on the back and disappears in the opposite direction.

It all feels so different from when I first showed up here last December. Better. People know me, and this time I know them too. Bodhi calls out my name as my friends spot me, and it is only then that I'm reminded of the one thing that is worse:

The person I most want to see is no longer in the building.

OCTOBER.

MAGGIE

"Never have I ever dated two people at the same time," my roommate, Tolu, says, followed by a gulp from her can of Natty Light.

There are seven of us crammed into our dorm room, and two others take a drink, including this guy Rory sitting next to me on my bed.

"That's so stressful," my frizzy-haired friend Gwen says. "I don't know how people do that."

"I found it exhilarating," Tolu says. "And fun."

We're almost two months into the semester, and I really like it here. It's honestly a little weird how comfortable I am—I just met Tolu and Gwen last month, but I already feel so close to them. Soon after meeting Gwen, I learned that she plays the violin, and we've been messing around with songs ever since. Earlier tonight, we did an insane cover of Katy Perry's "Never Really Over" at open mic night—me on piano, her on violin, both of us on vocals—and it truly killed.

"All right," Rory says. "Never have I ever made out with someone in a car." He takes a chug of beer with this smug look on his face, but I can barely take it in because I'm considering all the times *I've* made out in a car.

With CarCo.

I'd be lying if I said he hasn't been on my mind a lot.

I wonder how he's doing. How he's feeling.

Gwen and Tolu know I broke up with someone in the spring, though I haven't yet gone into the weird details. I save *that* for my voice memos to Shana and Ember.

Tomorrow marks two months till his birthday.

I wish I could talk to him.

Laugh with him.

Make out with him in a car.

But that would only be a recipe for more pain.

So I wait. I immerse myself in my new world, and I wait.

Two more months, and he'll forget me.

And then I will move on.

How will I even officially confirm that Carter looped back? I'll have to, like, reach out to someone who's still at Ridgedale. Probably Bodhi.

Ugh. It's all so depressing.

"Maggie?" Tolu says, nudging my knee. "Are you gonna go?"

"Oh," I say. "Go? You bet. Um . . ." I look at the faces of my new friends, all eyes on me. Why not? "Never have I ever dated a guy who's permanently sixteen."

I take a long sip, and everyone laughs.

They think I was speaking figuratively.

Three of the others drink too.

NOVEMBER.

CARTER

"Yo yo!" I say, immediately taking the FaceTime, even though I'm just leaving the soccer field and it's already starting to get dark.

"Hey!" Lincoln says, sitting in his dorm lounge. "Are you . . . in the woods? Searching for Bigfoot?"

"What else would I be doing on a Tuesday?"

Lincoln laughs. "Seriously, though. I can barely see you."

"I'm walking to my car. Just took photos of the last boys' soccer game of the season. Got some good ones."

"Oh man! Those pics you sent me from the skate park were unreal. Seriously, CT."

"Thanks, Link. That's . . . I'm really glad you're into them."

"Anyone would be. You're so good at this."

"Aw, stop." I arrive at my car, but I don't get into it yet. I'd rather keep talking.

"Look," Lincoln says, "I've gotta get back to my reading in a sec, but I wanted to check in. Since, you know, we're at the one-month mark. Are you doing okay?"

I stare at the high school, the soccer field, the parking lot. The tree I swung from when I shouted to Maggie. And thought her name was Lindsey.

All the moments I'll lose. This moment right now. Gone.

"Oh, I'm fantastic," I say. "Never been better."

"Yeah," Lincoln says. "It's not the best."

"You'll be there, right?" I ask, my chest tight. "The night before my birthday? I mean, I know you'll be home for Thanksgiving in a week. But then . . . You'll be able to make it back in time. Right?"

"Of course, yes."

I exhale. "Good. Hey, before you go, how are *you*? What's the latest with Terrell?"

"Oh, that boy." Lincoln rolls his eyes and grins. "Honestly, I feel like he's in touch with me more now than when we were together."

"I told you those Spaniards can't compete with you."

"Well. We'll see. I've been meaning to ask—have you reached out to . . ."

"Maggie? No." The sun has completely vanished. "I've thought about it. A lot. But I can't mess up her life again. The only messed-up life should be mine."

The parking lot lights blink on.

"I mean," Lincoln says, "I guess that's fair. But you should at least know that, whatever mess there was, you and Maggie *were* good together, you know? And I'm sure you're gonna find that again with other people."

"Yeah," I say. "Maybe."

"We can't always avoid the mess, CT."

"Right." I finally get into my car. "I guess not."

DECEMBER.

CARTER

"You were right," Bodhi says to me. "Those chocolate chip pancakes were next level."

"I do what I can," Dad says, clearing our plates.

It's the night before my birthday, and, for the first time ever (so I'm told), I decided I want to actually celebrate this year. Before it all goes away. So we're having a party, the four of us and Bodhi. Per my request, Dad made breakfast for dinner: eggs, bacon, potatoes, and, of course, his famous pancakes.

"Look how proud you are, Dad." Lincoln stands to help clear the table. "It's so cute."

"I think I'm being pretty chill about it!" Dad says, putting the plates into the kitchen sink.

"You aren't, honey," Mom says. "But I agree it's cute."

It's 6:47, and it's hard not to feel the minutes slipping away. I'm trying to just be here with everybody. To enjoy the right now.

"If you think this is a lot," Dad says, "just wait till I bring out my cake."

"Mom and Dad," I say, "can I ask you guys something?"

Everyone stops what they're doing. One of the about-to-loop perks.

"Of course," Mom says.

"How come you gave me the name of a president who didn't do much, and then gave Lincoln the name of a total legend?"

Mom and Dad laugh. "I was expecting a way more serious question," Dad says.

"It is serious!" Lincoln says. "I've always thought that was a weird move."

"I never even realized you're both named after presidents," Bodhi says.

"Well, they aren't," Mom says. "Not entirely. We liked the name Carter, independent of any associations. And then we thought Carter and Lincoln sounded good together."

"And also," Dad says, "Jimmy Carter was an incredibly underrated president! And an underrated person! He was still volunteering to build houses for people in need when he was in his nineties. Did you know that?"

"I did not," I say.

"It's true," Mom says. "Jimmy Carter was loved by many. And so are you, Carter."

"Damn right he is!" Bodhi shouts, putting an arm around me.

Dad gets the cake ready—it's his chocolate peanut butter one, which he has every right to feel cocky about—and soon it's in front of me, an aspirational eighteen candles (seventeen and one extra for much-needed good luck) flickering as everyone sings.

I've traditionally found this moment of being sung to incredibly awkward, but now I just feel grateful. Even with all the shitty parts, this was a great year. My throat clenches, and my eyes get wet. I smile through it.

"Make your wish," Dad says, once the song is done.

"What ever will you wish for?" Lincoln asks, with a hefty dose of irony.

I shrug. "New sneakers, I guess."

I blow out the candles and, as everyone applauds, the doorbell rings.

We all look at each other. No one else was invited.

"Delivery person?" Mom asks Dad as she glides away from the table to see who it is.

We're all silent, listening as she crosses through the foyer and opens the door.

"Oh my gosh," Mom says. "So good to see you."

"You too, Wendy."

My heart reacts before my brain, so by the time I realize who it is, I'm already up from my seat and headed to the door.

MAGGIE

"You sent me these," I say, standing on his front porch and holding up the photos.

Carter stares at me for a moment, sweetly confused.

"I did," he says finally. "But the post office said they weren't supposed to make it to your house until after I . . ." He's so adorably flustered.

"Well, they showed up today," I say. "My mom recognized your handwriting and figured it might be urgent. So she opened it. And told me. I came home a day early. Because I love them. The photos."

"Oh." Carter smiles. "Really?"

"Really," I say. *Love* is an understatement. The photos are gorgeous. The ones at the wedding, the ones of us in his room. As I sat on the couch with Mom looking at them, I couldn't stop crying. "And I never love pictures of myself."

"I felt like you should see them," he says, shivering a little in his blue sweater. "To have something to remember me. I had copies developed for myself too. So when I loop, Future Me will know who you are. Through my eyes."

I nod. This is every bit as painful as I thought it would be.

"Do you want to come inside?" Carter asks.

I want to say yes. I desperately do.

"Probably best if I don't," I say, wrenching the words from my own mouth.

"Yeah, no," Carter says. "I totally understand." He steps out from the doorway onto the porch and closes the door behind him. He's in just socks. They have little tacos all over them. It's easier to look down there than into those green eyes.

"You look really grown-up," he says.

"I think it's just this new jacket."

Dad took me to the outlet stores on Black Friday and got me this light brown trench coat. I'm still not sure if I can pull it off.

"Oh yeah," Carter says. "I dig it. You're like a sexy detective."

"Okay," I say, laughing. "Not exactly what I'm going for, but I'll take it . . . ?"

"You should. Sexy detective is the highest compliment I can give."

A gust of wintry wind blows past us. This jacket definitely isn't warm enough. Carter is stoic, but I see him shiver again too.

"Hey, I'm sorry," he says. "That I . . . stopped being around. After the wedding."

"No, I get it. I'm sorry I lied to you. And put you in that position."

"Nah," he says. "I understand. It all got complicated."

"Just a little."

We're silent for a moment, and I know I should leave. But once I do, I'll never see this Carter again.

"I'm pretty scared about tomorrow," he says, and I want to hold him. "I truly doubt I'll age. Obviously the Layla apology won't do it. And I never really apologized to your sister."

"I think that's kind of beside the point," I say. "Who knows what it would take to help you move forward? Maybe whatever it is has already happened."

Carter shrugs, and he looks like he might cry.

"Hey," he says. "I know you never really wanted to, but . . . Since I'm . . . Can you tell me about our relationship? The stuff from before this year?"

"Oh. If that's what you want, then sure."

"It is."

So I do. I tell Carter about the first time I saw him, when I was eleven. The time he balanced a ketchup bottle on his finger, and it careened into the Caesar salad. How thrown I was to be working with him at Scoops 'n' Sprinkles years later and how quickly I was charmed by him despite all my efforts not to be. Our first date, when we got the times wrong and ended up seeing just the last half hour of some Glen Powell movie. The afternoon I was goofing around on a piano and sang something and Carter was so blown away that it made me realize maybe I could start playing music for an actual audience.

There's so much more I could say, but I remember his time is short, and I should probably stop.

"Thank you," Carter says, almost inaudible.

"Sure."

A car drives by. Then another.

"Do you think I could . . ."

"What?" I ask.

"Kiss you. One last time?"

And there goes my pounding heart.

"Yes," I say.

Carter steps toward me, and I step toward him.

We kiss.

It is lovely and sad, and I don't want it to end.

But it does.

"I'm really gonna miss you," Carter says.

I nod, try to speak, but my face is wet and my words are jammed.

I put one hand on his stubbly cheek.

"Same," I finally whisper.

If I stand here a second longer, I might crumble into dust.

I turn and walk toward Mom's car, which I parked at the curb.

I've gone only ten steps when I turn back.

"Carter," I say. Thank god he's still standing there.

"Yeah?"

"Would you call me tomorrow? If you . . . You know."

"Maggie," he says. "If I turn seventeen, you will be the first person I call as soon as I open my eyes."

I take in Carter's smile. His shaggy hair. His crossed arms.

I won't forget this.

"Thanks, Coco."

"You got it, Maguel."

I hold his photos tight as I walk away for real, refusing to entertain any of the five hundred voices in my head screaming at me to turn back and look at him just one last time.

CARTER

Lincoln is the first one to see me when I walk back inside.

"Hey," he says, getting up from the table. "Are you okay?"

I look at him, feeling the familiar tight throat, the tears welling up.

I shake my head.

And I let the tears fall.

I let all of them fall.

Lincoln rushes over and puts his arms around me.

I can't see, I'm crying so hard.

Then Mom is there too, and Dad, all of them, forming a circle around me.

And then Bodhi's in there too, which is maybe embarrassing, for him to see me losing it like this, but he doesn't seem to care.

"I don't want to forget everything again," I say in between sobs. "I don't want to go back to the beginning of sixteen."

"We know," Dad says. "We know."

"I want you to tell me everything this time, okay? I know it might hurt, I know it might be confusing and painful and all the things, but that's what I want, all right?"

"We will," Mom says. "We'll tell you everything."

"Promise," Lincoln says.

"Okay," I say, catching my breath. "That's good." I wipe my nose with my sleeve, run the palms of my hands down my face. "You guys?"

"Yeah?" Dad says.

"This really is a horrible prank."

"It's just not our thing, Carter," Mom says, smiling through her tears. "You know that."

MAGGIE

He hasn't called yet.

This isn't good.

I mean, I'm not really expecting him to.

He's probably back to having no idea who I am.

But at least this time I'm prepared for it.

I take a deep breath.

I—

Ohmigod.

My phone is vibrating.

"Hello?"

"Hi."

My vision blurs.

"Coco?"

There's a pause.

"I prefer CarCo."

I scream. He does too.

"FaceTime me," I say. "I want to see you."

"Just come to the front door."

I pretty much fall down the stairs.

I open the door.

And there he is.

Looking exactly like he did last night.

"Nice pajama pants," he says.

And then I'm in his arms, and he is in mine, a jumble of messy kisses.

"Happy fucking birthday," I say.

"Thanks, Maggie Spear. So glad you remembered."

ACKNOWLEDGMENTS

Hi! For the complete *16 Forever* experience, I recommend immediately starting the book over again to create the full effect of what it's like to be stuck in a loop just like Carter.

I know, I bet you weren't expecting to get such an amazing thematically appropriate joke like that in the Acknowledgments!

Okay, no more goofin'. There are, as always, so many people I'm grateful for and without whom this book would not be what it is:

David Linker, my terrific editor, who—along with his equally terrific assistant, Lily Randall—helped shape and guide this story. It turns out time loop novels like this one aren't a breeze to get right, and David and Lily's spot-on insights challenged and buoyed me through many rewrites and outlines.

Catherine Lee, Jessie Gang, and Alison Klapthor, who created a cover that is so delightful; I first saw it as I was knuckling through one last rewrite, and it helped fuel a burst of enthusiasm that got me to the finish line. The rest of the wonderful team at HarperCollins, including Jessica Berg and the stellar copyediting crew.

Mollie Glick, my intrepid agent, and everyone else at CAA, especially Via Romano and Dana Spector.

Jillian Tucker and Todd Goldstein, who each had conversations with me that were incredibly helpful and heartening, especially Jillian's thoughts, as a clinical social worker, on sibling dynamics and how people can end up stuck in unproductive patterns because of seemingly small moments that have an immense impact.

Mariel Rubin (my sister!), who read a draft and offered encouragement at a point when I was feeling particularly insecure about what I'd written.

Abigail Marks of Harper Audio, whose thoughtful production and direction of the audiobook—and support of my very specific casting choices for Carter, Maggie, and Lincoln—made me so happy.

Dustin Rubin (my brother!), who, as one of the above casting choices, was beyond game to bring his considerable voiceover talent to the role of Lincoln.

The warm and generous kidlit author community, including Gayle Forman, Emily Barth Isler, Ross Burach, Greg Andree, Kathryn Holmes, Adam Gidwitz, Corey Ann Haydu, Adam Silvera, Amy Spalding, Alison Cherry, Lindsay Ribar, Natalia Sylvester, Diane Debrovner, David Levithan, and Eliot Schrefer.

My all-star parents, Halice Rubin and Jeff Rubin. I remain so grateful for how supportive they were when I pursued a career in the arts. The rest of my wonderful family: Dustin and Erin, Mariel and Brett, Jenny and Larry, Hannah and David, and Cormie, Niamh, Huey, and Junie.

The librarians, booksellers, teachers, festival organizers, bloggers, and influencers who keep the world of books alive and thriving, which honestly is no small feat these days. You are amazing. A thank-you also to ALL of the readers, including *you*. There's a lot competing with your attention, and you chose to spend your time getting immersed in a book. Written entirely by a human! Please keep on reading, ideally physical books in public, as that might inspire some other people around you to do the same.

My many wonderful and impactful teachers over the years, specifically those who nourished my love for the arts: Margo Crupi, Lowry Marshall, Nadine Greenspan, Gail Bauwens, Linda Viel, Janet

Bol, Judi Wandres, Mary Ann Oksen, Lisa Trent, Larry Goldstein, Janet Breslin, and John Emigh. Also Leon Britton, who was my cross-country coach and taught me a lot about persevering.

My kids, Sly Rubin and Roger Rubin, whose magic—both figurative and very literal—inspires me every day.

Linda Weiner, a dear family friend who died in November 2021, and who I think about often. She always loved when I brought my guitar to a gathering, so I gave her maiden name to the musician who Maggie's band opens for. Miss you, Linda.

Also: Stephen Boegehold (who is nothing like Soren). Zack Wagman. Ray Muñoz. Haim. Joe Iconis & Family. "Seventeen" and "Lost Boy" by The Midnight. The Brooklyn Public Library system. The Gang. Community Bookstore. CABA. That scene at the end of the 1960 *Peter Pan* TV musical when Peter comes back to Wendy's house, and she's old now, with a daughter of her own. The 1986 film *Flight of the Navigator*, which I saw around the same time, in which twelve-year-old David falls in the woods and wakes up eight years in the future to find that his younger brother is now his *older* brother.

And, finally, deep thanks to Katie Schorr, who talked about this book with me *a lot* every step of the way, offering up nuggets of brilliance and casually wielding her mammoth intellect in the service of making the story stronger and better. She did the same after reading a draft. Oh, and she dazzlingly voices Maggie on the audiobook. This isn't even to mention the fact that she's been the one getting our family health insurance for many years, which is NO SMALL THING. I'm so grateful and lucky that Katie is my partner. And that neither of us is stuck at age sixteen.